Sirens *of* Memory

a novel

PUJA GUHA

Cover and jacket design by 2Faced Design

ISBN 978-1-951709-37-2
eISBN 978-1-951709-64-8
Library of Congress Control Number: available upon request
First trade paperback edition June 2021 by Polis Books, LLC
44 Brookview Lane
Aberdeen, NJ 07747
www.PolisBooks.com

Sirens *of* Memory

For anyone who has been the victim of abuse, you need not suffer in silence.

2015

Chapter 1

Austin, Texas, USA - November, 2015

Mariam snuck down the stairs, her face damp with sweat. She was moving as fast as possible without making a noise, but this was her one chance—she couldn't let it pass. She crept past the door to her husband's room, where he had bedded his other women—two or three of them—not that she knew, or really cared. The door was open a crack, which meant that tonight he was alone, and her only chance was to get to safety before he realized that she was gone. As she moved down the hallway, his throaty snore faded, and she couldn't help but hope that tonight would be the last time she was subjected to that noise.

When she reached the stairwell, she sped downstairs, keeping hold of the straps of her overstuffed backpack so that it wouldn't bounce too hard against her spine. The carpet muffled the sound of her feet, so she moved faster, with each step the doorway to safety growing closer and beckoning all the more intensely. She stopped at the last step and moved daintily onto the ceramic tile—Tareq was a light sleeper, and even the faintest noise had awoken him in the past.

Her gaze darted between the kitchen with the door to the yard to her left, and the front door past the foyer on her right. Tareq's bedroom overlooked the backyard, so she elected for the front, picking up speed once again.

As she stepped into the foyer, her foot caught the edge of the thick rug, and she fell forward with a soft thud, catching herself on the carpeting on her hands and knees. She froze in place and looked up the stairwell, straining her ears. Had she woken him? If she had, her best bet was to stay quiet—she hadn't made much noise; he might simply turn over and go back to sleep.

Please, *she looked up at the ceiling and pleaded the universe to come to her aid.* This has to end; I *have* to get away.

After several moments of silence, she got to her feet, thankful that the Persian Mashad rug her father had given her as part of her wedding dowry had cushioned the fall. At least it was good for something. *She covered the last few steps to the door and opened it. The hinges squeaked slightly, but she was too close to pause again. She closed the door and made it to the gate at the end of the driveway.*

Her heart sank as she realized that the gate was bolted in place. Tareq must have noticed she had left the padlock open and locked it before going to bed. The stainless steel was cold to the touch, and her fingers felt like lead as she fumbled with the combination. She tried it once, made a mistake, and had to start over, her head pounding to the rhythm of her racing heartbeat. Before she could stop herself, her eyes wandered back to the house, and she messed up again, restarting the four-number sequence for the third time. "Twenty-two, sixty-seven, eighty-three, twelve," she whispered to herself this time. You can't make another mistake, this is your only shot. *The reminder was painful; the light at the end of the tunnel could be extinguished at any time.*

On the fourth try, she succeeded, and with padlock in hand, she moved the bolt handle back and forth to slide it out of the socket. She felt compelled to move faster, but knew the bolt creaked. A few seconds later, the bolt was free, and she was outside the grounds. Her backpack snagged against the bolt socket, and she had to slide the straps off to wrestle it free. It's going to be okay, *she reminded herself,* you're just a few steps from freedom.

Mariam pulled the gate behind her and jerked the bolt back into place. It squeaked this time, but she willed herself to move—all she had to do was get the lock back on. Once she got to the main road at the end of the block, she could hail a taxi, and she would be free. She clicked the padlock into place, grabbed her backpack, and ran. Almost there, *she could see the lights of the cars at the end of the street.*

*When she reached the corner, she doubled over panting. The backpack had never felt so heavy—*What did you pack in it, a bunch of lead weights? You should have left some of your books. *Mariam shook her head, silencing those thoughts, and waved for a taxi.*

The white cab approached; the half-block it had to cover to get to her seemed endless, like the stretch of the Kuwaiti desert. The cab pulled to a stop, and she reached for the handle.

The door opened, and the world changed.

"Did you think you were going to get away?" Tareq said to her with a cunning smile. He motioned toward the empty seat next to him. "This will always be your place, right next to me."

Mariam turned to run, but the asphalt beneath her turned to quicksand, and the more she moved her legs, the deeper she sank. Tareq emerged from the cab and held out his hand, "You pretend to fear me, to want to run from me, but I'm the only one who knows you."

Now waist-deep in the quicksand, Mariam surrendered, as tears streaked her dust-stained cheeks.

I can never get away from him, I can never get away from this life.

The quicksand sucked her in, and she gasped her last breath as it passed her neck. She closed her eyes, the congealed red mud enveloping her completely.

This is how I die.

Before the thought could register, the mud was gone, transformed into a thick cloud of ash, and she was falling. There was air around her again, followed by a loud crash as her body rammed into something glass. Her vision flashed red once again, this time a different shade, that of her own blood.

A ringing filled her ears and transformed into a high-pitched siren. She could see an ambulance a few paces ahead, coming toward her, but it wasn't slowing down. The sirens reverberated, and she realized that she had to get out of the way, the ambulance wasn't coming for her, it was coming at *her.* It's going to ram into me! *She tried to move, but her limbs refused. All that she could do was open her mouth.*

"Help me! Somebody help me!"

Ritika Ghosh bolted up, awake. She tried to catch her breath as tears streamed down her face. She squeezed her eyes closed, begging the universe to put a stop to the nightmare. As her breathing slowed, she slid out of bed to shut her window. The sound of distant sirens waned as the window slammed shut. The noise disappeared and she shuddered—even after so many years, sirens could still trigger her. They could take her back to that night, one that she wished with every fiber of her being that she could forget, that she could erase from history. She wiped the tears from her cheeks and crawled back into bed as her husband stirred and put his arm around her. She snuggled up against him, glad to have the comfort of his touch, although her pulse was still racing, and she resisted the urge to close her eyes.

Over the years the nightmares had grown less frequent, but their impact had worsened. Her life was so far beyond the events of that night, yet she was still haunted.

She practiced a breathing technique that she had learned in yoga class, and her body and mind started to calm. She had been through this cycle before—eventually sleep would take her, no matter how restless it would be.

THE NEXT MORNING, WHEN RITIKA opened her eyes, the first thing she saw was the window that she had closed the night before. Raj must have reopened it, there was a cool breeze coming in from the crisp November morning air, and the sun was streaming in. She sat up, looking out at the green grass and the leaves of the oak tree outside peeking over their chestnut wood pergola—there were no sirens this morning. She heard footsteps on the deck and saw Raj step outside holding a mug of coffee. He glanced toward her and smiled, gesturing for her to come join him.

Ritika gave him a quick nod and, after splashing some water on her face, took a long deep breath and looked at herself in the mirror. She was still reeling from the nightmare—her wrist smarted as if she could feel Tareq's grip, pulling her toward him. She looked down at it, the scars from the cuts and bruises were long gone, and her arm looked just like it always had. Yet she could see it in her mind, she could feel herself falling through the coffee table, see the glass shattering around her as her head hit the edge of the couch. She shuddered again before working up the courage to put on a smile and join Raj on the patio. He didn't know any of that part of her past, she had only wanted to forget it, never to share it. She didn't want him to look at her as a victim, she felt so ashamed she couldn't bear for him to know about it. He had done so much for her, raising Aliya as if she were his own daughter, saving them from a life as refugees.

Ritika pulled the patio door shut behind her and sat down next to Raj. He planted a kiss on her cheek and handed her his coffee mug, "Good morning."

"Morning," she took the mug and gave him a quick kiss before helping herself. "Good coffee. Is there any more?"

"I love that little Bialetti percolator, but it hardly makes enough. I left it out on the stove though—it should be cool enough to make another batch pretty soon."

Ritika nodded and savored another sip, keeping her eyes on the oak tree. She could see from Raj's expression that he was worried. She wondered how blatant her nightmare had been, but she hesitated to ask. Standing up, she handed the mug back to him, "I should go take a shower."

Raj frowned, and she knew what was coming and sighed, they had been together for too long for her attempts at avoidance to work anymore.

"Are you okay?" he asked in a quiet voice.

I'm fine, she wanted to say. She even opened her mouth to say it, but the words caught in her throat. Ritika sat back down, staring at the ground as her eyes welled with tears.

"It happened again, didn't it?" Raj reached out and touched her hand, "You can't keep living like this. This has to stop."

"I don't know what to do. I thought the nightmares would just go away..."

"I talked to Aliya about it, and she suggested you see a counselor." He raised his hand to stop her from interrupting, "I know you said you didn't need one since the nightmares don't happen as much, but they shouldn't be happening at all. It's been twenty-five years since we left Kuwait. You can't keep running from this, otherwise it will stay with you forever. Clearly burying them, pretending that these memories don't exist isn't working—you have to confront them."

Ritika met his gaze, she could no longer protest—he was right. Even if he didn't know what the nightmares were really about, perhaps especially because of that, they had to stop.

Chapter 2

Austin, Texas, USA - November, 2015

Ritika drummed her fingers against the armrest of the chair as she waited for her appointment with the therapist. In front of her, the table was scattered with brochures on neurological health, depression, and bipolar disorder—all of which made her even more nervous. Even though she had known Raj was right about needing to talk to a counselor, she had put up several last-ditch efforts at resistance. *They'll just find a problem that isn't there... What if all they want to do is prescribe me drugs? I don't want to take anything... I should be able to handle this on my own.* Raj had countered her arguments as best he could, but finally called their daughter, Aliya, who had flatly contradicted every point that she raised.

"You have to let go of this ridiculous stigma, Mom," she had said. "You and Dad fled Kuwait as refugees. It is understandable that you have some PTSD, you just need to get help."

Post-traumatic Stress Disorder. Even saying the words to herself seemed insurmountable. She wasn't a soldier, she hadn't lost a limb, nor did she have any lifelong injuries from what Tareq had done to her. Why couldn't she put it behind her?

She was still asking herself that question when the therapist opened her door and ushered her inside.

"Ritika, tell me what brings you here," the counselor asked after they had spent a moment on introductions.

Ritika hesitated. *Where should I begin?* "I've been having some issues, but I'm not sure where to start, Dr. Teresa," she finally said in a halting voice.

"Just Teresa is fine," the therapist smiled. "Your husband gave me a little background when he called to make the appointment. The two of you were refugees during the First Gulf War? I understand you've been having some nightmares."

"Yes." Ritika's voice caught in her throat, and she saw herself smashing through the coffee table once again. She looked up at the ceiling as her face crumpled, "But that's not what the nightmares are about. I was nineteen when…"

Ritika wasn't sure how she got through the rest of the session. She went through an entire box of tissues, but between sobs, she finally managed to tell the story. The story of where her nightmares came from, of her old life. Ritika wasn't her real name. She wasn't even Indian. *Mariam Al-Salem.* That session was the first time in years that she had even said the full name out loud.

1990

Chapter 3

Sabah Al-Salem, Kuwait – Twenty-five years earlier, July, 1990

Mariam Al-Salem smoothed the creases on her dress and smiled as she looked at herself in the mirror safely hidden at the back of her walk-in closet. The fuchsia dress revealed just a little bit of cleavage and hugged her curves in all the right places. She turned to the left and right to watch the silk of the floor-length skirt twirl with the movement. *It looks incredible on you,* her cousin Dinah had said, convincing her to buy it. Not that she'd needed much—the dress looked remarkably like the prom dress she would have bought two years before, had her father allowed her to go to her senior prom.

"Mariam, are you ready?" she heard from the hallway outside.

A chill ran up her spine, and she grabbed a black cardigan from a hanger and proceeded to fasten all of the buttons down the front so that it covered every bit of cleavage the dress so carefully accented. Once she reached the last, she opened the closet door and called out to her husband Tareq, "Yes, just one second."

Mariam reached for her purse, the faster that they could get out of the house, the less time she would actually spend with him. Theirs was hardly a conventional relationship—her father had married her off to him less than a year before, despite her protests. All Mariam had wanted to do was go to college and travel—to see the world that she now only escaped to through the books she read. She rearranged some of her shoes to hide the box of books that she kept hidden behind them in the back of the closet. Tareq knew that she liked to read, but the only books that she dared keep out were a few family dramas in which nothing remotely risqué ever happened. He would never abide her reading anything with a sex scene or men and women interacting openly—especially if it took place in the Western world. He had plenty of women on the side, but the thought of her interacting with *anyone* else, even just to say hello to one of her brother's friends threw him into a rage. Fortunately, he preferred not to sleep in the same room—his was at the end of the hall. While he could have her whenever he wanted, she was able to maintain a space to hide her books and grab some alone time when she desperately needed it.

She heard his footsteps in the hallway and stepped out, still hoping to minimize the interaction. "I'm ready," she said meekly.

"You aren't wearing your abaya."

Mariam froze at his tone, kicking herself for forgetting something that obvious. She stepped back into the bedroom where the full-length black robe was laid out on the bed. Just as she was starting to put it on, Tareq came in, and she looked over at him. One of her arms was still out of the robe, and she reached for it, fumbling in her effort to move faster. She recognized the look in his eyes, and it made her want to flee more than anything else. Perhaps if she could cover up fast enough, he wouldn't force himself on her? Her shoulders relaxed for a moment when he moved past the bed toward the closet.

Thank God.

Mariam pulled the abaya over her other shoulder and fastened it in front before peeping in the closet. As he had done on numerous occasions, Tareq inspected her closet. That was how their first fight started: she'd hung up two of her dresses with the top of the hanger facing out instead of inward. Her throat constricted. *Had she made the same mistake tonight?* He moved down the length of her clothing, sliding one item at a time, and she chastised herself once again for taking so long to get ready. *We could have been on our way there,* she thought. Instead, she'd basically invited him to come into her room for another inspection by forgetting to cover up. Once he reached the back of the closet, he picked out two items, a full-sleeved black shirt, and a long chocolate brown skirt.

"These shouldn't be next to each other," he said with a quick glance. He moved the hanger with the shirt toward the front of the closet where her black abayas hung, along with two black dresses. "Move the other one," he motioned toward the brown skirt.

Mariam brushed past him and grabbed the hanger. *Where should it go?* The items in her closet were more or less color sorted—the way he liked it—but she didn't have anything else that color. She looked back and forth between the skirt and the hanger and made a gamble. The closest color was maroon, so she might as well put this next to it. Her heartbeat sped as she stepped closer to him and made enough space to put the skirt, then reached up to hang it. "Is this okay?" she turned to ask, swallowing again.

He examined the hanger rod for a moment, then looked at her with a nod, "Yes."

His eyes narrowed as he looked her up and down and Mariam bowed her head in defeat. There would be no getting away from him now. Still, she glanced to either side, hoping to find a way to get past him or to encourage him that they needed to leave for the party. Before she could come up with anything, he was on her, shoving her against the closet wall. She tried to catch her breath, to at least get him toward the bed, but he grabbed her wrist and threw her to the side.

She wriggled and wanted to protest. *You're hurting me,* but he slammed her against the wall again. Mariam winced as her head hit the wall and she squeezed her eyes shut. He wrenched her arm, and then she was on the ground, and he was on top of her. *Just give in, it will be less painful that way.* She had learned that the hard way, so many times.

When Tareq finally rolled off of her onto the closet floor, Mariam stared at the ceiling to stave off tears. This time had hardly been the worst, but she could feel pain radiating through her left forearm. She took a deep breath and waited for Tareq to disappear to the bathroom as he always did without a word, either that, or—had they been in bed—he would fall asleep. *Small mercies,* she thought as he disappeared.

Mariam rotated her left wrist and tears welled once again. That wrist had already been sore from the last time he had grabbed her, and now she could barely move it without cringing. She slid to the side and rolled into the fetal position before using her hands to get up. Even the limited weight on her hands made her torso go rigid, but she breathed through the pain. She found her underwear on the floor and pulled it on, then struggled to fasten her bra. The bathroom door opened, and she could hear Tareq breathing heavily behind her, so she urged herself to move faster. *Where is my dress?* She looked around and spotted the fuchsia silk on the floor behind her, where Tareq must have tossed it.

Before she could pick it up, Tareq grabbed it. He held it out in front of him, letting it hang from the spaghetti straps and examined it, looking back at her several times.

"You were going to wear *this*?"

Mariam's heart almost stopped, his tone made her want to huddle in the corner of the closet in the dark.

"I had a sweater on top," she whispered, but she knew there was no use to her protests.

Why did I even buy it? What was I thinking?

"You were going to wear *this*?" he repeated, louder. She could see the fury in his eyes. "How *dare* you?" The veins in his neck were popping out, and he handed the dress to her, pushing her back a few steps. "Put it on."

"I'll…I'll wear something else."

"Put it on!"

Mariam slid on the dress and winced as she had to twist her left wrist to pull the zipper. After grappling with it for several seconds, she turned back to look at Tareq, her eyes wide with fear. She had never intended for him to see the dress without the cardigan. She'd known she shouldn't buy it, but it had looked so beautiful when she tried it on.

How could I be so stupid?

She hardly had enough time to make eye contact with him again before he was in front of her, slamming her into the wall once more. This time, though, all he did was rip off the dress, then pick it up and tear at the fabric. He stepped on the bottom and with a few strong tugs, two of the seams came apart and one of the straps tore off. When he was satisfied, he dropped it at her feet.

"I'll expect you downstairs in five minutes. I don't think I need to tell you to wear something else," he said and vanished out into the hallway.

Chapter 4

Salmiya, Kuwait – July, 1990

Mariam walked into the party at her sister's house and let out a sigh of relief as she and Tareq separated to head to the areas designated for men and women. He gave her a brief nod before he disappeared, he seemed in a better mood now. *I guess he calmed down with the thought of the alcohol he's about to consume*, she grimaced. His reaction to alcohol usually went one of two ways: either it increased his sexual desire and he would want to have his way with her again, or he would drop her off at the house, slap her around a few times, and head off on his own, most likely to find someone else to satisfy his urges. Both scenarios made her tremble. She didn't care how many other women he slept with, but the prospect of being slapped around again made her wrist sting even more. She stepped into the women's only section of the house and let the door swing shut behind her as she looked into the diwaniya style room which featured a long set of couches along the walls surrounding four small coffee tables. As usual, the women had shed their abayas, which were hanging on a portable wardrobe in the corner. As Mariam walked toward it, her heart raced. She'd applied cover-up to mask the bruises on her arm, but the redness of the fresh bruise would still be noticeable up close, and in her rush to leave the house, she had forgotten to grab a long-sleeved cardigan that would have covered them up for sure. She was fiddling with the zip on the front of the abaya when she heard her sister's voice behind her.

"Mariam, how come you're so late?"

Mariam turned around and forced a smile, "Hi, Reema." She greeted her sister with a kiss on either cheek.

"Aren't you going to take off your abaya?" Reema asked. "Dinah said that you bought a new dress. I can't wait to see it."

"I didn't wear it tonight. I think I'm actually going to return it. The fuchsia was just a bit too much for Tareq." Mariam scanned the room behind her sister and noticed Dinah sitting in the far corner, talking to one of her friends. She tried to make eye contact, but Dinah was too engrossed in the conversation.

"Oh, I see." Reema pulled her into another hug and whispered in her ear, "I'm so glad you're accommodating him. I told you it would all be fine between the two of you."

Mariam nodded, unable to trust herself to speak. She extracted herself from Reema's hug and sat down next to Dinah, careful to keep her arms straight down so that her three-quarter sleeves covered as much of her bruise as possible. On her way, she had greeted six other women who were friends of her sister's, interrupting a lively debate about whether one of them should take their next vacation in Switzerland or Paris. Mariam found herself switching off as she moved past them. Not that she wasn't interested in travel, she'd actually always dreamed of living in Paris—the movies made it seem so wonderful, every person in touch with their inner artist. She winced at the thought. She and her mother had talked about visiting Paris together many times before she'd passed. They had planned to travel there once Mariam finished university and got her degree in Interior Design. She'd even been admitted to Pratt, one of the premiere design programs in the U.S., but after her mother's death, her father had squashed that dream, instead insisting she marry Tareq. Mariam rubbed her eyes, less than a year later her father was gone too, although the legacy of his brooding stare and disapproval remained with her. They'd shared some tender moments, but most of his affections had been reserved for her brothers, and even on occasion for her sister, all of whom had stuck to the mold that he'd had in mind.

Dinah's voice jarred her from the memories, "Mariam, hi, you look lovely."

Mariam wrapped her arms around Dinah and lingered in the hug for a moment. She released her and broke into the first real smile of the evening, "It's good to see you."

"I love this dress," Dinah tilted her head to examine it, focusing on the sequins stitched onto the fabric, "but I thought you were going to wear the other one tonight?"

"Some other time," Mariam whispered, not sure if she could say any more about the dress. Her body went rigid as she recalled what Tareq had done to it.

Dinah put her arm around her shoulder, "I haven't seen you in a few days. How is that design class going?"

"Shh," Mariam glanced around the room, relieved that no one seemed to be paying attention to them. None of the other women knew that she had enrolled in a part-time class at Kuwait University. Frankly though, how else was she expected to pass the time? She could only go shopping so often.

"No one's listening."

"The class is great," Mariam answered, still keeping her voice low and her attention on the rest of the room. "It's hard, I'm not really that comfortable on a computer, and I have to keep all of the drawings hidden, but so far, I love it."

"I'm so glad. I wish I could do what you do—your sketches are magic." Dinah linked her arm through Mariam's and leaned toward her ear, "Do you remember what I told you before?"

Mariam nodded and waited for Dinah to continue, of course she remembered. The whole thing terrified her, but she also couldn't help but live vicariously through it.

"I'm still seeing him," Dinah's face flushed pink. "I know I shouldn't be, but Fahad and I barely speak anymore. He treats me with respect, but we rarely spend any time together. Once a month or so he comes into my room for the night, but most of the time it's just me alone. Maybe if we'd been able to have children it would be different...but it never happened for us." She looked down at her hands, "John is so wonderful. It's like he sees me and accepts me for exactly who I am. I don't have to be anything in particular: this perfect daughter or perfect wife, or a good Muslim, or any of it. I can just be me—with all of my idiosyncrasies and obsessions."

Aren't you scared that Fahad will find out?

Mariam bit her lip, imagining the beating that she would get if Tareq ever found her with another man, and a shiver went up her spine. She held her tongue though, she knew the answer to that question already. Dinah would never give up her relationship with John, not willingly anyway.

"Oh, I almost forgot, I brought you something," Dinah slid her purse open, removing a dark green plastic bag and placed it into Mariam's purse. "I know you haven't made it there in a while."

Mariam looked at her cousin, overwhelmed with gratitude. She knew exactly what was in the bag, another book that Dinah had picked up from the British Council library where she volunteered. It was where she'd run into John, he was a trade attaché at the British Embassy and had come in looking for a book a few months earlier. Mariam had never met him herself, but he'd actually picked out many of the books that Dinah had brought her. Once in a while she was able to sneak a purchase from the Family Bookshop on the Salmiya Main Street, but she had to be careful. Tareq didn't approve of the mysteries and suspense thrillers that she loved, he'd rather her read religious texts—or nothing at all. Books that had any reference to smoking, drinking, strong female characters, or especially sex, were completely taboo, even though he smoked two packs a day and drank several times a week, along with the nights he spent with other women or prostitutes. That said, she felt nothing but gratitude for his proclivities, a night with them was a night that he wasn't beating her up or forcing himself on her.

Mariam glimpsed into her purse but wasn't able to see the book cover without taking it out of the bag. "What is it?" she asked.

"*The Godfather*," Dinah answered, still speaking close to her ear. "John says it's an incredible book, but it's so violent. I'm not sure if I could get through it."

"He always knows what to pick," Mariam's smile widened. John had a real knack for identifying the books that she liked, she could sense that he might be a kindred spirit, especially because of how Dinah's face lit up when she spoke of him. *So dangerous though...* Mariam suppressed that thought and zipped her purse shut, she didn't want any stray eyes to catch a glimpse of the bright green plastic. Without realizing it, she tugged at her cardigan sleeve—Dinah's embrace had pulled it up slightly.

The expression on Dinah's face changed and she grabbed Mariam's arm, "Let's go for a walk."

Mariam followed her down the hall and out the back door into the small garden nestled on the east side of the house. This garden was secluded from the rest of the grounds. It was warm outside with the late July heat, even in the early evening well after the sun had disappeared.

"It's hot out here, and no one can see you," Dinah said in a firm but quiet voice. "Take off your cardigan."

For a split second, Mariam considered refusing, but the glare in Dinah's eyes was clear. She took a deep breath and did as she was asked. Dinah took it from her and stepped closer, examining her forearm and elbow closely in the dim light. She rubbed her hand against Mariam's skin and glanced at it, some of the cover-up now on her fingers.

"Did he do that to you?"

"Of course not," Mariam answered with a stammer. "I ran into a door."

"A *door*?" Dinah gave her a painful glance, her eyes moving between the bruise and Mariam's face. "I knew he was mean, but I never thought..." She handed the cardigan back, "I'll help you cover it up again, let's go to the bathroom."

They stepped into the bathroom, and Dinah locked the door behind them before turning the dimmer up to its maximum. She pulled up Mariam's sleeve and applied a fresh layer of foundation to conceal the bruise.

Mariam didn't know how to react to the silence, normally Dinah was so talkative. When she finally pulled the sleeve back down, Dinah met Mariam's gaze, "You have to leave him. This is only going to get worse. *Please*, Mariam, you can't stay with him."

The whimper in her cousin's voice caught her off guard. Mariam opened her mouth to protest again but was unable to find the words. The truth of what Tareq had done, along with who he was, was tomato-red against her skin. Her wrist and elbow were both tender, and it hurt to move her arm. Mariam hesitated again, *It's not as if I* can *even leave him.* He kept her passport locked in a safe in his office, and her sister had already refused to take her in when she'd confided in her after the first time it had happened. "It's really okay," she said softly. "I made a mistake. It won't happen again." The words didn't even sound convincing to herself, but she still chose to believe them. What other choice did she have?

"Why are you staying with him?"

"He's my husband."

Dinah finished dabbing Mariam's arm with more cover-up in silence. After she put her compact away in her purse, she let out a long sigh. "Mariam, I'm not a good example to follow. I don't dare leave Fahad, even though I have this wonderful person in my life now." She pursed her lips, "But flawed as he is, Fahad would never hurt me. You can't let this happen again."

Mariam snatched her arm away, "I told you it was an accident." Her eyes smarted with tears, the shame of her situation weighing on her. Tareq's actions, they had to be her fault. Why else would he be so harsh? She stormed out of the bathroom, she refused to talk to Dinah about this anymore.

Chapter 5

Sabah Al-Salem, Kuwait - July, 1990

Mariam rushed out of the bedroom and—willing her legs to move faster—sped down the stairs. She'd left her purse on the living room couch. Several weeks before she had left her purse out on her bed and gone to take a shower, only to find Tareq inspecting its contents when she emerged.

How could I leave it downstairs?

The question ran through her mind repeatedly as she reached the last step and went into the living room. Her shoulders relaxed, the purse was nestled in the corner of the couch, just as she must have left it. Tareq was nowhere to be seen, so she grabbed her opportunity, picking it up and heading back upstairs. When she was safely in her room, she entered the closet and shut the door. She let out a sigh of relief, she could hide the book along with the rest of her collection. She was about to remove the green plastic bag when she heard the door to her room open, and her posture stiffened.

Keep calm.

She dropped the purse on the floor and opened the closet door.

Tareq was standing in the doorway with his arms crossed. "Mariam, please join me downstairs."

Mariam followed him, trying to control her breathing on the way. They reached the living room and she almost tripped over the edge of her long nightgown as she stepped onto the area rug under the ornate glass coffee table.

"Sit down," Tareq gestured toward one end of the couch.

She stepped past him to take a seat and watched as he sat down in his armchair across from her.

He must have found the book.

Her heartbeat drummed in her ears as she racked her brain for any excuse.

"You left your purse on the couch," he said in a flat voice.

"Yes."

"You know how I like everything to be put away."

Mariam's breathing steadied.

This is just about leaving the purse out.

"I'm sorry," she answered. "I won't let it happen again."

"Good. Did you put the purse away in your closet?"

"I did," she gave him another nod, and her eyes looked past his head toward the staircase.

When will he let me go?

"I noticed there was a green plastic bag inside."

Mariam shrank back, she had no idea what to say.

Maybe he didn't look inside?

She clung desperately to that glimmer of hope.

"Do you know what was inside the bag?" Tareq's words shattered the last remnants of hope that he hadn't found the book.

Why did you leave it out?

Mariam rebuked herself again, unsure of what to say. Anything she came up with might make the situation worse. She finally made a feeble attempt at an excuse, "It was a gift from one of the girls. A friend of Reema's. I didn't open it, but I couldn't say no."

"Why do you lie to me?" Tareq's voice sounded even more eerie than usual, with an element of cunning, as if he were calculating his next ten moves and luring her into a specially designed trap. Mariam shut her eyes for a moment. She felt like the little boy in *The Jungle Book,* which she'd watched a few days earlier with Reema's three-year-old toddler. The snake was encircling her, just as it had in the movie, ready to pounce when its prey was most vulnerable.

"How many times have I told you that you aren't to read inappropriate books?" Tareq continued.

"I couldn't say no," Mariam repeated as a Hail Mary pass. Perhaps if she said it enough times, he would start to believe her.

Tareq approached and grabbed her left wrist to pull her into standing position. She winced, the bruise was still so sore. He towered over her, glaring at her, and the seconds protracted as he stared her down.

Mariam avoided eye contact, still hoping to defuse the tension somehow. "If you aren't comfortable with me reading it, I won't."

"You thought I would let you read *The Godfather*?"

"I heard it was a good movie, that's all," she protested. "I'm sorry. I won't read it, I promise."

Before she could say anything else, Mariam felt a searing pain across her cheek as he smacked her with the back of his hand. The heavy gold ring he wore cut into her skin, and she doubled over the couch. She touched her cheek gingerly, the open wound stung, and she could feel the drops of blood. *Maybe he's done for tonight.* She stood up, praying that the sight of the blood would get him to stop, "I'm sorry."

He stepped back from her, eyes narrowed, then grasped her shoulders and shook her. A few seconds later, he opened the sideboard to reveal the green plastic bag. He took out the book, handing it to her. Mariam looked down at the title, *The Godfather*, embossed in gold text on the maroon cover.

"Tear it up," Tareq said.

Mariam looked at him and back down at the cover. *Tear up the book?* Her mother had always said that books were precious, that they were to be revered. *How could I tear it up?* She closed her eyes, and a tear trickled down her cheek.

There's only one way to survive this.

Mariam opened the book in the middle. She tugged at one side, and a slim crack appeared down the spine. She pulled at it again, but heard her mother's voice in her head: *Books are always to be respected. Never forget that, Mariam… You can love them or hate them, but never disrespect them. When someone writes a book, they put a piece of their soul on paper.* Her hands froze, and her chest shook. *A piece of their soul,* the words echoed through her head again. Her voice quavered, "Please—don't make me tear it up. I'll give it back, don't make me destroy it."

Mariam saw the look in his eyes and tried to run this time, but before she could get more than a step away, another blow struck her head on the other side. She fell and crashed into the coffee table and the glass shattered around her. Her head slammed into the edge of the couch and then ricocheted onto the ground, smacking the joint between the carpet and the ceramic tile underneath twice before she stopped moving. Then everything went black.

When Mariam came to sometime later, the only thing she could hear was the sirens blaring outside. She squinted, "Where am I?" Her vision came into focus, and she saw a man next to her.

"Hold on, you're going to be okay," he said in Arabic. "You fell, but we're taking you to the hospital."

Who is this man? Where am I? Her head pounded, and she let her eyes close. The sirens were so loud… *Make them stop,* she wanted to shout, but the effort of forming the words seemed too daunting. She drifted back into the black, the sirens still screaming through her head.

2015

Chapter 6

Washington D.C., USA - December, 2015

Dinah Qatami hung up the phone in frustration and drained the last few sips from her coffee cup. The cold, bitter brew made her even grumpier, and she headed one floor down to the Nespresso machine to make a fresh cup, all the while pondering, *Why is Mariam always so stubborn?*

When Dinah reached the machine, she searched the cabinet below for the pods but came up blank. She rummaged through empty boxes—normally the cabinet was well stocked, but she had no idea where any extras would be kept. *That should have been lesson one for this job,* she pursed her lips and did a final sweep. *The hits just keep on coming,* she gave up and returned to her desk, bemoaning for the umpteenth time that the closest coffee shop in the embassy's vicinity was a Starbucks. While she didn't mind the atmosphere, she couldn't say the same for the coffee, a far cry from the Italian espresso shop she had frequented in London.

Dinah sighed and stepped into the bathroom to call John, she needed to vent before she could return to schedules and bureaucratic paperwork.

"Hi, darling."

"What happened?"

"How did you know?" Dinah's eyebrows scrunched, he could always read her voice, even before she had the chance to tell him that anything was wrong. "It's Mariam," she said before he could answer—the question had been rhetorical anyway. He was a former MI-6 case officer, so it was no wonder his observation skills were off the charts, although he had given up his commission a few years prior to his posting in Kuwait, before they had even met.

"Dinah, if she doesn't want to come to the event, you can't force her."

"It's not just the event—I don't care about that, I'd be fine if it were just you and me, but why can't she come visit? When we decided to move here, I thought I'd get to see so much more of her. Austin isn't far away but she refuses to make the trip." Dinah replayed her last conversation with Mariam in her head. *What could I have said?* She missed her cousin, missed how close they once were. "I even checked the list of attendees when she said that she was worried someone would recognize her. Big surprise—there's no one we know on the list! But when I told her she just came up with another excuse."

"I'm sure she'll come around, babe. It can't be easy though, especially if it means attending an event at the embassy."

Dinah let out another sigh, she knew exactly what John was referring to even if he would only allude to it on an open line. Her cousin had cut ties with her Kuwaiti identity, so coming to an embassy party seemed like something of a stretch—although Dinah had hoped the event's exclusivity would still be a draw. "Come on," she protested, "it's just a party. There'll be food and music, and it's not as if she didn't escape the invasion. Why wouldn't she be able to commemorate the end of the Gulf War?" Even as she spoke, she recognized that it wasn't that simple, but she couldn't help it. She wanted Mariam at the event, wanted them to be there together. "I just need her there with me. We got out of Kuwait together, we took care of each other, saved each other at that camp. Is it really too much to ask?"

"It isn't, but you know it's not easy for her," John replied with a deep tenderness in his voice. "You saved each other, but you also went through a huge trauma. People deal with that in different ways. You have to give her time, my love."

"Why are you always right?" Dinah said with a small smile.

"Thanks for letting me vent."

"Of course, silly. I've got to run to a meeting, I'll see you at home later, okay? Love you."

"Love you, too." Dinah hung up and was on her way back to her desk when she passed Nadia, a new hire. On the corner of her desk sat a box of Nespresso pods: exactly what Dinah had been craving. On a normal day, Dinah never would have said anything, but she was frustrated and overwhelmed by Mariam's behavior, so she stopped. *I need this.*

"Hi, I'm Dinah," she held out her hand. "I don't think we've met properly yet. When did you start?"

The woman at the desk looked up, meeting Dinah's gaze with pale hazel eyes, highlighted by a dollop of black eyeliner and silver matte eye shadow. "I'm Nadia, nice to meet you."

After exchanging a few pleasantries, Dinah worked up the courage to ask about the coffee. "Normally I would never ask…but I've had quite the morning, and they're out of Nespresso pods at the machine downstairs. Is there any way I could impose on you?" She gestured toward the box.

"Of course, please, help yourself. Actually, I'll come with you," Nadia stood and followed Dinah down the stairs.

Although she tried to make polite conversation, Dinah couldn't help but wish that she could have just taken the pod and gone on her way. She wasn't in the mood for mindless small talk.

After a few feeble attempts to break the intermittent silence on their way downstairs, Nadia asked, "If you don't want to talk about it, that's fine of course, but is everything okay? You seem upset about something."

Dinah hesitated, she probably shouldn't talk about it, but what harm could it really do? *It's not as if I'm going to use Mariam's real name.* "An old friend of mine, we grew up together, like cousins—I really wanted her to come to the Liberation Day party, but she keeps saying she's not up for it."

"Really? My whole family is vying for all of my invites—parents, crazy uncles…" Nadia rolled her eyes.

"Don't talk to me about crazy relatives, I've got more than my fair share."

"This one's different, he was a prisoner of war, released a few years after the liberation. I think he went mad in there, he gives me the creeps," Nadia shuddered a little.

Dinah relaxed, perhaps she *could* let her guard down a bit. She hadn't made many friends yet in Washington, and while John was wonderful, she was yearning for more female companionship. She considered talking about Mariam, but instead redirected the conversation to the move from London. As they both sipped their coffees, Dinah started to feel better—maybe Mariam wasn't the only woman she could connect with, after all. *Maybe John's right,* her optimism returned, *Mariam will come around.*

Chapter 7

Washington D.C., USA – December, 2015

Nadia drove home on Saturday morning, exhausted, with her stomach in knots. She had spent the last two nights on Tinder dates, a fact that she was now regretting since she could have used the extra sleep. Her mom had insisted that she come home for the weekend, which meant only one thing: another set-up. There wasn't much that she wanted to do less than meet whomever her mother had decided was a good match for her. On top of that, she wasn't looking forward to seeing her uncle either, who was also visiting. Her parents were conservative enough, they didn't like that she refused to wear a hijab headscarf or the fact that she occasionally wore mini-skirts, but he took it to a whole other level. One time when he'd been visiting, she had arrived at home in a button-down shirt with the top two buttons undone. Even though she hadn't shown much cleavage, he had given her a harsh lecture on the inappropriateness of her behavior. She'd been twenty-one at the time, in her last year of college, and had talked back to him, but the look in his eyes had silenced her. For a moment, she even thought he was going to hit her, but her mom had returned from an errand just in time. Nadia spoke to her about it later, but her mother discounted it as a figment of her imagination, "I know he would never hurt you, he just has strong beliefs. I agree he could express them better, that he could be more level-headed, but think about what he went through. We are so lucky that he's still alive."

Nadia paused at a stop sign and considered how fortunate she was that her family had been on vacation in New York at the start of the invasion. Her father had been able to find a job there with the help of a few contacts, and the family returned to Kuwait two years after liberation. A year later, her uncle was released, although Nadia was so young, she didn't remember much from that time. She and her parents finally moved to D.C. shortly after her sixteenth birthday, and he had seldom visited until her mom processed his immigration paperwork to move to the United States while Nadia was in college. He lived on his own in an apartment outside of Baltimore, but Nadia's mother was always trying to convince him to move in with them.

Hell no. Nadia pushed the thought aside, wondering why she had such a visceral reaction to her uncle's presence. Just as she'd told Dinah, there was something off about him—maybe the darkness had come from his time in a Baghdad prison, or from being captured in Kuwait. *Or he's just a misogynist, maybe even all of the above.* The prospect of bringing him to the embassy party in a few weeks left an even more bitter taste in her mouth. *We'll have such a great time if he comes along.*

The drive passed quickly as she turned onto Canal Road and sped away from D.C. When she took the Potomac exit off Highway 270, Nadia practiced her fake smile. *Why do I do this to myself?* she pondered, but she had started to accommodate her mother's extreme requests years ago, and she was not yet willing to deal with the inevitable tension that would come with re-establishing her boundaries. *I don't even live with them, so I don't have to deal with it every day.* Nadia chuckled to herself as she recalled how her mother had tried to convince her that she could live at home now that she had taken a job in D.C. *Oh, Mom...*

She parked on the street a short walk from the house, practiced her smile one last time and headed for the door.

Here I go.

During the initial spree of questions about her first two weeks at work, how she was adjusting to life in the "unsafe" atmosphere of Washington D.C., and exactly what she had eaten that week, Nadia had already drained her first mug of coffee. She fidgeted with the empty cup as the discussion shifted to whether she'd been able to procure tickets for the family to attend the embassy party alongside her. After explaining for the third time that this was difficult to request given that she had only just started at the job, she excused herself to the kitchen, claiming that she wanted to make herself a fresh pot of coffee.

Nadia leaned back against the wall as she waited for the percolator to brew, which would take about ten minutes. She couldn't smell the coffee yet, but the kitchen was already full of the enticing scent emanating from her mother's lamb stew that was slow cooking on the stove. *This is why I come home.* Nadia took in the aroma, imagining the deep Ras Al-Hanout spice, along with the saffron rice her mother had already put out on the table.

She was still basking in the scent when her uncle appeared in the kitchen. Nadia stood up straight, "Is there anything I can get for you, Uncle?"

"I'm fine," he turned to examine her mother's spice rack with a frown. After switching two of the bottles, he looked back at Nadia, "Make sure you put the percolator back in the cabinet when you're done. I spent three hours cleaning in here yesterday—your mother keeps her kitchen so disorganized."

Nadia waited until he departed to curse under her breath. *Who the hell does he think he is? And Mom wants him to move in?* She clenched her right fist, the leeway that her mother gave him was so ridiculous. After several deep breaths, her blood pressure had cooled, and she sipped on her coffee, prolonging the quiet as long as possible. She was almost through her cup when the doorbell rang, and her mother called from the living room, "Nadia, could you answer that? Maybe they will join us for lunch."

Nadia almost choked on her last sip, her mother was trying for a new level of deception with this particular set-up. She set the mug on the counter, conflicted—on some level this attempt was hilarious, but on the other hand the deception made her even more frustrated—and went out to the foyer. *Time to start the* Guess Who's Coming to Dinner *game.*

Chapter 8

Austin, Texas, USA - December, 2015

Mariam finished the story of how she had escaped from Kuwait and looked at her therapist. "That's how it happened. Raj told the officials that I was his wife, Ritika Ghosh, and I've been her ever since. I took some Bengali and Hindi classes after we got to Mumbai so I could get by. When I filed my name change paperwork with my citizenship, I filed it as Ritika Mariam Ghosh so that I can still go by Mariam."

The therapist looked up from her notes, "What happened to Dinah?"

"She went to the UK, she and John are married now and living in Washington, D.C."

"What about you and Raj?"

"We left for India together, and our relationship moved forward." Mariam shrugged, and her eyes brightened, "He's always been wonderful. We had this connection from the days at the camp, but we finally let ourselves be together in India. We spent two weeks in Mumbai, staying with one of his distant cousins before we got our own place. At first, he slept on the floor, he didn't want to put pressure on me, but I didn't have enough money to get my own place. Then after a while, he didn't anymore. Aliya was born there a few months later, and we applied for immigration to the U.S.—an old friend of Raj's from university sponsored us. When the paperwork came through, we looked at a few different American cities. We were in Colorado for a while—Raj's childhood friend was already there, but then we fell in love with Austin, so we moved here. With all of the construction, there's been plenty of work for him here."

"What about Raj's family? Do you ever see them?"

"I've only met them a couple of times. He told them about what he did to help me get out of Kuwait after Aliya was born. They didn't really understand, but I guess they accepted it."

"Did you ever tell Raj about your husband in Kuwait?" the therapist asked.

"He knows I was married before and that my husband died during the invasion, but he doesn't know that Tareq was…" Mariam hesitated before she could make out the words. "That he was abusive."

"Why do you think you never told him?"

"I don't know. I guess I didn't want him to see me as the victim, maybe I didn't want to be the victim *again*." Mariam's voice caught in her throat, "I don't want to go back there. I was so powerless, I let Tareq do whatever he wanted to me, over and over. I never fought back—and I can't be that person again." Tears trickled down her cheeks, "When I think of the life that Aliya might have been born into, how I would never be free of him if we hadn't gotten away when we did—"

The memories were in front of her in full force now, they had control as they ran her over like a bulldozer. She raised her hand to her mouth, "The woman that I was, I never want Raj to see me like that. I was weak and small, and I didn't stand up for myself, everyone walked all over me except for Dinah—first my father, and then Tareq."

"But you left him—isn't that standing up for yourself?"

"I was going to go back to him," Mariam whispered. "I was going to go back to him until I found out I was pregnant."

"*That's* when you found out that you were pregnant?" Teresa frowned. "You didn't tell me that before. So that means that Tareq is Aliya's biological father."

"Yes." Mariam shut her eyes, the memories swarming her, "When I came to at the hospital, I only knew about the concussion. Dinah was there, and she tried to convince me to leave him, just like she had before, but I was *so* sure that I had to go back to him." She ran her fingers through her hair and let it fall forward, partially concealing her face as she looked at the ground. "I tried to talk to my sister about it once, after the first time that Tareq hit me—I told her, and I thought she would help me, I thought she would stand with me, but she said she was sure that it wouldn't happen again. She said that the family would never accept me if I left him, that I had to find a way not to provoke him." Mariam placed her hand over her mouth.

How can the memory carry as much pain as it did twenty-five years ago?

"Even though you didn't get help there, you found a way out later. You have to give yourself credit—try to remember that, to affirm yourself. You may have let that situation happen at first, but eventually, *you* got out of that situation, *you* found a way to take care of your daughter. You should be proud of yourself, not beating yourself up for what you already overcame."

"Sometimes I wonder what would have happened if the Iraqis hadn't invaded, if I'd never met Raj. Would I still be that meek submissive girl who could never stand up for herself? Would I have raised my daughter to be like that?"

"Ritika, er—Mariam, I think the fact that you're asking that question gives me the answer. You're so aware of how far you've come, I can't imagine you wouldn't have been able to get here. Circumstances might have made that happen faster—you most definitely had to act because of the invasion, because you had to find a better situation for Aliya, but as I said before, *you* did all of those things. You could have chosen to be with a man who didn't treat you right, who didn't support you and your daughter, but you didn't do that. I want you to think about that, to affirm that part of yourself."

Mariam let out a long sigh, "I'll try."

The session wrapped up quickly after that, Mariam having spent so much time over their last three appointments going over the history that had led her to this point. The rehashing was taking a toll, burying her memories of Tareq and how difficult that time was seemed far easier than recounting it and reliving the trauma. Discussing the refugee camp was difficult in its own right, the mix of perpetual uncertainty and fear that they had all dealt with on a daily basis, along with the inability to connect with any of the others at the camp for fear of revealing their true identities.

Immediately after the session, Mariam went home and sat down on her porch, facing the old oak tree. Raj was still at work so she was alone as she slowly sipped on a cup of masala tea, one of the more pleasant things that had come from her time at the camp.

She stared out into the distance and tried to push past her memories of Tareq—he was dead after all, why shouldn't she relish that? Her home was a symbol of a new life, one that she and Raj had built together, a life that had raised Aliya to be a strong independent woman with a good head on her shoulders.

Mariam smiled and reached for her phone to dial her daughter's number. After a few rings, she picked up.

"Hi, Mom, how are you? Dad told me you were going to therapy today."

"You and your father aren't allowed to talk without me like that," Mariam exclaimed in a huff. "You spend all this time bonding, and I'm totally out of the loop."

"Come on, you know you love it."

Mariam chuckled, she did indeed love how close Raj and Aliya were, such a contrast to the relationship that she'd had with her own father. "You know me so well," she said, shaking her head.

Aliya chuckled as well, then her voice turned serious, "How was it?"

"I don't know, it was hard."

"I talked to Dinah Auntie yesterday."

Mariam sighed, and her shoulders sank. *Here it comes.* "What did she say?" she asked, knowing full well what they must have talked about.

"She told me about the event at the embassy in D.C., that you said you didn't want to go."

"That's true." Mariam could feel herself retreating into her shell, she had no intention of going to an event to celebrate the anniversary of Kuwait's liberation after the Gulf War.

"You should go, Mom. It would be such a good way to confront your past. Besides, isn't it worth celebrating? If the invasion had never happened, you and dad would never have met."

It's not the Gulf War that I don't want to confront. It had been so much easier to pretend that her identity as a Kuwaiti didn't exist. Being

Raj's wife Ritika had always felt simpler: no abusive ex-husband, no guilt to bear as a result of his death. She exhaled slowly, communicating her real identity to Aliya had been difficult enough a few years earlier, especially since that had to be kept a secret, and there was no way she would dare put that at risk by going to an event at the Kuwaiti embassy. Mariam held her tongue though, neither Aliya nor Raj knew about Tareq's abuse or the details of his death, and she wanted to keep it that way. "I don't want to go, Sona," she said, using a Bengali nickname for her daughter that meant "my golden one" in the hope that it would get Aliya to back off.

"Will you promise to think about it?"

After another sigh, Mariam found herself giving in. *What could it hurt?* Besides, it might get Aliya off of her back, and that had to be worth something. "All right, you win. I'll think about it."

A few minutes later Mariam hung up after redirecting the conversation toward her daughter, probing to find out more details on the master's program that she was about to start at UT in Austin. Mariam pitched Aliya on the benefits of living at home, how she could save money and spend more time with them, but after getting the runaround for the third time that month, she conceded and let her daughter get off the phone. *It's good for her to have her independence, anyway.* Mariam looked out at the garden with a wistful expression. *Something I never got to have.* She finished her tea, glad to have spoken to Aliya. Even though they hadn't agreed on the event at the embassy, the conversation made her feel lighter, as if all the heaviness of therapy was far behind her. Stretching her arms and legs out, she took a deep breath, her past was exactly that, just a faded memory.

Mariam dozed on the lawn chair for a few minutes, listening to the birds chirping and hum of the wind passing through the trees. The warmth of the early evening sun was on her face and her body drank it in, the darkness of her past long gone.

A siren went by and she woke with a start, gripping the armrests as if her life depended on it. *It's nothing,* she told herself, probably just an ambulance going by on South Congress Ave a couple of blocks away. She stared straight ahead and fought for control of her breathing. *Maybe Raj is right,* she thought, *I can't pretend that part of my life doesn't exist. Pushing it down it just lets it come back stronger.*

1990

Chapter 9

Farwaniya Hospital, Kuwait - July, 1990

Mariam groaned as she opened her eyes. Her vision was hazy, all she could see was white.

"Mariam?" a familiar voice made the blood drain from her face. "It's Tareq."

She let her eyes shut, she didn't want to wake up—not when *he* would be there to greet her. Perhaps if she pretended to be unconscious for long enough, he would disappear?

Another voice startled her into opening her eyes, "Mariam? It's Dinah. I'm here too. You're at the hospital."

"Dinah? Where am I?"

"You're at the hospital," Dinah repeated.

Mariam felt someone squeeze her hand before her vision became clear. The stark white of the hospital furniture still glared back at her, but now she could see Dinah in a pale blue hijab that matched her full sleeve shirt. She was holding her hand tight and looking warily across the bed. Mariam followed her gaze and suppressed the compulsion to flee—Tareq was sitting in a chair on the other side of her bed. His expression was hard to decipher, some part of it feigned concern. He stood and grabbed her other hand and Mariam fought the urge to wrest it free. *What's the point,* she reminded herself, *it'll only make things worse later.*

Her eyes moved between the two of them as she tried to recall how she had gotten there.

She remembered the party, and the fuchsia dress.

Walking to the bathroom with Dinah, where she'd explained that the bruise on her wrist was from a household accident.

Going home… Mariam shuddered, and her eyes closed as the sirens reverberated through her brain and it all came rushing back.

The Godfather and trying to explain to Tareq that they could just get rid of the book.

Her cheek as he smacked her across the head, then the glass splintering as her body rammed into the coffee table.

Her head hitting their ceramic floor once, then again, but after that—only sirens.

"What happened?" she asked, looking down at her arms. Her left forearm was a dark shade of purple, with a long white bandage that stretched upward from her elbow. Her other arm had two more bandages, but the exposed skin was a pale shade of red. Mariam drew in a long breath and her gaze fixed on Tareq, "What happened?" *He must have told Dinah something.* Whatever lie he had told Dinah, she would have to accommodate him—the beatings would only get worse if she didn't.

"You tripped, do you remember? You fell through the coffee table—that's how you got so cut up," Tareq answered. "I'm glad you're okay. You've been in and out of consciousness all night."

Mariam nodded slowly, "The last thing I remember is coming home from the party." His expression warmed, and he returned her nod, she felt so relieved she almost started to believe the lie.

He looked down at his watch, "It's getting quite late. I have to get to the office. Dinah, will you be staying with her?"

"Of course. Will you be back this afternoon?" Mariam caught the edge in Dinah's tone and wanted to beg her to keep control of herself. *You're only going to make it worse for me later.*

"I don't think so. The doctors are keeping you overnight for observation, but it's just a concussion and some stitches. You're going to be just fine," Tareq said as he touched her right hand.

Mariam cringed and her eyes widened, she had to cover up how scared she was of his touch. "I'm sorry," she said with a long exhale, "the cuts on my arm—they're still pretty sore."

"Of course." Tareq stepped back, "I'll see you tomorrow morning." He turned around, and she watched him disappear into the hallway.

As soon as he was safely out of earshot, Dinah leaned over and kissed her on the cheek. "My god, I'm so glad you're okay. What did he do to you? He's a monster. Mariam, I'm not letting you go home with him, not ever. You're lucky to still be alive."

"I'm fine, Dinah. It's like he said, I tripped and I'm okay."

"Are you insane? You hit the ground so hard that you could have cracked your skull open. Do you even understand that? You might have needed brain surgery." Dinah dropped her head in her hands. "Mariam, you could have died, or you could have been paralyzed if any of that glass had gone into your spine. I can't say it enough, you're lucky to be alive. Please, don't go back to him. I can help you, if you let me. *Please.*"

And then what? How would I get away? Mariam stopped herself from asking those questions, and instead repeated, "I'm really fine." There was nothing Dinah could say, she wasn't willing to leave her whole life behind. She hardly had any money without him, and her sister had already made it clear that she wouldn't help. *You married him, you can't just walk away from that.* Her sister had said those words, and she knew how true they were. *What kind of life could you expect to have without him?*

Before Dinah could say anything else, a doctor and a nurse walked into the room. They greeted them both, and the doctor went through her injuries and how she would need to care for them. "Three stitches in your left arm, eight in the right arm...some serious bruising on your rib cage, but no broken ribs...the concussion isn't severe, but you'll need to avoid excess physical activity..." His voice droned on, and Mariam nodded several times, although she didn't really register what he was saying. Dinah asked a few questions, but Mariam was unable to process most of it.

"Most importantly, we wanted to congratulate you. You're pregnant."

Those words forced Mariam out of her daze. *Pregnant? What?* She gawked at the doctor, "Did you just say—?"

"Yes, and before you get worried, the baby is just fine. I'll have one of our gynecologists come in and speak to you, but it looks like the baby is about six weeks."

The muscles in her torso relaxed, and she began to sob. Mariam let her head fall back onto the pillow and tried to catch her breath as the tears poured down her cheeks.

THE NEXT FEW HOURS WENT by in a blur, Mariam couldn't keep track of any of it. The only thing that she could focus on, the only thing she could think of, were the words: *Congratulations, you're pregnant.* The thought seemed unfathomable—how could that be? She'd been on birth control, having a baby at nineteen certainly wasn't something she had hoped for, but now that she knew, everything was different. A gynecologist came in and spoke to her briefly, the baby was fine and growing. After giving Mariam a prescription for some prenatal vitamins and indicating that she should come in for another checkup in about six weeks, she, too, disappeared out of the room.

Dinah kept looking at her, but she no longer wanted to talk. Mariam wasn't sure what to say. She had made up her mind to go home to Tareq, to do her duty as her father would have wanted, but now everything had changed. Could she go home to him? Could she bring a *baby* into that house? Mariam shut her eyes and tried to imagine what Tareq would be like with a child, perhaps he would love it the way he was supposed to? He couldn't be entirely darkness and insecurities after all. In a way, she was more worried about how he would treat *her* during the pregnancy—if he had another one of his angry fits, the baby might be in danger.

Mariam dozed for the rest of the day, but each time she woke up she was relieved to see Dinah still at her side. She shivered at the thought of waking only to the sight of Tareq's face. *It's going to be okay,* she told herself but was unsuccessful in placating her fears.

By the third time she awoke, she stared at Dinah for a few minutes, the silence finally grating at her. "Aren't you going to say anything?" Mariam looked at her indignantly.

Dinah raised her eyebrows and pursed her lips, "What can I say? You were pretty clear that you're going back to him, even with all of this." She gestured toward Mariam's injuries with her hand. When she spoke again, her voice was shaky, "Why would you do that? Why would you go back to him? Look at what he did to you, and now you're going to have a child. In that house? What if he hurts you again? You're lucky the baby's fine…and after? What if he hurts the baby?" Dinah squeezed her hand but refused to make eye contact with her.

Now you're going to have a child… Mariam felt tears well up in her eyes again and spill down her cheeks, she felt like a spectator, as if she was watching someone else's life. *This can't be me.* She wasn't sure how long she cried, Dinah holding her hand as if she couldn't possibly let go.

Chapter 10

Farwaniya Hospital, Kuwait – July, 1990

Mariam walked into her bedroom and rocked the bassinet where her baby daughter was just dozing off. Her beautiful big eyes opened and closed a few times before she finally fell asleep to the melody as Mariam sung an old Kuwaiti folk song.

With the baby asleep, Mariam took a few minutes to take a quick shower and change her clothes, tossing the shirt that she'd been wearing into the laundry pile. It, like many of her other clothes, now smelled like milk and it seemed impossible to get her laundry done fast enough to keep up with the burps and spills associated with new motherhood. Every fiber of her being was exhausted, but she couldn't imagine anything more wonderful. There was nothing like the joy of watching her sweet little Aliya smile, sleep, or even suck on her breastmilk.

She heard a car pull into the driveway outside and froze, then took a deep breath. Tareq had been in a better mood for the last couple of days, there was no reason to believe it wouldn't continue. Mariam had temporarily moved her stash of books to Dinah's, eliminating his most likely trigger—she didn't want to risk anything that might set him off, and so far, it had been working. They had had a few altercations, but nothing compared to almost a year ago when he'd thrown her through the coffee table. She glanced down at her left arm and rotated her hand, noticing the faint scar along her elbow. It was hardly visible unless you were looking for it, but that wrist still got sore more easily than the other one.

Mariam heard the door slam downstairs, and her heart skipped a beat. He must be in a bad mood today. *She looked around frantically, wishing there was something she could do to appease him, to cheer him up. He had shown little interest in Aliya, simply commenting that she didn't "do much" as a newborn, but secretly Mariam was just grateful that he hadn't been violent.*

For a second, she contemplated locking her door and not letting Tareq in, but she didn't dare do anything to provoke him. Instead, she checked her reflection to make sure that she looked reasonably put together and decided to head him off at the stairs.

She greeted him, and he replied tersely, then disappeared into his room. Mariam relaxed, relieved that the worst was probably behind her, at least for that day, and settled down on the rocking chair next to the bassinet with a fairy tale. She would have preferred one of her old books, but she was thankful that Tareq had at least allowed her to buy a few old fairy tales to read out loud to Aliya. Mariam had already read them so many times, but without any other options, she picked up Sleeping Beauty *yet again and proceeded to read about Princess Aurora being smuggled away to hide in the forest as a newborn.*

Her door opened, jarring her from the story, and she looked up to see Tareq in the doorway. One glance at his face told her she was in trouble; her earlier relief had been nothing but a mirage. She attempted to greet him again, but the next thing that she knew he had wrenched her up from the rocking chair and thrown her to the floor. He was yelling at her, but she couldn't understand what he was saying. Aliya awoke and started to cry, and Mariam struggled to her feet to go comfort her, but before she could reach the bassinet, Tareq had her on the ground again. He smacked her twice across the face, and Aliya cried even louder.

"Why won't she stop crying?" he yelled out.

"Tareq, stop, please," Mariam whimpered, trying to get to her feet when he stood and moved toward the bassinet, a thunderous expression on his face.

"Tareq, no!" Mariam screamed as she woke up in a cold sweat. She thrashed out with her hands and her torso convulsed with sobs. *My baby...*

"Mariam? Mariam, are you okay?" Dinah's voice came from her right.

Mariam opened her eyes, and her chest heaved—the hospital room felt like it was closing in on her, the stark white descending upon her like a cage she'd never escape. She put her hands on her belly and realized it had been a nightmare. She hadn't given birth yet...

"Mariam, it was just a dream," Dinah said, grabbing her hand again. "I'm sorry, I shouldn't have been so hard on you."

"No, you were right." She stared at the white ceiling, finally accepting what she had realized as soon as she'd woken up in the hospital but had been unable to admit to herself.

I have to get out.

She would never be able to trust Tareq not to hurt her again, and she certainly couldn't risk that around her child. Perhaps she could have stomached it before, out of some sense of duty or inability to break free, but everything was different now. Whatever else she might have wanted from her life, there was nothing more important. *My little Aliya.* Mariam allowed herself the tiniest of smiles at the name, her mother's name. *I have to protect her.*

"Help me, Dinah. You're right. I have to get away from him."

2015

Chapter 11

Washington D.C., USA - December, 2015

Nadia pretended to smile, *This should be a good thing.* "Thank you so much," she managed to say.

"Of course, it's my pleasure," her boss said. "I know how much you wanted to be able to bring your family along to the party. New employees don't usually get a plus-one, certainly not a plus two, so I had to pull some strings but luckily it worked out. It will be great to meet them—especially your uncle, you said he was a P.O.W.?"

Nadia feigned enthusiasm, "Yes. Taken in Kuwait after the invasion, then held in Baghdad for three years before he was released."

"Wow, what a story. I can't wait to hear more."

When her boss walked away, Nadia shrank down into her armchair and let out a long sigh. At her mother's urging, she had requested tickets to the twenty-fifth anniversary celebration for her family shortly after accepting the job. She'd regretted it immediately—introducing Uncle Tareq to the people that she worked with only seemed like a good idea if you had never met him. Nadia had been relieved when her boss said he wouldn't be able to acquire extra tickets, but now that he'd walked that back, she had no clue what to do.

He's such an ass, everyone thinks he's a hero because he was held prisoner, but he's awful. She shivered, he had been so mean to her when she'd last seen him. After her parents' friends had arrived with their twenty-nine-year-old son Bassam in tow, of course, Nadia had, of course, suffered through the interaction. While his parents were actually quite interesting—they told funny stories and were clearly well-read—Bassam couldn't string two sentences together.

By the time they left, even Nadia's mother was in agreement that she shouldn't give him the time of day. That, however, had sparked a full-on argument about how Nadia wanted her parents to have nothing to do with her love life, and had to stop meddling. The discussion—not that it could really be called that given how much shouting had been involved—had dissolved into a highly emotional rant that had severely hurt her mother's feelings. While they had spoken over the phone since, the hurt and scars remained, although Nadia refused to capitulate to her mother's wishes. There would be no more set-ups, that much she was sure of.

Her uncle's involvement, though, had been the most painful. After the argument had erupted, Nadia had retreated to her old bedroom to stew, while her parents attempted to take their normal afternoon siesta—one of the benefits of being retired. Once her emotions had cooled, Nadia returned to the living room to watch a show on Netflix until her parents woke, which is when her uncle had cornered her. The conversation started with him castigating her: "Respect for your elders is of paramount importance," "What worth do women have without a man," etc. Her blood was boiling by the time he was done, but somehow, she had kept her mouth shut—she couldn't imagine how her mother would react if she raised her voice to him, especially after how poorly the afternoon had gone. When he was done, he asked, "Do you agree with everything I said? I want you to tell me you understand."

His voice, the eeriness of the look on his face alarmed her enough to stifle her anger, but apparently, it was visible anyway. Nadia shuddered, wishing she could forget how he had come toward her and shaken her by the shoulders; he'd seemed about to scream, but instead, he had whispered, "You will show me the respect I deserve, little girl. Do you think you can challenge me? That you can stand up to me? You are nothing without men like me. You deserve nothing and will never have anything unless another man supports you."

Nadia shut her eyes tight, the memory was still incredibly painful.

She had always thought she would be able to stand up to someone if they came at her like that—not that she'd ever had occasion to test it before. *I should have said something,* she thought, still unsure why her mouth had been sealed shut, all of her inner strength gone in the moment that she needed it the most. Prior to that encounter, her uncle had made her uncomfortable many times, but she had never experienced anything like that: the complete powerlessness and loss of her own agency.

She'd been saved by her father coming into the living room. Nadia had considered telling him about what had happened or speaking to her mom, but she couldn't bear the thought that she would be told to live with it, or that her feelings would be dismissed. *Did I imagine it? Would he really have hurt me?* She wiped her eyes and deliberated what to do, she couldn't imagine bringing her uncle to the event, although her mother would be there to run interference. *It would make Mom so happy, and maybe it would show him the respect he deserves,* she rationalized. Before she could second guess her decision, Nadia sent her mom a text message to tell her the good news.

Once the message was gone, she took a deep breath. *It's going to be okay.* Taking her uncle would show him that she didn't disrespect him, that she was trying to honor him, and hopefully, he would never have occasion to speak to her like that again. *Thank God he said he doesn't want to move in.* She couldn't imagine having to interact with him every time she made a visit home.

Nadia's phone buzzed with her mother's reply, "That's wonderful! Tareq will be so happy. I'm so glad we can go as a family."

With another shudder, Nadia locked her phone screen and stepped away from her desk to make herself a cup of coffee, hoping that it would squash the trepidation in the pit of her stomach.

Chapter 12

Austin, Texas, USA - December, 2015

Raj looked at Mariam and did his best to control his pent-up frustration—she had been going to therapy for weeks now, yet he still felt as if they were spinning their wheels. He had originally pushed her toward therapy for *her*, as a route to get past her nightmares, and to accept her past. Her initial reluctance had exposed a key vulnerability in his own logic on the subject: if he thought that *she* needed therapy to deal with the trauma of the Gulf War, then why didn't he? Until recently, neither of them had ever spoken to a therapist about their experiences, about the sudden invasion, and their time at the refugee camp. Most importantly for him, he had never addressed his emotions around the death of his first wife Ritika, whose identity Mariam had assumed upon their evacuation from Kuwait. The logic that had compelled him to take Mariam to therapy had, in turn, pushed him toward doing the same, especially combined with the persuasive capabilities of his daughter Aliya. Raj sighed, Aliya didn't even know that she wasn't his biological child. *She is one hundred percent my daughter, but she deserves to know that Mariam was married before.* It seemed like such a half-truth that Aliya knew about his first wife yet nothing about Mariam's first husband.

In his therapy sessions over the last month, Raj had finally opened up on the subject. He had so many questions, most of which had never been answered. When he had tried to address them in the past, Mariam had tactfully dodged them, and after that had happened enough times, he'd stopped asking. Despite that, the questions had remained, in fact, they had grown, doubled in size because of their suppression over the years. Why wasn't Mariam willing to tell Aliya about her first husband? Why had she decided to live her entire life under someone else's identity? He had never loved Ritika, had never had the opportunity to develop that intensity of emotion for her in the short time that he'd known her, but a sense of responsibility remained. *She died during the Gulf War.* Ritika had died and he had moved on, and everything had happened so fast. He understood exactly why Mariam had used that identity to leave Kuwait, how that had been the start of a new life together for the two of them. *But why continue it? Why not use her real name once the evacuation was over? Once the invasion had ended?*

At the heart of all his questions was guilt, as he had discovered somewhere between the extra reflection he'd been doing and his therapy sessions. *I feel guilty...I* am *guilty.* How could he give someone else Ritika's identity, allow someone to compromise her memory, even if it was the person closest to him in the world? And why on earth did she *want* to do that? *There has to be something she's not telling me.* Whenever he thought about it, he came to the same conclusion: it was too late for it to stop, too late to change the paperwork that said she was Ritika M. Ghosh, but he needed to hear the whole story. *Whatever it is, she has to tell me.* He could feel the secret, palpable in the air between them—from his side, the fact that he hadn't shared any of these bubbling emotions, and from hers, the answers that she continued to hide. A few weeks ago, he'd been hopeful, when he first confronted his feelings—she was in therapy already, it was only a matter of time until she opened up.

But that day had never come.

Raj resisted the urge to slam his fist on the dinner table and zeroed in on his plate, applying tremendous focus to cut his slice of lamb roast into tiny bite-size pieces without saying a word. He didn't trust himself to start the conversation—at least not today—he was far too likely to lose his cool. Friday night at the end of a long work week was hard enough under normal circumstances, but this week had extended far beyond tough—his crew'd had two near disasters in as many days, and their client was threatening to pull the entire project if they billed for any of the extra hours.

Mariam shot him a look from across the table, "No conversation over dinner today?"

Her voice sounded testy, much like he felt, so Raj set down his knife and fork and took a deep breath, "Sorry, darling, it's been a hell of a week. How are you? How was your day?" *Don't lose it, not right now,* he reminded himself. He had only just reached his boiling point after realizing that she seemed less and less likely to bring it up, and he wanted a chance to talk about how he would broach the subject before he blew the lid off the whole thing. *Stay on target,* the quote from Star Wars echoed through his head.

"The day was okay," Mariam shrugged. "This season is crazy, but nothing unusual. Everyone just wants to buy gifts for Christmas, so we're all working extra hours restocking books, talking to customers, stuff like that. I'm pretty tired too, from being on my feet all week, and I wish I didn't have to go in tomorrow."

"That's too bad, I forgot you have to work Saturdays now," Raj felt his shoulders relax, he wanted some alone time in the morning. This would be his first day off in a while, and he had scheduled a therapy session for midday—having the morning to himself beforehand would be perfect, even though he would never have wanted to hurt Mariam's feelings by asking for that had she been at home.

"It's okay, I love the job. Do you want to talk about what happened this week? Did anything else happen today?"

"Not really, I'm exhausted."

They sat quietly for a few minutes, Raj forking the meat into his mouth and chewing slowly. He only broke the silence to comment on how delicious the lamb was, roasted in the oven with a ton of flavorful spices—he couldn't distinguish all of them, but he could detect the cumin, cardamom, and cinnamon melding together with the onions and garlic to bring the best out of the meat. Helping himself to another bite, Raj couldn't help but sigh—Mariam seldom cooked Arab dishes, even though she could clearly prepare them to perfection. *Is that another sign of her forcing herself to be Ritika?* She cooked Indian food far more than Arab, but in the last couple of weeks she had made more Arab dishes—was that a sign of change? Was he expecting too much too fast to know all the details of her secrets right now? He meditated on that, wondering if he should bring up his discomfort with her use of Ritika's name and identity. *I just want her to tell me why, is that really too much to ask?*

He was lost in thought when Mariam thumped her water glass down on the table, an obvious attempt to get his attention. "Raj, what is going on with you? You've barely said two words to me this evening." She gave him another one of her looks, usually only reserved for Aliya during her rebellious teenage years, "Talk to me. There's clearly something going on, and I don't think it's just about work."

"Can we talk about this tomorrow? I'm so tired," Raj stood and picked up his mostly empty plate, glad that he had wolfed it down.

Mariam's eyes narrowed, and she looked both angry and hurt, "Sure. Do whatever you want."

Something in her tone struck a nerve with him, "Whatever *I* want? Do whatever I want? We've been doing what *you* want for the last twenty-five years."

Her eyes started to tear up, "What are you getting at?"

"You make all the decisions—you wanted to immigrate to the U.S., so we left India. You wanted to live in Boulder, so we did, then you decided that you liked Austin, so we moved here. You wanted to keep living as Ritika and Raj, so we did!" The last phrase burst from his mouth before he could stop it and he felt a pang of immediate regret as her face contracted.

"If you had such a problem with it, you didn't have to marry me!"

Raj pulled his chair closer to hers, sat down, and grabbed both of her hands, his anger already starting to dissipate. He didn't want to hurt her, and he did love her, he just wanted her to talk to him. *I need to understand.* "Mariam, you and I never got married. We never got to do that—because you were living under Ritika's name. We have all these secrets, you don't see anyone in your family, and Dinah is the only one who even knows that you're a whole different person now. My parents still don't understand what's going on, I tried to explain it to them, but—how could I? I don't understand myself."

"So, what do you want? You want me to change my name back to Mariam Qatami? That will go over really well with the U.S. government—it won't cause any confusion at all."

Raj touched her face with his right hand, "No, of course not," he said with a smile. "Especially in this political environment. I just want you to talk to me—tell me why. Why did you want to live as Ritika?"

"I'm sorry I'm not as wonderful as she was," Mariam looked away and stared at the wall.

"That's not fair," Raj leaned back in his chair, the weight of her words sinking in. "You know that's not true, I barely knew her, never had the chance to develop real feelings for her. I have always been honest with you about her, about my past, but I don't know anything about yours. I bet Dinah does, and I don't begrudge you that for a second, I want you to be close to her. That's why Aliya and I have been trying so hard to convince you to visit her and go to the event at the embassy." He tried to meet her eyes, to catch her gaze, but she kept it fixated on the wall, "I don't know what it is, Mariam, but there's something deeply wrong, something that you're not telling me. What is it about your past that you can't share? What is it that you can't face?"

Raj waited several seconds, hoping that she would answer, that she would say something, but she remained silent, a few tears trickling down her cheeks. He could tell how much what he'd said had hurt her, and he wished that he had done it differently, especially after speaking to his therapist about it. He sighed. *What's done is done.* Standing up, he reached out and squeezed her hand, "I love you and I always will, but I need you to talk to me. At some point, you need to answer my questions."

She looked up and finally made eye contact, "I'll go to the event in D.C."

That's it? "I'm glad, but that's not enough, and you know that. I still need to know why." Raj turned around to walk away, then glanced back, "I'll sleep in Aliya's room tonight."

Chapter 13

Austin, Texas, USA - January, 2016

"How are you doing, Mariam?"

Mariam gave her therapist a short rundown of what had been going on that week, skirting the subject that they most needed to discuss. She mentioned that while she and Raj had had their fair share of disagreements, the extra hours at BookPeople had become a welcome distraction, and in general she was doing well.

Teresa nodded, then did a run through of her notes from their previous session and asked, "Have you spoken with Dinah this week?"

"We played phone tag but haven't managed to talk properly yet," Mariam shook her head, at the same time amazed that Teresa was able to identify the most important issue so immediately.

"Are you still on the fence about attending that event in Washington?"

"I told Raj I would go, last night after we had this huge fight, but I don't think I want to." Although she had avoided the subject earlier, Mariam reluctantly spent a few minutes explaining the fight, how she still couldn't bring herself to tell him her whole story.

"We'll come back to the fight, but first, can you tell me why you still don't want to go to the embassy party?"

Mariam shrugged, wishing that she could string together a more believable answer, *If I couldn't convince Aliya, then how on earth am I going to convince a trained therapist?* She sighed, "I left that part of my life behind—Kuwait, the Gulf War, Tareq…all of it."

"You did leave Tareq—but why do you feel like you need to separate yourself from the rest of it?"

"I don't know." Mariam examined the curtains, looking carefully at how the sky-blue pattern framed the picture window which looked out onto Town Lake. *I could be out there, walking the trail, but instead, I'm in here, in therapy.* She ran her fingers through her hair, Teresa was still waiting for an answer, and from experience, she knew that she wouldn't be able to avoid responding to the question. "I feel guilty," Mariam finally said, a broad headline that covered some of what they had discussed in their prior sessions.

"You've mentioned that before. Can you tell me more about why?"

"I feel guilty about his death, I feel guilty for being glad he's gone." Mariam rubbed her right eye, "I know he was a monster, but I hate to think of myself as someone who would want to kill another person—so it's even worse that I'm responsible for his death."

"Is that why you don't want to go to the event? You feel like you'll be held responsible for that?"

Mariam tilted her head to the side, considering the possibility, "Maybe."

"But what happened wasn't your fault."

"None of it would have happened if it hadn't been for me—if I'd left Tareq months earlier, or if I'd reported him to the police—maybe he wouldn't have been there that night. Maybe he wouldn't be dead."

"It's understandable you feel that way," Teresa offered. "But the maybe game is endless—you aren't responsible for everything that happened. You're right when you said he was a monster, at least to you, and he put you and your daughter in danger. It is okay for you to be glad that he isn't here to terrorize your life anymore, the same way that it's okay for you to feel a little bit guilty about what happened to him. What you can't do though is let that stop you from experiencing your life. You talked about Dinah before, how she never stopped being herself. She left Kuwait the same way you did—but went on to London where she and John got married. Could you tell me how you feel about that, how you feel about her?"

Mariam frowned. "I'm not sure what you mean. Dinah is the only family I have—I love her, and she's like my sister," she hesitated, "certainly more of a sister than my actual sister, not that I've spoken to her in years."

"Dinah's the only one in your family that knows you've been living as Ritika Ghosh, correct? You mentioned last session that she even checked the event guest list to make sure that there wasn't anyone who'd recognize you."

"That's right on both," Mariam clarified.

Teresa crossed her arms, "Have you ever thought that you might be jealous of her?"

"Jealous of her? Of Dinah?" *Why on earth would I be jealous?*

"She has this life now, with John, but she still gets to be the same person that she always was."

"But I'm happy with my life—I have Raj and Aliya, I have my job at BookPeople which means I get to spend my whole day managing books that I love..." Mariam let her voice trail off, what could Teresa be getting at?

"Do you think you *had* to give up being Mariam Qatami to have this life?"

Mariam's shoulders sank as what Teresa was saying finally hit home. *Could she be right? Am I jealous of Dinah for still having the same identity?* "What do you mean?" she asked.

"Well for starters, don't you think Raj would love you anyway—if you were Mariam? He and your daughter love you for who you are, which is a combination of Mariam Qatami and Ritika Ghosh. Even if you're not ready to admit it to other people, you have to at least acknowledge that who you *were* helped get you to who you are now. Once you let yourself believe it, you might even be able to share it with those closest to you."

"But Mariam Qatami was a victim, a girl who couldn't fight for herself... a woman who let her family and husband bulldoze her into every decision they ever made for her. She never stood up to them, just let them run the show." *That's not who I am,* she felt like shouting to the world.

"You were nineteen, your family should have protected you instead of marrying you off to a dangerous man. They should have stood by you when you tried to walk away from him; when you told your sister about what he had done to you. It's not your fault they didn't do that, and you still managed to find the support you needed to walk away. We've been going over this for a few weeks—*you* made the decision to leave Tareq."

Teresa took a sip from her water bottle before she continued, "Sure, it was influenced by Dinah and your pregnancy, but it was also because of you. It was your decision, and you took it, so give yourself credit and acknowledge that doing that took strength and courage. You talk about Mariam Qatami as if she's a weak woman, and Ritika Ghosh as if she's strong and powerful, exactly who you want to be. Those two women are the *same* person—they're *you*, and you are strong and powerful and vulnerable and emotional. You feel guilt and fear, and none of that is anything to be ashamed of. You owe it to yourself to confront all of that reality—you can't keep disassociating from half of who you are. Keeping that part of your life a secret will always follow you, and suppressing that identity is only going to hurt you and the people that you care about—"

"But I can't go back to being Mariam Qatami … that's not even an option—all of my documents, everything here is in the name of Ritika Ghosh. That's my life now."

"I'm not saying you need to file a name change with the government, this is about *internal* acceptance and acknowledgment, not external. Mariam Qatami is still part of who you are now, not some forgotten identity that doesn't matter. You are the whole sum of who you were, and that includes growing up in Kuwait, the Gulf War, your time as Ritika, and even your time with Tareq. Pretending that that past doesn't exist doesn't serve anyone, and you can already see the pressure it's putting on your marriage."

"I don't think that I consider myself separate from who I was—I think of myself as Mariam, and it's not as if I don't remember that time," she protested. *This is going nowhere,* she thought, recalling the number of times that she had considered walking away from therapy. *It's not easy confronting some parts of yourself,* Aliya had said once as one of the takeaways from a psychology class that she'd taken during undergrad. *Dammit,* Mariam realized how much truth there was to that statement. "So, what do you want me to do?" she asked with obvious frustration.

"If you still consider yourself Mariam, and you can accept who you are, then why not share that with Raj? Why not visit Dinah and go to the embassy party? You should celebrate the end of the Gulf War, that's when your life turned around. You went from being an abused, pregnant woman, struggling to escape a terrifying husband, to a woman in a refugee camp in search of a new direction, and look who you are now. Why not revel in that? This goes back to so much of what we've been talking about, you aren't willing to affirm yourself for getting past that life. Giving yourself credit doesn't mean that you did it on your own, but it does mean that you succeeded, on your own merit and with the help of others, and I think you know that. You have a good life now. Don't you think you deserve to celebrate it?"

1990

Chapter 14

Farwaniya Hospital, Kuwait - July, 1990

Mariam awoke after her second night at the hospital—the pain made it hard to relax, even with the painkillers she was taking, but more importantly, Tareq had said that he would return this morning. She allowed herself a moment of relief when she opened her eyes to an empty room—*Maybe he can't make it today?* Immediately, she let go of the idea, not wanting to hold onto something that would only disappoint her. *He's probably just running late,* she noted the clock on the wall in front of her, which read just after seven fifteen. Tareq normally liked to be at work at exactly eight—another manifestation of his OCD. *Obsessive Compulsive Disorder.* That's what Dinah had called it anyway, she had read a book at the British Council library on different mental health problems a couple of months earlier. At first, Mariam had dismissed it as some weird psychological mumbo jumbo that couldn't be real, but when she'd started to observe Tareq's behavior in the context of what Dinah had said, the picture became clearer. She'd never told Dinah about her suspicions, only asked questions about what she had read. Enough questions that eventually she had started to believe it might actually be part of his diagnosis.

Her doctor walked into the room and snapped her out of those thoughts. "Good morning, Mariam. How are you feeling?"

"Like a herd of elephants ran over me, but better than yesterday."

"I'm glad." He picked up a clipboard at the base of her bed and flipped through the pages to review her chart. "Everything looks good. You should be all set for discharge this afternoon. And you spoke with our gynecologist Dr. Sharma yesterday? Did she answer all of your questions?"

"Yes, doctor." *If only she could tell me how to get away from the baby's father.*

"Great."

He stepped out moments before Dinah appeared. She greeted Mariam with a kiss on the cheek. "It's all set," Dinah said in a voice that sounded out of breath. "I have our guest room ready for you. I called Tareq and told him that Reema and I were both here and that the doctors want you to stay another night at the hospital. You know how he hates being around too many women… He was already running late so he said that he'd try to visit you in the evening after work, but before that, we're going to get you out of here. They said you're ready for discharge, right?"

Mariam opened her mouth to respond but was unable to process what Dinah was saying.

Dinah waved her hand in front of her face, an inch from her nose, "Earth to Mariam, we have to go. *Now.* You're ready for discharge but they haven't done the paperwork yet—that will at least create some confusion and give us a window to get you out of here before they call Tareq. But we have to leave now." She placed a plastic bag on the bed, "I brought you some clothes and a new abaya. Get dressed."

Mariam took a deep breath, a thousand thoughts running through her head. She had decided to leave Tareq, but she hadn't expected the moment to be upon her so quickly. Now that it was here, she couldn't help but hesitate before she leapt off the cliff. She bolstered her resolve and nodded. *It's now or never.*

An hour later, Mariam flopped down on the bed in Dinah's spare room, finally allowing herself to relax. She stared at the ceiling until her cousin came into the room carrying a tray with two cups of piping hot tea and a plate of biscuits. Mariam placed her hands on her belly and the realization struck her in full technicolor, *I left Tareq.* Whatever happened next, she had taken the first step to protect her baby...and herself.

Dinah set up a foldable table in front of the bed and picked up one of the teacups, after pulling up an armchair for herself. "I made hibiscus for you, with honey."

Mariam grasped the cup, searching for the words to thank her cousin, but nothing she could think of would do her feelings justice. Gingerly, she took a sip of the tea and set the cup back down.

"Dinah, I don't even know what to say. I can't thank you enough. I'm sorry I was so stubborn—you were right about Tareq—to tell me to leave him, you were right about everything." A lump formed in her throat, "Thank you for helping me. If it weren't for you..." *I'd be back with him now, probably about to get slapped again.* She couldn't bring herself to say those words aloud—at least not yet.

"I love you so much, I couldn't bear to see you suffering." Dinah stood and wrapped her arms around Mariam, squeezing her tight, as if she would never let go. When she stepped back a moment later, she rubbed her eyes before she sat down again. "Now, all we have to do is figure out what's next," she said, her eyes still wet. "What do you want to do? If you let me tell Fahad what happened, he might help us if you want to report him."

Mariam gulped a mouthful of tea, the floral sweetness offering a welcome distraction from the conversation. She knew that Dinah was right, that they couldn't afford to wait to figure out what to do. Time was on their side right now since Tareq didn't know where she was, but it wouldn't take long for him to figure it out once he realized that she had left the hospital. There were only a couple of places for her to go. She had thought about asking Dinah to take her to a hotel, but she didn't dare spend any of her money on something like that. She had kept a bank account of her own, with money that her mother had given her over the years. Tareq didn't know about it, and she hadn't touched it, so while it wasn't a lot of money, she at least had some. She looked over at Dinah, "You should tell Fahad, but I don't want to report him."

"Are you sure?"

"I just want to get out. If I can leave the country before Tareq finds out I'm pregnant...then I have a chance, a chance to be free of him. If he ever finds out though—" *He'll be after me forever.* "But you have to tell Fahad. Tareq will come here once he realizes I'm not at the hospital." She hesitated, "Do you think Fahad will help us? Help *me*?"

"We don't have much of a marriage anymore, but he's not a monster," Dinah answered in a quiet voice. "If I tell him what Tareq did to you, he'll help us."

"Thank you, thank you both."

Dinah gave her a quick nod before changing the subject, "Now where's your passport?"

Chapter 15

Salmiya, Kuwait - July, 1990

Mariam stretched her arms overhead and winced at the pain. Still, that was nothing in comparison to the last few days, she could feel her blood pressure shoot up just thinking about it. As they'd expected, Tareq had indeed come to find her. The first time, Fahad had sent him away, stating clearly that she wasn't there. He'd accepted it, but the next day he had returned.

"I checked everywhere else she could be—at Reema's and her brothers'. She has to be *here*."

When Fahad denied it again, Tareq had demanded to speak to Dinah and started to get violent. Fahad had held his own, barring him from entering the house, "I'll have Dinah call you." Fahad was several inches taller than Tareq and an intimidating figure, so, eventually, Tareq had shrunk away, only to return two days later. This time he wasn't going to take no for an answer, and he and Fahad almost came to blows until Dinah threatened to call the police.

Mariam had stayed hidden upstairs although part of her wanted to give up. Tareq had her passport locked in his safe, and without it, they kept moving in circles. She had to get out of the country, but she had no way to do that. She could try to get a new passport, but Tareq was listed as her emergency contact and she didn't want to risk the passport office informing him of the proceedings. That was still probably the only way, but Mariam was hesitant to start down that path—besides she couldn't travel until her stitches were removed. She had already used that excuse a few times, but her time would be up that afternoon. Fahad had arranged for a doctor from the hospital to come to the house to remove them, off the books.

Mariam sighed and forced herself out of bed as a wave of nausea overcame her. Morning sickness, again. She groaned and groped her way toward the bathroom where she spent the next few minutes crouched with her head over the toilet seat. Most of the time she didn't actually vomit, the wave of nausea would hit, she'd sip some soda water and it would pass, but every few days she'd find herself like this on the bathroom floor. Ten minutes later, she used the vanity to pull herself up and flushed the toilet. After a quick shower and some time in front of the mirror, she felt slightly better—enough to make the trek downstairs to the kitchen.

The rest of the morning passed quickly. Fahad left for work, and Dinah chatted with her over breakfast, then headed off to the British Council. Mariam walked around the house, realizing that she was alone—Dinah's housekeeper had gone out to run some errands and wouldn't return for another hour. She tried to find distraction with the morning paper, but found herself drawn to the window, watching the street below as her heart raced.

When will Tareq come back? She steadied herself against the windowsill, certain that he was going to return, that he would corner her in the empty house. She grabbed a knife from the kitchen, her knuckles turning white as she gripped the handle. With the knife in hand, she made her way back upstairs and locked her bedroom door. She set it on her bedside table and turned on the television—she had to pass the time somehow. Her eyes moved to the clock on the bedroom wall, Dinah would be home in three hours, she only had to make it until then.

Mariam spent some time watching *The Young and the Restless*—anything to keep her away from the window—before she gave up on the tumultuous soap opera and settled into one of Dinah's books. Not having to keep her reading hidden from anyone had been the best part of the week that she'd spent there, and she wanted to take advantage of every minute. Alone in the house, though, even reading felt like torture, she could hardly keep her attention focused for more than a page.

She heard a noise downstairs and picked up the knife and pressed her ear to the door; a wave of relief greeted her as she heard Dinah's housekeeper, Janhvi, call out, "Hello," from the stairwell.

Mariam loosened her grip on the handle and let the knife slip from her hand onto the bedside table, then slid off the side of the bed to the ground. Today was the first time that she'd been alone in Dinah's house, she'd never realized how comforting the housekeeper's presence was. She wiped her eyes and scrambled to her feet, then settled onto the bed and picked up the book again, still overwhelmed by the sense of relief. Finding the story totally unfamiliar, she had to turn back several chapters before she noticed something she recognized. She reached one of the more scandalizing scenes and had to stop to take a deep breath and drink a glass of water as she envisioned the sensual moment. *Is that what sex is supposed to be like?* Her cheeks flushed at the imagery and she read through the scene again.

Dinah finally returned around one in the afternoon, and the two of them chatted over a long lunch while they waited for the doctor to arrive. Once he did, he looked over Mariam's stitches and made quick work of removing them. Mariam asked about the pain in her left forearm that continued to plague her, and he explained that the wrist was sprained from the impact of the fall, which would take another few days to heal. The doctor asked several questions about Mariam's other symptoms—if she was having any trouble with reading or watching television. "Those are the symptoms to watch out for after a concussion," she explained.

Mariam chuckled, "The only thing I'm having issues with is morning sickness. I've had a couple of headaches, but nothing severe."

"Good," the doctor nodded. "Keep taking Panadol if you need it for the headaches and rest up. Don't do any strenuous activity until the headaches are completely gone, and if you do start to exercise, do it gradually."

"Do you think the scars will fade?" Mariam looked down at the gashes on both her arms, now more or less healed, but heavily scarred.

The doctor took a second to examine them again, then took out a prescription pad and scribbled something illegible. "This cream should help," he said as he handed the prescription over. "Don't worry, the scars will fade—eventually."

LATER, STILL ABSORBED IN HER book, Mariam heard a commotion downstairs. She made it to the edge of the stairwell before she stopped, frozen in her tracks. She could hear two voices downstairs yelling at each other in Arabic. One was Fahad's and the other—Tareq was here, *in the house.* Her blood ran cold. Her breathing turned shallow. Part of her wanted to run away, but there was nowhere to go. She couldn't help but inch forward, she had to know what was going on.

She crouched behind the upstairs railing that offered a view of about half of the entrance foyer and resisted the temptation to move to a better vantage point, lest he notice her. So far, Fahad seemed to be holding his own, shouting repeatedly that Mariam wasn't there and that Tareq needed to get out of his house. She could see Tareq in profile, and based on his stance, she guessed that he had been down one of the bottles of Scotch he kept in a hidden cabinet in the pantry. Her body quivered—Tareq angry was bad enough, but the addition of alcohol amplified the violence.

"I know she's here," Tareq yelled for at least the fourth time.

"Get out of my house," the volume of Fahad's voice had dropped now, he wasn't shouting anymore. "Get *out.*"

For a moment it seemed as if Tareq might listen, especially given Fahad's superior size, but Mariam felt as if she was watching a car about to drive over a cliff.

He won't leave. She knew it deep in her bones.

Tareq threw the first punch, a right hook to Fahad's jaw that caught him by surprise. Mariam couldn't keep track of much after that, there were punches and elbows and then the two of them fell to the ground, knocking over an antique Egyptian vase on display in the foyer. The alabaster shell exploded as it hit the floor, but the two men didn't notice. Eventually Fahad managed to pin Tareq to the ground with his forearm pressed against Tareq's neck. "Now, get out of my house," he repeated in the same cold voice. "If I see you here again, I'll have you arrested." Fahad waited a second before he released his hold on Tareq, who slid slowly across the floor and stood up with the help of the door frame. He was gone a moment later, with the sharp slam of the front door.

Mariam turned around, her back to the railing, hyperventilating and trying to get control of her breathing as black spots appeared in her vision. Her skin crawled. All she wanted to do was escape him, to never see him again—yet some part of her felt as if she should run after him, go with him and defuse the situation. She blinked away tears.

Why does this man have so much power over me? Why do I let him? She had to get away.

Mariam took a deep breath, and at that moment, resolved to go out and get a new passport. Whatever the risks, she had to take them.

I have no choice.

Chapter 16

Salmiya, Kuwait - August 1, 1990

Mariam tossed and turned into the early morning. She both relished her increased resolve and feared it. She had no idea what might be around the next bend, how she would get away from Tareq if the passport office informed him of her application. If Dinah was so convinced that they could do it, then she had to be right—there would be a way out of this. *I'll find a way,* she repeated to herself.

After Tareq had left, Dinah had tended to the cuts on Fahad's face, while the three of them sat together in the living room in silence. Mariam had thanked Fahad several times, had tried to express her gratitude for what he had done and for their help in letting her stay, but he'd responded with only a few grunts. Luckily, none of the cuts were severe, and after Dinah placed a Band-Aid on the worst of them on his forehead, he stood up, gave them a brief nod, and retreated to his study.

"Don't worry about him," Dinah said in a quiet voice, looking back at Mariam. "He's always been the strong silent type."

Mariam could see the forced chuckle; Fahad's silence was certainly one of the reasons that Dinah and his marriage had broken down. Mariam remembered vaguely from about three years earlier: Dinah in tears after a second miscarriage, how she couldn't understand why Fahad wouldn't talk to her anymore, how she'd hated the whole world. Mariam had been too young to really understand, but she had seen Dinah as she sobbed on her sister Reema's shoulder.

After a long sigh, Mariam turned on the light, giving up on sleep and grabbed the copy of *Coma* from her bedside table. She tried to read, but couldn't make much progress. She was about to turn the light out to go back to sleep—some version of "fake it till you make it"—when the ring of the telephone broke the night silence.

Who would be calling now?

Three rings later the phone stopped, Fahad or Dinah must have picked it up. Mariam turned out her bedside lamp and pulled the covers up to her chin. Even though it was peak summer with the dry desert heat of early August, the house was actually cooler than it would have been in December, with the air conditioning running at full blast. She was finally starting to relax when the bedroom door flew open.

"Dinah?" Mariam sat up and switched the light back on. The expression on Dinah's face told her that something dire had happened.

"What is it?"

"The Iraqi army just crossed the border."

2016

Chapter 17

Washington D.C. area, USA - February, 2016

Mariam looked at her watch for the fifteenth time as her flight touched down at Reagan National.

I can't believe I'm doing this, I should have let Raj or Aliya come with me. She took a deep breath and had to remind herself to let it out. *How on earth did Dinah convince me to do this?* Following the last few months in therapy, Mariam had finally felt strong enough to confront her old identity by attending the Liberation Day celebration at the Kuwaiti embassy, but now she wasn't so sure.

Over the year and a half since Dinah had come to Washington after several years in London, Mariam had considered visiting her cousin many times, each time managing to find an excuse to stay put. Dinah had come to Austin once, and they'd had an incredible time together, picking up as if no time had passed, but Mariam still struggled with the idea of touching the embassy with a ten-foot pole. Her paperwork as Ritika Ghosh was in order, and Dinah had checked and rechecked for anyone on the guest list who have known her in her past life, but Mariam's battle was entirely internal: she wanted to distance herself from her past. Her therapist, along with Raj and Aliya, had been firm though, this part of confronting her old identity—the good and the bad, of accepting that she was still a Kuwaiti and that her past would always be a part of her—was essential for her to get past her fear and nightmares. *It's the right thing,* she repeated to herself. Deep down she knew it, even if she would have preferred to hide under her blankets.

She had still been unable to open up to Raj about Tareq's abuse or how he had died—how could she be so close to Raj and yet so closed off at the same time? Her last few sessions had focused on this point, along with her fear of her old self. Rationally, she recognized that Teresa was right, that Mariam Qatami was part of who she was now, but emotionally, Mariam couldn't be more disconnected from her. That identity belonged to someone else who had died during the Iraqi invasion, a submissive woman, a victim who had let her husband hurt her and stayed with him anyway. Despite her breakthroughs in therapy, including the realization that part of her decision to leave Tareq had indeed been her own, she was still struggling with the emotional aspect of it all. Her intellectual self had caught up, but her emotional self remained leagues behind.

Regardless, Mariam clung to the hope that Teresa was right. By attending the event at the embassy and celebrating the twenty-fifth anniversary of Kuwait's liberation, she might be able to reintegrate that part of her identity into her new life. *It's only taken over twenty-five years.* She couldn't help but smile, human beings were far too complicated for their own good. The plane came to a halt in front of the gate, and she stood up as the fasten seatbelt light turned off. "At least you'll get to see Dinah," Raj had said to help convince her, although what had really propelled her forward was his other point, the one they were still dancing around.

Mariam forced herself to keep breathing, even though weeks had passed since his first outburst, she found herself incapable of processing what he had said. She had barely had the courage to talk to Teresa about it, instead focusing on work stress, her secrets, nightmares, memories—anything but the fact that the bedrock of her marriage had become unstable.

I can't believe he's felt that way all this time.

Raj's words continued to echo through her head.

...I never understood why you didn't want to take your old identity back. Dinah did and she's happy...

I've never regretted helping you. Pretending to be Ritika was so important for you to get out of Kuwait, but since then, you could have been yourself again...

I fell in love with you, Mariam—and I want to be married to you, not you pretending to be my first wife. I love you, *and that will never change, but why can't you be yourself?*

Her eyes stung as she kept her gaze ahead and pulled her carry-on bag toward the exit. Although she had vacillated on attending the event several times since first agreeing to it, those were the words that had finally pushed her over the edge, compelled her to take this trip and confront her past.

Mariam stepped onto the jet bridge. It all went back to the same point which she and Teresa had beaten to a pulp in therapy. *I have to tell him about Tareq, who we were... what he did to me. But most importantly, how he died.*

She followed the signs for ground transportation down a long corridor and onto an escalator past baggage claim, keeping her eyes out for Dinah. *I'm going to tell him,* Mariam vowed as she waved at her cousin who had just pulled up along the curve a few feet away. *But not today.* Her face burst into a smile. First, she'd get to remind herself that being Mariam Qatami might not be so bad after all.

Chapter 18

Washington D.C., USA – February, 2016

Mariam smoothed out the skirt of her floor-length burgundy dress, considering whether or not she should put on a cardigan. Her long dark hair was pulled into a low French twist that hung at the base of her neck, just off-center. She had only worn that hairdo a couple of times before, but it was one that Raj really liked—she had chosen it specifically so that he would notice when she called him on FaceTime earlier, right after she and Dinah returned from the hair salon.

"You look lovely," he'd said with a smile, although he'd neglected to comment specifically on her hairstyle. Under normal circumstances, she would have teased him about it, reminding him why she had chosen that style, even if he had forgotten that he'd once mentioned how much he liked it. With how strained things were between them, she remained silent, and they spoke only about a few mundane topics—his work, some family logistics, and their last conversations with Aliya. *Better than nothing,* Mariam rationalized, but the lack of real connection with her husband was wearing on her with every moment it continued. Raj had been such a big part of her life since they left Kuwait, even before that, and the loss of that connection left a tremendous gap, as if she were trying to walk after losing a leg.

Mariam wished Raj was standing next to her, maybe she could open up to him, tell him everything. She had no doubt that he would be kind, that he would be empathetic and understanding—along with angry that anyone could have treated her that way, much less her husband and her family.

They should have protected me, not hurt me, she repeated the words from her therapy session. She could even have let herself be angry at them, she could imagine confronting them and cornering them to tell them how much better she had, and still did, deserve.

Why wasn't I enough? What did I do to deserve to be treated that way? Did I deserve it?

Why couldn't you just love me?

With a deep breath, Mariam pushed those questions aside and ventured down the hall to Dinah's room. John had already left for poker night at a friend's house, so she opened the door immediately after knocking.

Dinah was dressed in a flowing evergreen gown that skimmed the floor, and she turned around to look at her. "Mariam, wow, I don't think you've aged at all. Do you know when the last time was that I saw you dressed like this?"

Mariam tilted her head to the side, considering when that might have been, "I don't think so. It must have been back before the war? I guess we haven't been to a party together in a while."

"I think it was when we went shopping together." Dinah broke into a wistful smile, "You tried on this incredible dress that I convinced you to buy—it was stunning, this brilliant fuchsia color." She gestured toward Mariam's dress, "Maybe a little bit more revealing than what you're wearing now." Dinah paused, "Actually you came to a diwaniya at Reema's house, maybe a month before the invasion. I think you were supposed to wear the fuchsia dress, but in the end, you decided to wear something else."

Mariam returned her smile tentatively, she remembered that diwaniya well, more than she cared to admit. She drew in a quick breath, that was when Dinah had first explicitly told her that she should leave Tareq, after he had severely wrenched her wrist because she hadn't properly organized her closet. *And then he tore up that dress because it was too revealing....* It was also the night she had crashed into the coffee table. *I'm so glad he's gone,* she thought, relieved to find that the recollection was no longer accompanied by a deep sense of guilt. *I wish he hadn't had to die for us to get away.* She looked at Dinah, grateful that they had both escaped him and built new lives for themselves after the Gulf War.

"Are you okay?" Dinah asked. "You look like you're lost in thought."

For a moment, Mariam considered telling Dinah more about therapy, about the range of emotions that she had been grappling with but decided against it. She didn't want to ruin this moment, this celebration for the two of them. "I'm fine," she answered, letting her smile widen. "Thank you for inviting me here, and for letting me use John's ticket. I know I was a pain because I wasn't sure I wanted to face all of that past, but I'm really glad I'm here. I'm so thankful we're here together."

Dinah wrapped her arms around her and squeezed her tight, "Mariam, I couldn't do this without you. This is our history, no one else's—at least not in the same way. I talked to Janhvi the other day, by the way. She's still in Mumbai, doing pretty well, and she said to say hello. Did I tell you she got a new job teaching English at a tutoring center? I'm so impressed by how well she's done—she grew up with so little."

"I thought she was working as a nanny?"

"That's the first job she got after finishing her English course, but now she's a real full-fledged teacher. She said she can't believe she earns enough money to support her daughter in university. Isn't it wonderful? After saving up over so many years as a housekeeper… You know, I'm sure she'd love to talk to you. Maybe we can call her together tomorrow?"

"Sure," Mariam agreed, uncertain if she could handle that.

Dinah hugged her even tighter, then stepped back and wiped a tear from her eye, "You're going to ruin my makeup. We better get going before I have to redo it."

"Okay," Mariam stood up with a chuckle. "One second, I'll grab my coat. Meet you downstairs."

Mariam returned to her room quickly and picked up her coat along with gloves, apprehensive about the cold February weather. She was about to head downstairs when she realized that she'd left her cardigan out on the bed. Shedding her coat, she put the cardigan on and looked at herself in the mirror. She was tempted to leave it off—while it was sleeveless, the dress wasn't very revealing—but chose not to, she felt too exposed without it. Mariam smiled at her reflection, reaffirming her decision to attend the event. She put the coat back on, her heartbeat drumming in her ears and sped downstairs to meet Dinah.

Chapter 19

Washington D.C., USA – February, 2016

Nadia paced up and down the foyer at her parents' house, glancing at her watch every couple of seconds. She considered calling out for her mom and uncle again, but her father shot her a glance from the sitting room. Nadia sighed. He was right, she had told her mother to hurry up barely five minutes earlier, and another prompt would only stress her out even more.

"All of you women fit the stereotypes so well." Uncle Tareq shuffled past her and sat down in an armchair across from her father. "You're either running late or stressed, or both."

Nadia detected his attempt at levity. She had noticed him trying to make things lighter between the two of them in their few interactions since her mother had told him that she'd secured him a ticket to the embassy party. After a quick nod to acknowledge it, she retreated into the formal living room on the opposite side of the foyer, mumbling an excuse about needing to check her shoes. She dreaded every encounter with her uncle after the way he had spoken to her that day after her mother's last set-up—the look on his face still sent a shiver up her spine. *I should have told Mom.* She sat down on the couch. She'd hesitated to sit down earlier, not wanting to wrinkle her dress any more than the car ride already would, but at this point, she had given up. Given up on the dress, on her mother, and on having a good time at the event—*Not if Uncle Tareq is coming. I just have to get this night over with.*

Nadia mulled over how hesitation had cost her the chance to tell her mom that morning. *Now it's too late,* she looked up at the ceiling, at the ugly popcorn surface above the ceiling fan. This was the only room in the house her father refused to renovate, "We never use it," he'd explained repeatedly. Nadia smiled as she remembered how many times her parents had relived that same discussion: her mother claiming that they would use it if they liked it more, and her father insisting that formal living rooms were useless pieces of the property that real estate agents used to con buyers into thinking their lives would be full of pomp and circumstance.

Tonight is actually a night of pomp and circumstance. She had heard several of her friends at the office discussing how epic the Liberation Day parties usually were. Since this one was for the twenty-fifth anniversary, everyone was expecting even bigger things. Nadia knew for a fact that there would be two live bands, a massive buffet with at least four courses of Kuwaiti specialties, and a set of dance performances, along with several songs to be sung by a famous Kuwaiti singer. While she hadn't recognized the name initially, a quick google search had confirmed how much of a big deal the singer really was. *They've spared no expense,* her father would say, quoting *Jurassic Park,* one of the movies they had watched together during her childhood. *It's too bad he's not coming,* he would have been far better company. He was also much better at cajoling her mother into getting ready on time—a trick Nadia had never managed to master. Besides, her father was more than happy to stay home, put his feet up, and watch a movie on his own, he had no interest in this sort of fancy event. He considered them more of an annoying requirement of being a prominent businessman and had welcomed the opportunity to bow out and give his ticket away.

Nadia heard footsteps coming down the stairs and almost leapt to her feet, catching herself just in time before a landing on her three-inch stiletto heels caused an accident. She rolled her eyes and gathered herself. *Let's get this over with.*

"I'm ready," her mother called from the foyer. "I don't see anyone else here who's ready, I already have my coat on."

"Very funny, Mom," Nadia returned to the foyer and pulled on her long grey overcoat.

"Is that a coat or a bathrobe?" Uncle Tareq asked as he joined them, gesturing toward the front knot tie closure on Nadia's overcoat.

"Actually, this kind of coat is quite fashionable," Nadia snapped before she could stop herself. Between her mother and him, she had lost patience with that side of the family. "Let's go, we're already late."

NADIA PULLED UP IN FRONT of the Kuwaiti embassy and glanced at her watch. They were an hour late. Sighing, she handed her keys to the valet and helped her mother out of the front passenger seat. Uncle Tareq emerged and bent over slightly, then straightened up with a grunt.

"Tareq, are you all right?" her mother asked.

"I think so," he answered with another grunt. "My stomach was hurting, Nadia's driving was rough, but I'm sure it's nothing. I'll just get something to eat inside."

If you weren't feeling well, you could have decided to stay home. Nadia reprimanded herself for being so hard on him. She inhaled and forced a smile, "We'll get you some tea and food and I'm sure you'll be okay."

His eyes narrowed, clearly not taking her statement as kind. Nadia shrugged it off, she couldn't blame him, not with how she'd been responding to his poor attempts at jokes. *Oh well.* She had no control over his reactions, she just had to make sure she was never alone with him again—she didn't want to picture what he might have done if her father hadn't appeared in time on that afternoon a month earlier.

They ventured inside, lingering in the front hallway which featured a photo exhibition on the Iraqi invasion and liberation. Nadia felt her heart skip a beat as the weight of the photos became clearer, she'd regarded this event only as a party and a celebration instead of realizing exactly what they were celebrating. She took her mom's arm as they paused in front of a photo of the oil fires set by the Iraqi troops as they retreated from Kuwait, a last blow to strike down the colony that they hadn't been able to hold onto. "I think I remember seeing that on the news," Nadia said in a quiet voice, "but I didn't understand what it was."

"You were only three years old, of course you didn't understand," her mother gave her a warm glance. "Why don't you go on inside, Sokar? I'll stay with your uncle, I think he might need more time here, but you should go in and see your friends."

Nadia hugged her mom, touched by her usage of the Arabic word for sugar, a term of endearment that her mother hadn't used since her childhood. For a moment, she pondered their relationship; her mother was able to see a side to her uncle that she didn't. "Were you close to him, when you were growing up?" she asked.

"Not really—honestly, we're not even close now, but he's lost so much. The least I can do is take care of him, show him some respect. He lost his wife during the war too…."

"I can't imagine him with a wife. I wonder what she was like," Nadia looked over at him wondering if she should perhaps show him some more consideration. *He must have had a heart back then, maybe that's why he's so jaded. He lost his wife and his freedom all at once.*

"They were only married a short time, I only saw her once, at their wedding. I can't imagine what he's been through." Her mother gestured toward the end of the hallway exhibit, "Go on, my dear, have fun. We'll be all right."

Nadia was about to disagree, but she discarded the idea—perhaps she should be kinder to her uncle, but she didn't trust herself to do that. Besides, she did need to greet her boss and co-workers. *And maybe even enjoy the party…*

"If I don't see you inside in a few minutes, I'll come back to check on you. I love you, Mom." After giving her mom a kiss on the cheek, Nadia turned around to head into the main hall for the party.

Chapter 20

Washington D.C., USA - February, 2016

Dinah raised a glass of sparkling apple cider and clinked her glass to Mariam's, "It's not as good as champagne, but it's still quite nice." She leaned in to whisper, "A colleague of mine hid a few bottles of the real stuff in the audiovisual room down the hall if you want some."

"I'm okay," Mariam chuckled. She adjusted her cardigan, playing with the button in the front.

"Why don't you take off the cardigan? It's so warm in here with all these people."

"No, it's fine." Mariam took two sips of the cider and shrugged, "It's not bad, actually. I think it's similar to what I used to drink once in a while when Aliya was little. Raj would get these bottles for me from the grocery store in Boulder."

"Are you all right?" Dinah sensed something off in the way her cousin mentioned his name. "How are you and Raj doing?"

"It could be better, I guess. I've been struggling, honestly—he can't understand why I kept on using his first wife's name, and I don't know what to tell him."

Dinah's frown deepened, "You never told him about Tareq? Why not?"

"I don't want him to see me that way—Tareq made me the victim, you know." Mariam held back tears and looked away, "Sometimes I wonder if it was my fault, if I'm the reason he behaved that way." She gestured to stop Dinah from interrupting, "Look, rationally, I know that's insane, but I can't help feeling that way. It's something I've actually been talking to a therapist about."

"I didn't know that." Dinah recognized how much her cousin was opening up, "John and I saw one too, you know—not recently, but a couple of years after I moved to London to be with him. In a way I resented him, and we needed to deal with those feelings."

"You resented him?"

"He got out of Kuwait so much faster, and I couldn't go with him. The British embassy evacuated their staff immediately, so just like that, he was gone. I know we got to speak once in a while, but I felt like I had been through so much more, especially with those months you and I spent at the camp together. It was hard for him to understand how traumatic that was, and I had trouble accepting that he couldn't have taken me with him. We were in love, but we weren't married. Plus, I felt guilty about Fahad, what he did for us—and how, in a way, it was easier for me to be with John because of that." Dinah stopped, feeling raw, talking about Fahad was still painful. "Do you mind if we talk later?"

Mariam took her hand, "Of course. It's probably for the best, we're both so weepy."

"Let's focus on enjoying the party." Dinah gazed around the room, "Oh look, there's my friend Nadia, she's lovely. Come on, I'll introduce you."

Dinah greeted Nadia with a kiss on either cheek and stepped back to admire her gown, "You look beautiful, I love this dress. This is Mariam; Mariam, this is Nadia, a close friend of mine from the office. She's the one who keeps backup Nespresso pods for when they run out upstairs."

"It's great to meet you," Mariam said to Nadia with a smile.

"Where's your family?" Dinah asked. "Didn't you say your mom and uncle were coming? I want to meet them."

"Sure. Did you see the exhibition hall? They're back there."

Dinah shook her head, "Actually, no, we came in from the back entrance, so I forgot all about it. Mariam, you should see it, I saw some of the photos while they were setting it up yesterday, it's pretty amazing."

Mariam gestured toward the far side of the hall, "That sounds wonderful, lead the way."

"I didn't realize my family was that exciting, but I know my mom would love to meet you, Dinah. I've told her a lot about you," Nadia agreed. "Follow me."

1990

Chapter 21

Salmiya, Kuwait – August 2, 1990

The Iraqi army just crossed the border.

Fifteen minutes after hearing the news, Mariam was sitting in the living room with Dinah, trying to process what had just happened. Fahad had appeared for a moment, then disappeared into his study, on the phone with his business partner.

"Are you sure?" Mariam asked, looking at Dinah. Maybe asking the question would make it less of a reality.

"They came across the Abdali border an hour ago. Fahad spoke to one of his site engineers who works near there. They moved quickly… came in and took Bayan Palace."

"And you're sure the Emir and his family are gone?"

How could they abandon us? Mariam squashed her urge to ask the question. The Emir and the royal family had fled, for better or worse, leaving Kuwait's population to fend for themselves under the occupation.

"I'm glad they got away," Dinah answered. "They would only have been killed if they'd stayed. Maybe this way, they can get help…maybe the UN can get the Iraqis to leave…" Her voice trailed off, neither of them had any idea what that would mean.

Mariam stared at her hands, kicking herself for not getting out of the country when she'd had the chance. *If I'd only applied for a new passport like they told me to.* She bit her lip, thinking of her baby. *I need to get her out of here. She has to grow up safe.* Mariam was acutely aware how much her dream had influenced her. The baby was already a girl, and her name was Aliya. She shrugged off the possibility it was a boy. Regardless of whether the baby was a boy or a girl, she would love it more than anything in this world, and somehow, she would get her to safety. This was not the world her baby was going to be born into. Mariam let her imagination run for a moment, recalling the travels that she and her mother had joked about taking together. *I will take them.* An image of her mother appeared in her head. *I'll take them with your granddaughter, Mom.* The memory comforted her, and Mariam reassured herself as she was sure her mother would have. *This is not going to defeat me. I won't let it.* There was a way out, and she was going to find it.

Chapter 22

Salmiya, Kuwait - The next morning, August, 1990

Mariam awoke with a crick in her neck, curled up in a ball in the corner of the living room couch. She moved slowly, wincing as her stiff muscles reacted. She stood quietly and padded out of the room toward the bathroom, Dinah was still asleep in the armchair at the coffee table, and she wasn't sure where Fahad had gone.

Once she reached the bathroom, Mariam splashed cold water on her face and stared at her reflection hoping to retrieve her determination from the night before. *This is not going to defeat me,* she said to herself again, first in her head, then aloud, but the words didn't have the same power they'd had at three in the morning. She sighed and returned to the living room, where she was about to wake Dinah when she heard a commotion outside.

Reacting to the noise, Mariam stepped out into the garden, ignoring the wave of heat that greeted her. Without the insulated doors blocking out the noise, she could hear the soldiers on the street bellowing triumphantly. *"Hadha al Eiraq"*—"This is Iraq now," they exclaimed in Arabic. "Long live Saddam. Kuwaitis, this is Iraq now."

Mariam shuddered and crept toward the garden wall, grateful that it stood at over six feet. Behind the solid cement, the soldiers wouldn't be able to see her, but she could see through the joint in the wall. There were four trucks laden with soldiers going up and down the street.

She looked up to see a helicopter flying low in the sky. It descended so far that she could see a group of soldiers carrying machine guns, circling the neighborhood three times. It drowned out the chanting, then rose again and faded into the distance.

Mariam's stomach was in knots as her attention returned to the street in front of the house. The soldiers had restarted their chant, this time with even more gusto. She watched transfixed as a group of about ten jumped to the ground and forced through the gate of a house across the street using a pair of boltcutters to get past the lock. She couldn't see much more, they disappeared behind the walls, but she could hear the screams from the house. Dinah joined her in the yard and grabbed her hand, the two of them watching in horror.

Mariam wasn't sure how long she stood there, glued to the spot as another group of soldiers repeated the same process to get into the next house and then the next, moving down the street toward them. Mariam turned to her cousin. *We should leave*, she thought to say, but fear had stolen her voice and the words wouldn't come.

Dinah's housekeeper Janhvi ran out into the yard and grabbed Dinah's other hand, "Madam, we have to go. Sir said we should go. We need to get out of here. They'll be at this house any second."

Mariam heard the words, but she was still unable to react. She had to be dreaming, how could there be Iraqi soldiers approaching their doorstep? The situation was so far from any reality she could ever have imagined. A second later, the meaning started to register, and she repeated Janhvi's words.

"We have to go. Dinah, we need to get out of here. Is there anywhere we can hide?"

Dinah looked as stunned as Mariam had felt moments earlier, so she nudged her hard, "We need to leave."

Before Dinah could react, a gunshot woke her from the spell, the crack echoed through the air from across the street. Janhvi yanked Dinah's arm and gestured for Mariam to follow her. She led them to the side gate of the garden and out into the narrow alley that ran between their house and the neighboring one. Large dumpsters and trash cans lined the walls and they crouched behind one of them. With the narrowness of the alley and the size of the dumpsters, the soldiers wouldn't be able to see them from the street ahead.

Mariam peered around the side of the bin, attempting to discern what was happening on the street. She could hear the shouting which had continued more or less nonstop, "Kuwaitis, this is Iraq now," like a video playing on loop.

A truck pulled up in front of the alley and Mariam's heart stopped. She had convinced herself that Dinah's house was somehow invisible to the soldiers. Some part of her still felt as if this was some sort of nightmare and that she would eventually wake up.

Mariam heard her cousin's breathing turn even more shallow. She placed her hand on Dinah's shoulder and gave it a gentle squeeze, wishing there was something that she could say or do.

"Where's Fahad? Where's Fahad?" Dinah whimpered, her eyes moving frantically between Mariam and Janhvi. "Where is he?"

"Madam, shh," Janhvi hissed. "Sir is back at the house, he said to help you both hide."

"He'll be okay," Mariam said softly to Dinah, wishing she could be more convincing.

Chapter 23

Salmiya, Kuwait – August, 1990

Fahad looked down at the backyard from the window of the second-floor landing and let out a sigh of relief as Dinah, Janhvi, and Mariam disappeared into the alley. *Thank God.* He had no idea what the Iraqi soldiers on the street would do to them, and his one thought had been to get them to safety. Now that they were at least hiding, he could consider what to do next. Perhaps he should run himself, join them in the alley? The soldiers would move along once they had ransacked the house.

A surge of panic gripped him, and he bolted toward the steps; flying, panting as he reached the first-floor landing. He willed his legs toward the backyard just as a loud creak came from the front yard where the soldiers had pushed through the gate. He'd been meaning to have the joints oiled so that it wouldn't make such a jarring noise, but now he thanked his procrastination as he rushed toward the back door. *Just a few more steps.*

That thought was his last before he found himself faceplanted on the living room floor. He cursed the unanticipated step and sprung to his feet.

They're here! Move! he commanded himself. The living room

suddenly seemed immense as he fought for breath. Finally, Fahad reached the back door and fumbled with the lock. He jerked it several times. *Come on, you son of a…* finally the bolt gave. He was just about to step outside when a shot rang out and a bullet embedded itself in the drywall inches above his head.

"Freeze, Kuwaiti!" a voice demanded.

FAHAD KNELT ON THE GROUND with his hands clasped behind his head, trying to maintain his composure as a group of soldiers spread out throughout his house. He couldn't see them all, but there had to be at least five. A loud thud reverberated from the floor above. *Six,* he realized there must be at least one more upstairs.

The two in the living room—besides the one pointing a gun at him—had torn apart the cabinets that ran alongside the dining table. He'd heard the sound of glasses shattering as they threw them to the floor, just for fun. They had found his liquor collection, in a hidden compartment behind the glasses, and were passing a bottle of what looked like Johnny Walker Black Label back and forth, along with several bags of Nice Kitco chips from the cabinet below. The table was already covered with the crumpled-up remnants of four or five other empty bags. Even from his precarious position, Fahad was amazed by how much they seemed able to consume—in what couldn't have been more than five minutes they had already eaten and drunk what would have taken a month for him and Dinah to get through. *They could have gone for the quality single malt, and they went for Black Label.* Fahad dismissed the point, wishing that was all that he had to worry about, he could always get more liquor, but not if he was in prison. *Or dead,* he repressed the bitter thought.

He looked out the corner of his eyes toward the backyard. He wasn't sure if Dinah and Mariam were still in the alley outside or if Janhvi had taken them elsewhere. He wasn't sure which was better—three women found wandering the streets could be just as bad as being found at the house, he had to hope that they would get away. He had to keep the soldiers from searching the backyard, if they did, they might find the side gate to the alley. If the girls were still hiding out there, that would be the worst possible outcome. Fahad suppressed a shudder, he didn't want to find out what would happen if the soldiers found them.

Chapter 24

Salmiya, Kuwait - August, 1990

Fahad cried out as his right shoulder slammed into the ceramic tiles of his living room. His left eye smarted from the impact of the blow, and it stung as he blinked, but it was nothing compared to the searing pain running through his shoulder. His right arm hung limp; he could no longer hold it over his head.

The beatings had started only a few minutes before, but he could hardly remember what his body felt like when it was pain-free. The soldier who had punched him—Fahad had lost count of how many times—looked like he had barely gone through puberty, he couldn't be older than sixteen or seventeen. His superior, the lieutenant—Fahad heard the soldier call him Mulazim—who had been barking the orders, appeared to be in his early thirties, but barely seemed more intelligent than the one dealing the punches.

Fahad found his focus coming in and out of consciousness. His chin bounced off the tile and his head spun, coming into focus on the swollen big toe of one of the younger soldiers, standing a few feet away. Fahad realized that the soldier wasn't even wearing real shoes, just what looked like a pair of bathroom slippers. The stream of normal thoughts dissipated an instant later as he jolted forward from another punch.

Fahad spat out blood and tried to form words, the pain in his jaw was agonizing as he opened his mouth. "I'll give you anything you want," he finally managed. "What do you want?"

The lieutenant drained the bottle of Black Label, tossing it behind him. It snickered and he shattered. "We already have what we want, Kuwaiti. All that's left is for you to admit that you're an Iraqi now, that we have control."

Fahad flinched, even in his beaten state, acquiescing seemed unfathomable. He realized now what the lieutenant wanted: submission and control.

The lieutenant leaned over, bringing his face close to Fahad's. His breath stank of raw onions and Fahad had to stop himself from recoiling. Instead, he shut his eyes, anticipating the next punch.

Footsteps on the staircase distracted the lieutenant as another soldier appeared and spoke to him in a quiet voice. Fahad strained his ears to pick up what they were saying—what were they planning to do with him? Could he bring himself to say those words?

The lieutenant looked at him with a cunning smile. "Private Rahim here was upstairs. You have quite the lovely house, beautiful bedrooms." He paced up the foyer and stopped as his smile widened, "And lovely windows. Do you know what you can see from one of your windows?"

The question felt like a knife to the heart. They could see Dinah and Mariam hiding in the alley outside.

Any strength that Fahad still had disappeared, he felt it seep out of him, still clinging to the hope that they might have gotten away. *Please. Please, God.* His mind flashed back to several years ago, one day when he and Dinah had had lunch together in the backyard. They were happy then, before all of the difficulties conceiving and the subsequent miscarriages. He knew she didn't love him anymore, that he no longer felt as he had then, but he still cared about her. She didn't deserve to be raped by these soldiers, and Mariam was barely more than a child. *Please, God,* he begged the sky again.

The lieutenant's eyes narrowed, "You won't answer? I'll tell you. It looks like there's an alley that runs alongside this house. But that's not the only thing hiding in the alley—there are some trash bins and three lovely ladies. It's so hot outside, they must be having a difficult time." He fanned his hand at his face, "Maybe we should go out and get them? Bring them in here to the air conditioning?"

Fahad trembled. "Have mercy," he whispered. "Let them go. They've done nothing wrong. I'll give you anything—anything—you want. There's a safe upstairs with gold jewelry, you can have the rest of my liquor collection—I have more in a cabinet in the kitchen. Just please, don't hurt them." He swallowed again, then repeated, "I'll give you anything."

The lieutenant drummed his fingers against his pant leg for a few seconds before he spoke to one of the younger soldiers, "Get him upstairs." He turned toward Fahad, "Show me the jewelry. Maybe it's enough to buy their sanctuary."

Chapter 25

Salmiya, Kuwait - August, 1990

Fahad watched as the Iraqi lieutenant dumped Dinah's jewelry boxes out onto the bed and rifled through them. He picked up a white gold necklace with a series of diamonds nestled in the band and pocketed it, then examined a ruby pendant. Fahad felt the pinch, recalling how his mother had given that to Dinah shortly after their wedding, a piece that had been given to her by his father before he died. *I was supposed to give that to my daughter.* He hadn't seen it in so long he had almost forgotten it.

"Seems as if you like this one," the lieutenant let it dangle from his hand. He glanced at his pocket, then pursed his lips and inspected a makeup bag from Dinah's dressing table. "This will do nicely," he emptied its contents onto the bed, and stuffed the pendant along with several more pieces of jewelry into it, before shoving the whole thing into his jacket pocket.

"Is this all?" the lieutenant gave Fahad a stern look. "A rich man like you, with this house—I would have thought there'd be more."

"The rest is at the bank…my wife has a safety deposit box." Fahad considered saying more, telling the soldier about the other safe, the one in his office but decided against it. There was only one piece of jewelry in there, and he would have gladly given it up, but the other items in that safe were far too valuable—that was where he kept their passports. Their Kuwaiti ones were apparently useless now, but their British ones still had to be worth something. Fahad had lived in London as a teenager; his father had worked at Barclays Bank there for several years. He'd rarely used his British passport other than to avoid visa restrictions when traveling in Europe, but now those documents were worth more than all of the jewelry they owned. He had to protect them. *It's too late for me, but not for her.*

The Iraqi lieutenant seemed to debate that point in his mind for a second before he rolled his eyes. "Get him out of here," he shouted to one of the junior soldiers.

A FEW MINUTES LATER, FAHAD'S skin went prickly as two soldiers dragged him out the front door onto his patio where the sun was beating down. He squinted, it took his eyes a few moments to adjust to the bright sunlight. When his vision began to clear, he kept his gaze focused ahead of him, other than a short glance toward the side wall out of the corner of his eye. The girls were probably just on the other side, although he prayed that they had taken the opportunity to run. *If only.* He resisted the urge to sigh, it's not as if there was a safe place for them to go. All they could do was to run and hope.

Fahad's stomach did a flip as he wondered if he had done enough to satisfy the Iraqi lieutenant. *They'll take the jewelry and the alcohol, and let me and the girls go,* he wanted so badly to believe.

"It's time, Kuwaiti," the lieutenant said, snickering. "You still have to say it—you're an Iraqi now, and you serve me, you serve Saddam. Say it, or I'll send my men into that alley right now."

Fahad opened his mouth and shut it for a second, gathering his determination. *You have to do this… for Dinah.*

"I'm an Iraqi," he whispered.

"Louder."

"I'm an Iraqi now. I serve Saddam."

"Again, louder."

"Ana Eiraqi…"—"I'm an Iraqi. I serve you, and I serve Saddam," Fahad coughed, almost choking on the words.

"Good. Now lean over and kiss my boot." The lieutenant moved closer to him so that his boot was less than a foot from where Fahad was kneeling on the ground.

Fahad shut his eyes and leaned forward, a tear mixing with the sweat and grime that covered his face. *For Dinah,* he thought as his hands grasped either side of the colonel's boot. *For Dinah,* he brought his lips to the stiff leather toe and pushed himself back into his upright kneeling position. *Don't spit,* he could barely stop himself but somehow maintained control. He made eye contact with the lieutenant. *Please, let this be over now.*

The lieutenant sniggered and motioned to one of his men, "Search the alley, find the women and bring them to me." He turned back toward Fahad, "Your luck has run out, Kuwaiti. Those women are mine for resisting arrest, and there's nothing you can do to save them." He pulled a revolver from a holster at his waist, pointed it toward Fahad, and cocked the hammer.

"Dinah, run!" Fahad shouted as loud as he could before the lieutenant pulled the trigger.

Don't let me die for nothing.

2016

Chapter 26

Washington D.C., USA - February, 2016

Nadia looked around when they entered the exhibit hall searching for her mom and uncle. They continued down the hall past the painting of the oil fires she had been looking at earlier, then on into the extension. When they reached the end of the exhibit, she frowned, "Hmm, maybe we passed them on our way here?"

She turned back toward the other entrance and stopped to glance at her phone, "Huh, it seems like we just missed them," her brow furrowed. "My mom just sent me a message that she decided to take my uncle home, he's not feeling well. I'm surprised she didn't let me know beforehand, I would have driven them."

"She probably wanted you to stay and have a good time. I'm sorry we didn't get to meet them." Dinah gave her a considerate look, "I definitely want to meet her some other time. I hope your uncle's okay."

"I think so—he said his stomach hurt a little, but it didn't seem like anything serious. Maybe things got a little too emotional for him?" Nadia glanced at Mariam and explained, "My uncle was a P.O.W. so he wanted some extra time in here. It's an amazing exhibit, but it's incredibly sad."

"Of course, I'm so sorry," Mariam said.

"It's okay, he's fine, I guess. She just sent another message not to worry," Nadia looked up from her phone with a relieved expression. "He's just a bit worn out, so he needs to rest at home. She sent me three messages repeating that I should have fun." Nadia shook her head. "Moms are so sweet."

"They are," Dinah agreed, giving Mariam a knowing glance.

"I have to admit, I don't mind that they left," Nadia continued. "I'm not that close to him. Honestly, he can be a bit of a control freak, and I'm not really the best at handling it. Mom says I should take it easy on him, but that's easier said than done, sometimes. I shouldn't speak too poorly of him though, I know he's been through a lot, more than I can imagine. He's just a little intense."

"I understand, we all have those relatives," Dinah nodded. "Let me know if you need anything for him, tonight or this weekend. It's not always easy to take care of family."

"Thank you." Nadia raised her glass. "Anyway, we should celebrate, that's what tonight is for."

"Absolutely, we'll meet another time," Dinah touched her glass to Nadia's.

"Definitely, I bet she'll like you more than she likes me. Anyway, let's take some pictures together. You both look amazing."

Chapter 27

Washington D.C., USA - Three days later, March, 2016

Mariam was on a high as she raised her glass across the table from Dinah and Nadia. "To both of you," she beamed, "thank you for showing me such a good time in D.C." She took a sip, savoring the earthy tones of the Nero D'Avola wine. "Have I told you how much I love this wine?"

Dinah and Nadia both burst out laughing, and Dinah said, "Yes, my dear, I think you have... maybe a few times."

"What can I say, I'm a lightweight," Mariam giggled and looked sheepishly back at her glass before taking another swig.

"Don't worry, we're not far behind you," Nadia continued to chuckle. "Hopefully they'll be ready to seat us soon."

Mariam craned her neck to look around the Il Pizzico restaurant, "I think so—they said it would be about thirty minutes and it has to have been that long. I can't wait to try the food; this place looks incredible." She drained her glass and set it down with a pouting expression. "We should *not* order another bottle, right?"

"I think we should," Nadia placed her empty glass on the table as well.

"Not until we get some food in us," Dinah insisted. "Ugh, I sound so old." She turned to Nadia and smiled sadly, "Next to you, I guess I am. How's your uncle doing?"

Nadia shrugged, "He's okay—really hard to read. He's staying with my parents this week, so I went home last night to see him. He seems fine, but my mom is still worried. She just worries about him—he won't see a therapist but obviously, he's been through hell, he was held prisoner in Baghdad for three years. He also lost his wife during the Gulf War, so he's had a really tough life."

Mariam nodded, "If there's any way to convince him to go to therapy, it's worth it," she said in a soft voice.

Dinah squeezed her hand and explained to Nadia. "We had a tough time getting out of Kuwait. We stayed at this Indian refugee camp for a while, and eventually managed to get out."

"Wow, I didn't know that. So that's how you two know each other?" Nadia asked.

"We also grew up together, but yes." Dinah answered.

"I didn't realize—here I've been talking about my uncle, but you've both been through so much, too," Nadia looked startled. "Dinah, I'm surprised you never told me, all you said was that you were evacuated through Jordan. How long were you at the refugee camp?"

"A couple of months. That's actually where Mariam met her husband."

"That's so romantic," Nadia exclaimed. "It's nice to hear stories like that—that people can meet even in those sorts of crazy circumstances."

"It *was* pretty romantic," Mariam agreed, wishing it hadn't also been so complicated.

Before Nadia could ask for more details—the fact that she wanted to hear the whole story was written all over her face—a waiter approached to take them to their table. Mariam placed her credit card on the bar and tried to catch the bartender's eye. "Could you close out our tab?"

Nadia picked up the card and waved it closer to the bartender. She glanced at it before handing it to him, "Is Mariam your nickname?"

"It's actually my middle name, my first name's Ritika, but I usually go by Mariam. I don't know why—it's always been that way." *This is no big deal,* she consoled herself, *she knows your real name, so what?*

Chapter 28

Washington D.C., USA – March, 2016

Nadia stopped in front of Dinah's desk to say hello to her and Mariam. "Are you leaving for the airport soon?"

"We're going to grab some lunch first. Would you like to join us?"

"I wish I could," Nadia answered. "I promised my mom and uncle I'd give them a tour of the building today, so I'm on my way to greet them. If you're still here, I'll bring them over? My mom was so disappointed that she didn't get to meet you both at the party."

"We're a little tight on time, but yes, definitely, if they're here right now. Dinah's just finishing something up before we leave."

"Amazing," Nadia beamed, "I'll go get them." She sped downstairs, grateful for any opportunity to incorporate distractions into her interactions with her uncle. *At least he's not so bad when Mom's around,* but she still wasn't looking forward to spending any time with them. Uncle Tareq was such a control freak, he noticed if even the most minute detail was out of place and turned it into a big deal. When she had gone home to see him the day after the Liberation Day celebration, her mother had requested that she make coffee for everyone, which Nadia had done. Afterward she'd forgotten to put the Bialetti percolator back into the cabinet—it had been too hot to clean when she poured the coffee—so she left it to cool on the stovetop instead. The admonishment she received from her uncle was worse than all the arguments she'd had with her parents during her entire teenage rebellion period combined. He had the same chilling glint in his eyes when he spoke to her, but this time her parents were in the next room, so she didn't have to suffer through it for long. Nadia shuddered, suspecting she would never be over the menacing look. She steadied herself against the stairwell railing and covered the last few steps to the entrance.

Just a short tour, no big deal, it'll be over soon enough.

"Hi Mom, hi Uncle," Nadia said after she signed them in with security. After some small talk in the lobby, she motioned toward the elevator. "Normally I'd take you around this level first so that you can see the big hall where the party was, but Mom, I know you wanted to meet my friends. A couple of them have to leave pretty soon, so how about we go up to my cubicle first?"

Chapter 29

Washington D.C., USA - March, 2016

Mariam glanced at her watch, then looked over at Dinah who was still in the midst of typing out a long email. *Looks more like an essay.* She nudged Dinah, "I have to leave for the airport soon, and I'm hungry. Can you finish the email later?"

Dinah looked up with an apologetic look, "Sorry, sorry. I'm almost done—besides, didn't you just tell Nadia we'd meet her family?"

"I didn't realize how late it is. My flight's in less than three hours, so with the time to eat, come back here to grab my suitcase, then get to the airport, it cuts things a little too tight. Would you mind meeting them later? You can blame me, of course."

"All right, let's go," Dinah stood and grabbed her coat. They were halfway toward the stairwell when Dinah patted her pocket. "One second, I left my phone on my desk." She darted back, picked up her phone and walked toward the stairwell to meet Mariam. As she passed the elevator, she pointed toward the floor meter climbing toward them. "That must be Nadia," she called out to Mariam, who was a few feet away at the entrance to the stairwell. "Why don't we just say hello?"

Mariam shook her head. There was no such thing as a quick hello in Kuwaiti culture. She gestured toward the stairwell door, indicating for Dinah to hurry.

"Okay, okay, I'm here," Dinah said when she reached her, pretending to be out of breath.

As the door was closing, Mariam heard the elevator chime. She was glad she didn't have to greet Nadia's mother and uncle. *The inevitable discussion—Kuwait before the Gulf War, the refugee camp, etc., etc.*, she had no desire to treat it as a normal conversation topic. *I just want to go home.*

1990

Chapter 30

Salmiya, Kuwait - August, 1990

The gunshot jolted Mariam out of her panic.

We have to get away.

As if she could read her mind, Janhvi jumped up and pulled Dinah to her feet, "Madam, we have to go. *Now.*"

Dinah's face was ashen, and she seemed unable to speak, but they didn't have time to console her. Mariam grabbed Dinah's other arm and dragged her along, letting Janhvi lead them down the alley. She had no clue where they were going, but Janhvi looked as if she had some idea. Mariam compelled her legs to move faster. Dinah was essentially a deadweight, but at least she wasn't on the ground sobbing.

"This way," Janhvi said. At the end of the alley, she turned left and went past four houses. She stopped at the fifth, opening the back gate and ushering them into the yard. "This house is under renovation so hopefully the soldiers won't bother with it." She gestured toward the rundown home, which looked empty—scaffolding on both sides of the structure blocked the view from the road.

Mariam and Dinah followed her into the house through a door which was slightly off of its hinges. They all collapsed onto the living room floor and Janhvi plugged a conveniently nearby fan into the wall outlet and turned it on. Fortunately, it worked. Mariam sank to her knees in front of it, letting the cold air blow straight into her face for a few seconds before she felt functional. She moved aside so that Dinah could take her spot and squeezed her cousin's shoulder gently. *I'm so sorry,* she wanted to say, but the words would have so little impact that she didn't bother. Dinah knew that she was there for her, the gesture and the touch had already told her as much, and there was no point in forcing the onslaught of emotion that would be coming soon enough. Mariam had to admit to herself that she wanted to stave it off as long as possible. Dinah couldn't be an emotional wreck if they were going to get through the rest of the day. *Not that I have any idea how to do that.* Mariam felt a wave of panic about to descend and tamped it down as much as she could.

Mariam shifted her legs and stretched out, then repositioned herself against the wall and wiped her hand across her forehead. Even though the house wasn't air conditioned, simply being out of the August sun was a blessing, and a few moments later she was able to regain coherent thought. She looked around the room and noticed that there were several spots along the wall that were considerably less dusty than the rest and glanced at Janhvi. "You've been her before," she realized. "That's how you knew to bring us here."

"The owner stopped renovations last week because he was waiting for some fixtures to arrive from Switzerland. Some of the other maids and I came here to chat a few times."

A different kind of hideaway, for happier times. Mariam sighed. She shut her eyes, realizing how exhausted she was for the first time in hours. She and Dinah had been up most of the night after the news had come in, so it was no wonder the exhaustion had hit her now that the adrenaline was wearing off. Mariam started to gag and stumbled outside to the garden wall where she retched into the bare soil between two wilted palm trees.

Fahad is dead. He died to protect us.

When the vomiting ceased, she fell back onto the ground, panting.

When Mariam awoke a few hours later, the sun hung low on the western horizon—the worst of the midday heat was now past. She rose slowly, careful not to make too much noise. Dinah was still fast asleep, and she wanted to talk to Janhvi alone. *We need a plan.*

She placed her hand on Janhvi's shoulder and gently shook her.

Her eyes fluttered open, "Madam?"

"Oh for goodness sake, you saved us, call me Mariam. Thank you, for bringing us here."

Janhvi lowered her eyes and Mariam asked, "What do you think we should do? Where can we go?" She gestured around the living room, "We can't exactly stay here."

"I don't know, Madam Mariam."

Mariam sighed, not bothering to restate that there was no need to call her "Madam" as she racked her brain for ideas. The first step was for them to find somewhere they could stay that actually had resources. She glanced outside. The backyard was eerily empty and quiet, and she wondered whether the danger of the day had passed. Would there be bodies beyond the boundary wall? What would greet them when they left this spot of relative safety? An idea occurred to her: once darkness fell, there was an old bakala convenience store not far from Dinah's house where they could get food and water. But then where? They'd have to find a place to take shelter—perhaps Reema's house? It was in a different neighborhood, so maybe it had not been raided? It would be a long walk, but they could make it.

We have to—it's not like we have anywhere else to go.

Mariam attempted to think of alternatives but came up blank. *We'll make it, the soldiers can't be executing* all *the Kuwaitis, we would have heard more gunshots, even from here.* The rest of the day had been remarkably quiet, especially in comparison to that morning—she had heard the soldiers chanting when she'd come in and out of her nap, but there'd been no more gunshots. She exhaled, relieved at the semblance of a plan, "We'll go to the bakala down the street, then get to my sister's house. We can stay there for a few days while we figure out what to do."

"Okay, Madam—"

"Just Mariam, Janhvi. And thank you again, for bringing us here. You really *did* save us."

"Welcome."

Mariam woke up Dinah, running over the plan quickly. Dinah looked at her with a blank expression.

"We have to go back to the house."

"Why?"

"My passport, Fahad kept it in the safe in his study. I have to get it."

"Your passport, why?" Mariam frowned. *Why on earth would Dinah want to go back to the house?* At best, Fahad had been taken prisoner—*or worse*—and the soldiers could have taken refuge at the house.

"My British passport, Fahad wouldn't have let them find it, I know it. I have to get it. Besides, I'm sure the bakala is closed." Dinah stood up, "I'm ready," she said in a quiet but firm voice.

Mariam considered protesting but examined her cousin's face, impressed at the determination she saw there. She nodded and they headed for the backyard.

Chapter 31

Salmiya, Kuwait – August, 1990

Mariam fought to keep her calm as Janhvi opened the side door into Dinah's backyard. The streets had been quiet on their return, and the soldiers appeared to have dispersed, but she still felt as if they could be lurking around any corner. She had to keep it together for Dinah.

"Wait," she whispered to Janhvi. "We have to make sure the soldiers are gone." She shut the door behind them and listened. After several seconds, she exchanged a glace with Janhvi and nodded toward the house. With the soldiers gone, it might even be safe to stay there until they could come up with a better plan. That thought brought her a moment of comfort until she remembered what had happened to Fahad.

And where.

Once inside the living room, Mariam was struck by how much the soldiers had destroyed in such a short time. Evidence of the ransacking was everywhere, in the broken glass that crunched under their feet, to the bags of chips and empty bottles strewn across every empty surface. Taking it all in, she realized that what little supplies had been at the house were now gone. She turned and addressed them both, "Dinah, I want you to go upstairs and pack some things. Janhvi, I want you to do the same." Her voice trailed off as she recalled Fahad shouting followed by the gunshot, she didn't want to consider what had happened to him. She trudged on, "We can't stay here. We have to go somewhere safe, somewhere with supplies, and access to food. With the bakala closed, there's nowhere nearby to restock. For now, I think we should go to Reema's until we can come up with a better plan. Her house isn't that far, and we can hide out in her cellar for a while." Reema kept her basement stocked with canned goods and water; she had always been paranoid—now that paranoia seemed like a blessing.

Mariam waited until Dinah disappeared up the stairs, thankful that her cousin had listened. Once she was past the first-floor landing, Mariam braced herself and made her way to the front of the house. The shot they had heard from the alley had come from the *front* yard. She had to see what had happened.

THE SIGHT THAT GREETED HER when she stepped out of the front door was worse than she could have imagined. Fahad's body was splayed out against a step on the patio, a single shot through his head. Mariam grabbed a blanket from one of the outdoor chairs and moved quickly, she had to at least cover the body before Dinah saw it. She made her way to the edge of the patio and tossed the throw, doing her best not to look at him. Not that she would have recognized him anyway; his face was so obscured by cuts and bruises and his shirt was torn and covered in dirt and dust.

With a deep breath, Mariam touched his eyes to force them closed. She whispered the prayer from the Quran her mother had taught her before her grandfather's funeral. When she reached the end of the verse, her voice caught, and she let the tears stream down her face.

"Thank you, Fahad. For everything." Memories hit her like a freight train: how he had shielded her from Tareq just a day earlier, how he had protected them from the soldiers today. "Thank you," she said again before she pulled the throw up over his face.

Mariam was about to go back inside, she had to pack her things as well so that they could get to Reema's, when she heard the front door open. She looked up and saw Dinah standing in the doorway. "He's gone, isn't he?" she asked, trembling.

Mariam met her gaze, "I'm so sorry, Dinah."

What else can I say?

Dinah grasped the doorframe to steady herself. "He was a good man."

"He was." Mariam walked to the door and moved past her, guiding her back inside. "Help me pack my things?"

"Of course."

Mariam didn't need help, and they both knew it, but Dinah would welcome any chance to get away from the body. The faster they were packed, the faster they could both leave all the horror behind.

Chapter 32

Salmiya, Kuwait - August, 1990

Mariam took the last five steps in one set and dumped her suitcase at the bottom of the stairwell. She looked down at the medium-sized suitcase that contained all of the possessions she would be taking with her. She had left so much behind when she'd gone from her house to Dinah's, and now she was relinquishing even more of her belongings.

Whatever I do, I have to protect my baby. She placed her hand over her belly and took a deep breath; even with how dire their situation was, the fact that they were about to move made her feel like there was a chance.

Mariam dragged the suitcase a few more steps and deposited it in front of the back door to the house. She wiped her palm across her forehead, glancing at the other two suitcases already there. Janhvi had finished packing first, and Dinah had already brought her suitcase downstairs with her help. Mariam had sent her to take a quick shower before they left—she was hoping that it would help her to keep processing what had happened, especially since they had spent the entire day outside of the air conditioning that normally protected them from the sun and the heat.

After catching her breath, Mariam ventured back upstairs to grab the small wad of emergency cash that she had withdrawn from her personal bank account. She'd thought of putting it in the suitcase, but felt it was better to keep it on her person. A wave of sadness overwhelmed her and she gripped the bed's footboard to push past it. Her gaze returned to the cash in her hand. *Is it even worth anything anymore?* She stuffed it into a tote bag—if she didn't take it, then she would be sure to need it—and returned to the stairwell. On her way out, she paused, letting her gaze linger on the first place that had given her sanctuary since her marriage to Tareq. In all likelihood, she would never see it again.

Mariam heard Janhvi's voice from downstairs. At first, she was scared, but then realized the conversation was one-sided and walked toward it, wondering who she could be talking to. When she reached the kitchen, she saw that Janhvi was on the phone speaking in what she vaguely recognized as Hindi—she had learned a few words from her childhood housekeeper. Janhvi sounded concerned, and Mariam waited a minute or so for her to hang up.

"Mada—Mariam, I know where we can go."

MARIAM SAT DOWN ON THE couch and looked at Dinah, who said, "She's right."

"I never really wanted to go to Reema's anyway, so yes, that's what we'll do," Mariam agreed. She felt conflicted about Janhvi's plan: there was a group of Indians gathering at an office nearby where they could seek shelter. The Iraqi soldiers weren't hunting Indians, so they would be much safer there than at Reema's—but they would have to pretend to be Indian and she wasn't sure if they could pull it off. Janhvi pulled a few pieces of clothing out of her bag—two salwar kamese, each with a long loose tunic and a pair of balloon style pants.

It's not like we have much choice, she grabbed one of the garments and went to get changed. Mariam pulled the tunic over her head, but couldn't silence her internal voice that clothes wouldn't be the issue.

I barely remember any Hindi and Dinah doesn't speak a word of it.

Several minutes later she and Dinah had discarded their clothes in favor of the salwar kamese. Mariam looked her cousin up and down and asked, "What do you think?"

"It's a little short on me, but I guess it'll do," Dinah said, gesturing toward her salwar which stopped an inch above her knees. Since Mariam and Janhvi were about the same height, the outfit fell lower on them.

"It's okay, Madam—the shorter ones will be fashionable in a few years, I'm sure," Janhvi reassured them. "You look like you could be Kashmiris, you're both so fair."

Dinah shrugged, "I'm just glad India has so many different languages—it won't be that unusual that I can't speak Hindi so long as we keep to ourselves and don't speak in Arabic." She turned to Mariam, "Do you remember any?"

"A couple words maybe, but not much." Mariam gathered her resolve and grabbed the handle of her suitcase, "Let's go."

MARIAM WAS WAITING FOR JANHVI and Dinah to drag their suitcases into the backyard when she heard a car at the front of the house. She froze.

They're back.

The noise ceased, and she rejected it offhand—there was no chanting from the street, so it had to be her mind playing tricks on her.

A second later, she knew she hadn't been wrong. The doorbell sounded several times—a shrill ring, followed by a loud knocking. They could leave and try to get away before they were seen, but they didn't have much of a chance with the bags in tow. Dinah and Janhvi were already in the yard, along with all but Mariam's suitcase, but if they left hers by the door, the soldiers would know the house had only just been abandoned and search for them. She motioned toward them.

"Hide the bags in the garden. Run, let's go." She tugged on her suitcase, just getting it through the doorway, then reached to shut the door behind her.

She had a grip on the handle and was pulling it toward her when a voice calling her name stopped her in her tracks.

No, no, please. It can't be.

"Mariam!"

Mariam let go of the handle and the suitcase tipped over and crashed into the doorframe, the glass door clattering as it collided with the suitcase. With all of the chaos she had hardly thought about Tareq since they had received the phone call about the invasion the night before, but now he was here.

I will never be rid of him.

She looked down at her hands, down at her feet, she should move—she still had a chance to get away—but she couldn't. She was paralyzed.

Dinah hissed at her from behind, "Mariam, come on, *run*," then shoved the suitcase from the side, and as soon as it budged, yanked her out of the doorway into the yard. Mariam stumbled, and her suitcase fell onto its side with a soft thud, followed by the loud slam of the back door to the house. "Get up," Dinah cried out, trying to help her.

Mariam was scarcely on her feet when the back door opened.

2016

Chapter 33

Austin, Texas, USA - March, 2016

When Mariam got off the plane in the late afternoon, sunlight streamed in through the windows on the jet bridge. She was tempted to stop then and there and bask in the sun's rays—the contrast with D.C. underscored by the heavy overcoat she had draped over her arm—but the line of people moving behind her kept her moving until she reached the terminal.

Her phone buzzed. Raj was on his way to pick her up, she would just have enough time to grab her suitcase at baggage claim. A few minutes later, Mariam headed for the exit as her stomach did several flips in nervous anticipation. *I'll tell him everything today,* she decided with a smile. The time with Dinah had done wonders, and she had to admit that he, Aliya, and her therapist—all of them—had been right about attending the event. She'd had a great time.

When Raj drove up, he got out of the car to greet her and pulled her into a long hug. Mariam rested her head on his chest and inhaled his scent—her decision to go had been right, but being back in his arms had never felt better.

"I'm sorry I pushed you so hard," he said in a quiet voice, planting a kiss on her forehead.

She gave him a peck on the lips. "You were right. Let's go home."

The twenty-minute drive passed quickly as they sped along the highway, Mariam taking in even more of the warmth with her window down. She spoke a little about the event and told Raj how wonderful it had been to see Dinah—all things she *wanted* to talk about, but distractions before the main event. When they pulled into her driveway, Raj wheeled her suitcase into the house, and she took his hand, leading him out to their back patio. She would need the late afternoon sun to keep rejuvenating her to get through this conversation.

I should have told him years ago.

Mariam grabbed one of the deck chairs and turned it to face him instead of looking out at their beautiful live oak tree as she usually did.

"You've asked me a question several times over the last couple of months, and I couldn't answer you.... There's something I need to tell you—really, a *lot* I need to tell you."

Chapter 34

Austin, Texas, USA – March, 2016

Mariam blew her nose, tossed the tissue into the wastebasket under the patio table, and looked up at Raj, her heart beating at a mile a minute. She had never felt so raw and emotional, not even in therapy, but at the same time, she couldn't be more relieved. Telling Raj her secret, letting him in on what Tareq had done to her, made her feel as if a tremendous weight had been lifted off her shoulders. She let out a long exhale. She had stopped him from interrupting while she was speaking, but when she started to sob, he had put his arm around her until she was ready to continue. Now that she was done, she was apprehensive about his reaction.

"I'm sorry I didn't tell you earlier."

Reaching out to grasp both of her hands, Raj met her gaze, "I—I'm so sorry, Mariam. I'm so sorry for what that monster did to you." He sighed, "I only wish you had told me earlier, that you'd felt you *could* tell me. I can't imagine how hard this must have been for you." He raised his hand to his mouth as he looked over at the garden. "That's Aliya's father, that monster."

"No," Mariam shook her head, "*you're* Aliya's father."

"That's why you never wanted to tell her…that she's not mine?"

"It was always to protect *me*. I didn't want her—either of you, really—to see me differently. That's how I justified it, at least. All these years, I didn't want you to think of me as a victim."

"Are you worried I'm not going to let you run the house anymore?" Raj gave her a small smile.

Mariam chuckled in between her sniffles—they both knew that she ran the household, that had never been a question, not in all the years that they had been together. When the laughter subsided, she spoke again, recalling what he had said about her continuing to use Ritika's name. "There's more to it though, I didn't realize it until I talked about it in therapy. I feel guilty, that's why I kept using Ritika's name."

"*Guilty?*"

"Guilty that he's dead. That I might be held responsible. That's why I was so reluctant to go to an embassy event, why I never wanted to be Mariam again." She hesitated, "I needed other people to help me to get away, I couldn't do it on my own. I didn't want to be that person anymore."

"Mariam, we've been together for twenty-five years, and you're the strongest person I know. You have nothing to feel guilty about, and I think you know that." He cupped her face in his hands, then leaned forward to kiss her. "Tareq is gone now, and he can't hurt you anymore, he's just part of your past. Now that that's not a secret anymore, he can never hurt you again."

Chapter 35

Washington D.C., USA - March, 2016

Nadia set her wine glass down on the table, chuckling.

"All right, I give up, I'll show them to you." She made a face, pretending to be bothered by her mother's repeated requests for pictures from the Liberation Day party. Her father rolled his eyes, and she ignored him; unlike her mother, he could see right through any of her attempts at drama—he always had, even when she was a teenager. He had an uncanny ability to get to the core of an issue, even before she knew what it was. She'd once had a huge fight with her mom about a gift that she had sent her in college, some kind of specialty cheese *grater* even though she had asked for a cheese *knife*. Nadia's mother had been taken aback by the argument, but her father had seen right through it—the fight was actually about her mother not listening to her—it had come shortly after her first attempt to set Nadia up on a date.

You'd think she would learn, Nadia thought as she recalled that moment. She wasn't clear where her father stood on the whole thing, he was far too content to accommodate her mother's desires on the subject. She shrugged off the memory, they would probably have another fight about that same issue again sooner or later, but there was no point wasting any time on it beforehand. For now, she was content to tease her mom a little bit, especially after her second glass of wine. Uncle Tareq was once again over for the weekend. He never seemed to be at his own house. Fortunately, he'd already gone to bed so she could enjoy time with just her parents.

She connected her phone to their Chromecast so that her pictures would show up on the TV. "The first few are the ones we took together," she paused on one of her and her mother. "Mom, that dress looked amazing on you," Nadia shot a glance at her father out of the corner of her eye. "I bet Dad thinks so too."

Her father grunted, opening a newspaper in front of him, but Nadia could tell that he was actually looking at the picture. Her smile widened, and she continued, going through two pictures of her mom and uncle, followed by three different shots of the Gulf War exhibit. "This is the main hall," she said as she moved on, "where most of the party was. I'm so sorry you missed it."

Her mom looked captivated by the photo, "Me too, but maybe we can go with you next year."

"I hope so," Nadia agreed, keeping how difficult it had been to get the extra tickets to herself.

She continued with the pictures, showing off the decorations in the main hall, but moving through them quickly. "This is me with my friends Dinah and Mariam," she stopped on the first picture of the three of them. "I'm sorry you didn't get to meet them when you came by the office the other day. Mariam was running late for her flight home, so they were in a bit of a rush." Nadia swiped to the next one, "That's my boss Faisal, who you met when you came in—"

"Go back to the last picture," a raspy voice said from behind her.

Nadia turned and saw her uncle standing in the doorway to the living room, "Sure."

How long has he been lurking there?

"Tareq, I didn't realize you were up. Did we wake you?" her mother looked over at him.

"I'm fine." He took a seat at the other end of the couch from Nadia and leaned forward, focusing on the television, "Go back to that picture."

Nadia went back to the picture of Dinah, Mariam, and her, and waited for a response, but he said nothing. Rather, he walked in front of the TV and examined the screen even closer. After what felt like a long second of silence with him staring at the television wide-eyed, she asked, "Are you all right? Do you know them, Uncle?"

"I thought I did," he shook his head, "but they can't be who I thought."

Nadia frowned, there was something cunning and deceptive in his tone. *What is with you?* she wanted to ask but held her tongue and thumbed through the rest of the pictures quickly. When she got to the last one, she stood and stretched, "I'm exhausted. Good night."

She left the room quickly before her parents could raise any objections and turned out the light in her room. Something about the interaction with her uncle felt off—well most of them did—but he had clearly recognized either Dinah or Mariam. *Or both.* The real question was, why would he lie? She wondered if her mother had noticed, but was skeptical about bringing it up without telling her about how he'd behaved a few weeks earlier.

She was in the midst of pondering that when the door to her room flew open.

"Who are the women in that photo?" Uncle Tareq's voice pierced the darkness, his silhouette in her doorway.

Nadia swallowed. She opened her mouth, and a voice in the back of her mind told her not to give him their names. *Something is wrong with this picture;* her heart skipped a beat. "They're friends, one of them works on my floor," she answered, trying to keep her voice as nonchalant as possible.

"What are their names?"

Nadia's torso went rigid, she didn't want to tell him anything, but she also didn't want to fuel his curiosity. *Maybe if I tell him something basic, he'll go away.*

"The one in the middle is Dinah, she's the one I work with."

"What about the other one?"

Uncle Tareq's question confirmed her suspicions, he did indeed know Mariam. Nadia's mind raced, she shouldn't tell him anything about her—he was far too dangerous. *If I don't say anything though, he's going to hurt me.* "She's one of Dinah's friends, I don't know her," she made her tone as convincing as possible. *Ritika M. Ghosh,* Nadia remembered the name on Mariam's credit card.

Don't tell him that. She had no idea why, but she knew it deep in her gut.

The silhouette moved toward her and Nadia lay there in bed, frozen.

I should move, I have to do something. She opened her mouth to scream, but less than a second later his hand was at her throat, squeezing her airway.

"Tell me her name! Now."

1990

Chapter 36

Salmiya, Kuwait - August, 1990

Mariam stared at the hunting rifle in Tareq's hand.

How can this be real? She wanted to pinch herself, to wake up from this nightmare so badly. She looked over at Dinah, also on her knees next to her against the wall of the living room.

This can't be happening.

"You thought you could get away from me?" Tareq yelled, turning quickly from side to side and brandishing the rifle as if it weren't dangerous at all. "Now you're going to pay, bitch."

It took several seconds for Mariam to be able to speak.

"Tareq, I'm sorry," she whispered. "I'll go with you, I will. Just put the gun down and let them go. They didn't do anything."

Dinah shot her a look that clearly told her to shut up, and her gaze darted toward the door to the backyard. Janhvi'd had the presence of mind to hide before Tareq had ushered Mariam and Dinah inside, so perhaps they still stood a chance. Mariam had no idea how, though. *It's not as if Janhvi's a vigilante with a gun of her own to defend us with.*

"Please, Tareq," Mariam implored. "I'll go with you, I'll do whatever you want. Just let Dinah go."

His eyes narrowed, and she felt as if he was boring into her soul.

He had taken so much from her already, she could never fight him, she would never be free.

How is this my life? The thought ran through her brain resonating in the corners of her mind, the hopelessness of her situation stretched out in front of her like a desert wasteland.

But my baby. That recollection jolted her out of the despair, she had to find a way out.

"Tareq, let's leave," she said softly. She unclasped her hands and lowered them to the ground, using them to help her stand up, "We can leave now, just you and me. I've missed you."

He scrutinized her and wavered for a moment before he took a step back. "Mariam, I would never hurt you. Why did you run away? You belong with me, you belong *to* me. I do everything for you, I take care of you."

Mariam tasted bile in her throat and coerced a swallow, then took a step toward Tareq. She could see Janhvi at the back door, now open just a crack. The only chance they had was to distract Tareq long enough for her to get the jump on him. Reaching out with her right hand, she touched his forearm. "I shouldn't have run, but I panicked. I know you didn't mean to last time, but you really hurt me. I was so scared." She focused on the last phrase, the only part of what she was saying that was true. Somehow, she had to make him believe it. She raised her other arm so that she was grasping both of his forearms, "Tareq, please, put the gun down." At the same time, she pushed down, leading him to lower the gun and set it down on the coffee table.

He released his grip on the rifle and glowered at her. "Mariam, you will always be mine." With his left hand, he grabbed her by the throat and pushed her against the wall. "You make it seem as if you didn't enjoy every second of the time we've been together—I know how much you like it rough. I would never actually hurt you—that gun wasn't even loaded." He leaned forward and kissed her, shoving his tongue down her throat.

Mariam fought the urge to gag, especially with the continued pressure of his hand on her throat. Instead, she responded to his kiss, linking her arms behind his neck and intertwining her fingers.

Janhvi, Dinah, please do something. She wasn't sure how long she could keep this up.

Almost on cue, Mariam heard a loud crash and shut her eyes

as shards of ceramic fell to the floor from the vase that Janhvi had shattered over Tareq's head. He stumbled, landing on the ground hard.

"Run!" shouted Mariam. She had no idea how long he would stay down, but she wasn't going to miss her chance. Janhvi and Dinah were already almost at the door, and she jumped over Tareq. The door was so close, her escape was just within her grasp.

Suddenly she felt something grip her ankle and before she could process what was happening, she was falling forward. Her wrists hit the floor first, bracing against the impact, the pain doubly strong because of her recent injury, as she was dragged backward toward Tareq. She kicked out with her other leg once, hitting only air, and then again before her left foot managed to connect. Tareq cried out at the impact, and she struggled to regain control of her other foot. He pulled her back farther and before she could land another kick he was almost to his feet. She flailed as he yanked her back into the wall, then straddled her hips and pinned her to the ground as she fell.

Tareq smacked her across the side of her head, and she saw stars. Dinah jumped on his back, but he was easily able to throw her off. She hit the ground and went silent.

Mariam's chest heaved, she could see his expression, one that she had seen so many times before. He was about to rape her, and there was nothing she could do. Whatever hope she had had for her baby, whatever life she had wanted for herself—all of it was gone now for a life of beating and submission. And once the baby was born, she would never be free of him.

This is my life now.

MARIAM LOST COUNT OF THE number of blows that followed. He dealt repeated punches to every part of her body; she couldn't be sure what was real or what wasn't anymore. Her cheeks and eyes were on fire, and as he reached for the waistband of her kamese, she felt more like he was touching someone else, as if she no longer inhabited her body. She had no more fight left, he could do as he pleased.

The air moved, followed by a bang that resounded through the air. The pressure on her hips eased, and Tareq's weight fell to her left. Mariam's vision took a few seconds to clear—Tareq was lying on his side next to her, his head bleeding profusely, with Janhvi in front of her brandishing what had to be a cast iron saucepan. She blacked out a moment later, surrendering to the darkness.

Chapter 37

Salmiya, Kuwait - August, 1990

Janhvi sank to the ground, struggling to believe what had just happened. She dropped the pan, and it clattered against the ceramic tile as she attempted to catch her breath. Pulling her feet into her chest, she wrapped her arms around her knees with tears pouring down her cheeks.

This didn't happen, this didn't happen, she said to herself over and over again.

She wasn't sure how long she stayed like that, but eventually, she unwrapped her arms and managed to get to her feet. Dinah and Mariam were both still unconscious, and as far as she could tell, so was Tareq. She fumbled her way toward him and felt around his neck haphazardly in search of a pulse.

Do I want him to be alive or dead? She didn't know what the right answer was—she couldn't imagine being responsible for his death, but if he wasn't dead, how were they going to get away? The thought of him attacking again made her tremble, and her memory flashed to her uncle. She had rarely thought of him since she arrived in Kuwait over a year earlier, but her recollections had never been more vivid, or more tangible. He'd tried to touch her when she was young, before she had known anything more than the fact that it didn't feel right, that she didn't want him to do it anymore. A picture ran through her head: wielding the cast iron pan at his head just as she had with Tareq. Her fingers moved around on his neck, still unable to find a pulse. This man was slime, just like her uncle, and she had to bite her lip to shake off the image.

He was dead. They were rid of him.

But he was dead because of her.

I killed him.

The very concept was incomprehensible. Her chest swelled, and without thinking, she reached for the saucepan and slammed it against the side of his head again. Her arms gave way under the pan's weight, the adrenaline of the fight had given her the strength to swing it, but now it felt heavier than her entire suitcase.

Janhvi dropped the pan and let the tears fall for a moment before getting up once again. Dinah and Mariam—she had to help them.

She made it to Mariam first and touched her shoulder, "Mariam?"

Mariam groaned as she opened her eyes, which were filled with fear. "He's gone," Janhvi said quietly.

Mariam looked like she was about to speak but remained silent as she struggled to stand. Once she was upright, she broke away and went straight for Tareq's body. She kicked him in the torso, sobbing and shouting at the same time. Janhvi couldn't make out everything that she was saying, but she caught the stream of curse words masked partially by tears. Janhvi shuddered, then pulled Mariam away from the body, still sobbing. Mariam collapsed on the ground but eventually allowed Janhvi to help her to her feet.

With one arm still around her shoulder, they moved toward Dinah, who was lying on the other side of the room. "Madam, wake up," Janhvi said in an urgent tone. "Wake up." She smacked Dinah's cheeks.

Dinah's eyes flickered open and closed before they shot open wide, and she jumped. "What happened? Are you okay?" She looked frantically at Mariam before she noticed Tareq's body. "Is he—?" her gaze moved between Janhvi and Mariam.

"Yes," Mariam answered, her tone cutting through the air like ice.

Dinah remained silent, and together Janhvi and Mariam supported her as she stood, and they made it out into the backyard. After a moment to catch her breath, Janhvi reached inside to shut the back door to the house. The noise she heard felt as if someone were stabbing her in the back: a moan coming from the corner of the living room.

He's still alive. She checked behind her in the yard to see if either Dinah or Mariam had heard anything, but they seemed oblivious. They were almost to the gate, each lugging a suitcase forward, and seemed completely occupied with the effort.

Janhvi took a couple of steps to get a glimpse of him. He was still on his side, and he didn't appear capable of moving. There was blood forming a small pool next to his head. In a split second, Janhvi made a decision: this was their chance to get away. With that much blood on the floor from a head wound, even if he wasn't dead yet he would be dead soon enough.

Leave and he dies. She faltered, and the memory of her uncle washed over her again. Her jaw set and after one last glance toward Mariam and Dinah, she stepped into the yard and slammed the door shut.

He deserves to be dead; she had never been more certain of anything in her life.

We said he was dead, and no one needs to know any different.

He is *dead.* She wouldn't do anything to help him.

2016

Chapter 38

Austin, Texas, USA – March, 2016

Mariam gaped at Teresa, at a loss of how to answer her therapist's question. She had expected her first session since returning from D.C. to feel more like a triumph, but instead, she shifted in her seat in obvious discomfort. *I'm not scared,* she wanted to protest, but the phrase felt too pathetic to say aloud.

Teresa continued, "I don't say this to put you on the spot, or to push in one direction or the other, but I do think it's important that you know the answer. For the last couple of months, we've been working on getting you past the trauma of your relationship with Tareq, on letting that fear go. So, I want you to really think about why you're still scared of him, because I believe you are, and I think you know the answer."

Mariam's gaze darted around the room, wishing that by remaining silent the question would dissipate as if it had never been asked. Deep in her gut, she did indeed know the answer, although she had never admitted it out loud.

I should have killed him myself, and I wish I had. Even though the notion had been right there all along, this was the first time she'd realized it. Yet there it was in front of her, in black and white. She opened her mouth and hesitated, what kind of a person did it make her that she wanted to say those words? That she believed that?

"I don't know, I guess it's like I already told you. He made me the victim, and I didn't fight back. I never want to be that person again, I never want to feel that weak again."

"But why do you feel weak when you look back? When you think about what happened?"

She knows... Mariam was tempted to try another dodge, to only partially answer the question, but after a few more moments of debating, she acquiesced. *What harm could it do?* She had already told her therapist more than she'd ever shared with Raj or Aliya, or even Dinah, put together. She had let her in on the whole story, every detail on the number of times that Tareq had beaten her, and how Dinah had finally convinced her to leave him. She had even divulged how she had almost let him have her, how she'd given up that last day when she thought that she would never be free of him. Mariam trembled, she could still feel his left hand groping her as his other arm pinned her at the throat. Letting the tears fall she looked at her therapist, and the words burst from her chest.

"I never walked away from him on my own, I never stood up to him. With Tareq I was *always* the victim. You've been telling me to affirm myself, to give myself credit for walking away, but I don't deserve it. I don't deserve any of it!"

Teresa handed her the tissue box and waited for Mariam's tears to ebb before she asked, "You said earlier that you finally told Raj the truth about Tareq. Do you think he sees you as a victim?"

"He didn't say that, but I *was*. He said he sees me as someone who's strong, who has nothing to feel guilty about, but that's not true."

"Why do you think you're being so hard on yourself? Even if other people helped you, you still decided to leave Tareq after you woke up at the hospital."

"But I never would have left him if I hadn't found out that I was pregnant."

"You told me before that you reached out to your sister for help, but she refused. Even then, you were trying to find a way out."

"But after that I just gave up—I believed her when she said I had to go back to Tareq," Mariam bit her lip.

"Are you angry with her? With your sister?" Teresa asked softly.

"I don't know."

"You know that it's okay to be angry with her, right? It's okay to be angry with all of them. She should have stood by you, she should have protected you, but instead, she sent you back into the lion's den. Of course, you're angry, and you have every right to be."

Mariam felt the tension in her chest start to ease. "I *am* angry." Saying the words out loud felt so anticlimactic, yet so significant at the same time. "I am angry," she repeated. "I'm angry at her, and at my father, and my family. I'm angry at my mom for dying before she could stop my dad from marrying me off without a second thought. I'm so angry, but really, I'm angry at myself more than anyone else. I'm not the one who stopped Tareq—I left him because of Aliya, because I had to protect her. I knew I'd never be free of him after she was born."

Mariam stopped, shocked as she realized what she had said. "I mean, I knew I'd never let him get his hands on her, that I had to keep her away from him," she backpedaled.

Teresa looked at her with kind, empathetic eyes, "Mariam, it is okay to acknowledge that part of why you left Tareq was also because of you. You wanted to be free of him, you couldn't let yourself be tied to him for life, *and* you had to protect your daughter. Those two things are not mutually exclusive. You do know that, right?"

Mariam's gaze lingered on the ground, staring at the zig-zag pattern on the blue and gray carpet. "Maybe, maybe you're right."

"It doesn't make you less of a mom that you wanted to get away from Tareq for yourself as well as Aliya. Isn't that the personal initiative you said that you didn't take? You wanted to give credit for getting away from him to Dinah, to Aliya, even to Janhvi since she was the one who stopped him from hurting you, but you just said it yourself. You knew that you would never get away from him if you didn't do it at that time, so you had to do it. *You* did that, no one else."

Teresa took a sip of water before she went on. "I also want to make something clear—going through that kind of abuse doesn't make you weak, and neither does being here in therapy. We've touched on this before, but I think it's worth revisiting. *Anyone* can become a victim of abuse, it doesn't matter how strong you are, or what background you come from. No one is immune to it. In fact, by recognizing that, and coming in for treatment, you made a decision from a point of strength, not weakness. If you'd fallen down the stairs and broken your ankle, you would see a doctor and a physical therapist without missing a beat, and none of that would make you feel weak. Coming to therapy is almost the same thing, you're taking your life back. You recognize that you need help and you're taking the initiative to get the care that you need. You made that decision, even if Raj helped you get there, just like you made the decision to leave Tareq that day at the hospital."

The words sank into Mariam's head slowly, could that really be true? She had indeed been the victim, Tareq had victimized her every day, but Teresa was right. *At least part of the decision to leave him was for me. It wasn't just for Aliya.* Tears formed in her eyes once again, but this time she smiled in relief, "You're right. Part of the decision was for me." She could hardly believe it, but now it seemed clear as day—she had indeed walked away from Tareq, even if she'd had help, even if her pregnancy had nudged her over the edge. What Raj had articulated suddenly registered in a way it never had before.

I am *strong.* Mariam drew a deep breath and for the first time had the courage to voice what she had been unable to earlier.

"I wish I was the one who had killed him," she said, barely above a whisper.

"I can understand that, that adds another facet to the guilt that we've been talking about, you feel responsible, but at the same time wish you had done more. It is okay for you to feel that way. That man terrorized you, beat you, hurt you. He took your dignity and trampled on it every day that you were together. When you finally left, he came for you and you were ready to do what you had to do to survive, but someone else stopped him. It's not a huge leap that you would wish that person was you, but that's not your fault. You were doing what you had to do, to survive, and your friend saw that—she saw what you were going through, and she stood up for you. It's as simple as that."

Is it really? Mariam fiddled with the pendant on her necklace, realizing once more that Teresa was right. *It* is *as simple as that.*

"I really want to emphasize that point—you shouldn't blame yourself for letting him touch you that day. You weren't capitulating to him because you wanted to be the victim, you were doing that because it's what you thought you had to do to survive. Besides, I don't think Janhvi would have been able to take him out if he hadn't been distracted. Think of it that way. You weren't the one that dealt the final blow, but you were instrumental in getting rid of him."

When the session was over, Mariam made her way to the parking lot and stopped in front of her car. She closed her eyes and turned to face the afternoon sun, drinking in the warmth. She felt somehow lighter, as if her soul was free now that she had left the burden of truth in Teresa's office.

I wasn't just the victim, I was instrumental. *I made the decision to get away from him, for Aliya, and for myself.*

Her past was behind her, and she was free.

Chapter 39

Washington D.C., USA – March, 2016

Tareq used his thumb and forefinger to zoom in on his phone's screen and examine the picture more closely.

It has to be her.

There was no question, the woman in the picture was his wife Mariam. *Even if Nadia said her name is Ritika.* A smile crept across his face, he had believed this day would elude him, that he would never be able to exact his revenge for what she had done to him. But now the wait was over.

I've found her. I will find her.

His smile faded as he considered the different options, how he could use her name and her picture to locate her—he could squeeze Nadia further, but he had to be sure his sister never found out. He had broached the subject with a younger woman at the bank where he worked, saying he wanted to see if he could get back in touch with any of his old friends from Kuwait, and she had recommended using social media. He'd never thought of it before—he wasn't even on Facebook himself—but now Nadia had accepted his friend request. *As if she would dare refuse,* he smirked. Unfortunately, neither her account nor a search for people who had listed their hometown as Kuwait had yielded anything.

Tareq crossed his arms, recalling how he had searched for Mariam when he had first been released—the internet was still in its infancy, and his only option had been to hire an investigator. *Do they still exist?* He opened a browser window and typed "private investigator near me" into Google and a number of results came up. He scrolled through the list, noting down several phone numbers. He grinned, she was within his grasp.

Switching back to the picture, he ran his hand over his head, starting at the ridge just above his left ear and traced the scar along his jawline to the base of his cheek. His jaw clenched. He could still remember the blow that he'd sustained there from the woman who had hit him, some friend of Mariam's. *To stop me from being with my wife?* The very idea made the veins in his neck start to pop. His wife was *his* to have whenever he liked, *his* to control, and she had been away from him for over twenty-five years now.

Twenty-five years, seven months, and two days. Tareq's eyes seared into Mariam's picture, the audacity of spirit that he'd always seen in her taunting him. There were a few lines on her face, around her mouth, by her eyes, and her cheekbones were more filled out than he remembered, but she looked much the same, still beautiful. She wore a long burgundy dress, and he ached to see her figure, her curves move in the soft fabric, but that part of the picture was hidden by the other two women.

In turn, Tareq glared at them, first imagining driving a knife into Dinah's gut. The other woman next to Mariam ceased to be his niece Nadia. She morphed into the woman who had hit him the night Mariam got away and he grimaced, visualizing the same knife stopping her heart.

If it weren't for you, Mariam would never have left me, this is all your fault. His eyes narrowed, he would deal with both of them when the time was right, after he had Mariam back in his arms.

They will pay.

Bolstered by his resolve, Tareq let his desire level, and the picture in his hand returned to normal. He fixed his gaze on Nadia, and his smile returned—he had all the power over her. His expression sobered, and he retraced the scar. He would have to make sure that she didn't warn Dinah. His threats against her had remained a secret thus far,

Nadia was too much of a lamb to say anything, but he had to keep it that way. Perhaps it was time for him to agree to his sister's offer, the one that he'd refused for the last few months. He couldn't afford to risk anything that might spoil the surprise for Mariam, she would be so overjoyed to see him. He rubbed his chin, recalling how much she had enjoyed his touch, even when she had fought and cried. They deserved to have that again, they *would* have that again.

My Mariam, my wife.

Tareq stood up, widened his smile and practiced speaking to his sister in the mirror. "I've changed my mind. I'd like to try moving in with you for the next month." Once he had tried it a few times, he was content with his performance, ready to put on a show. Nothing would stop him from having Mariam back, and he wasn't going to allow Nadia or anyone else get in his way. He repeated the words to himself before heading for the door to speak to his sister.

She will always be mine.

1990

Chapter 40

Salmiya, Kuwait - August, 1990

Mariam cowered in the fetal position and rocked back and forth. After staring at the ceiling for what felt like hours, she'd given up on sleep—it's not as if a bed sheet on the floor of the office that they had been assigned offered much comfort. She still couldn't believe it, Tareq was dead.

He's dead because of me.

Her body quaked as she grappled with that reality. If only she had left him months earlier, none of this would have happened. *I could already have been in Europe, and my baby would be safe.* With her hands on her belly, her torso racked with sobs. Tareq was gone, but her life was still as bleak as ever—she would never be free, she would have to explain what had happened, how he had died. The recollection of him touching her, the movement of his tongue down her throat as he tore at her underwear—she could not get away from it. Each time she would have to recount, and *relive,* what he had done to her. As she lay there on the floor, she doubted she would be able to survive that. She had to be strong, she had to take care of her baby, but Tareq's ghost would follow her forever.

I will never be free of him, I will always be weak and at his mercy.

Her diaphragm pulsed uncontrollably as she curled in a ball and surrendered to sobs, desperately trying to be as quiet as possible.

MARIAM EVENTUALLY DOZED OFF, HER body finally granting her a temporary respite from the series of traps that her memories had become. When she opened her eyes, sunlight was streaming in through the office windows, and she shifted in her spot, realizing how much of an impact the day before had had on her. In the morning, the world, and her future in it, seemed a little less dire, even though nothing about the situation had actually changed. She rose slowly and made her way down the hall in search of the restrooms past a myriad of people she didn't recognize. There were several different clusters in the various rooms that she passed, some still sleeping under conference room tables and corners of the hallway in front of her. She could make out what sounded like at least three different languages. *At least Janhvi was right when she said that we didn't necessarily have to speak in Hindi to blend in.*

When she got to the end of the hallway, she made a guess and turned right. She could hear more people talking that way than to the left. The hallway opened out into a massive canteen, and the echoing chatter filled her ears as soon as she stepped inside. If she hadn't known better, she would have thought it was any old workday, the canteen was packed to the brim with people seated at a series of rectangular and oblong tables set along the windows. The discussion sounded lively even if she couldn't understand a word, although there were some terms that seemed vaguely familiar, jogging her memories of her housekeeper and reflecting the similar roots that Arabic and Urdu shared. She craned her neck to see the back of the room and was relieved to see Dinah and Janhvi sequestered at a high-top table in the far corner. Mariam exhaled and waved, then made her way toward them.

MARIAM WAS IN THE PROCESS of wolfing down half of a paratha from Janhvi's plate when she noticed Dinah and Janhvi looking past her. Mariam gulped down the morsel before she glanced to her left, where a tall Indian man was standing. He said something in what she recognized as Hindi, although she only understood a fraction of it. *I think he asked if we're okay?* Mariam gave him a puzzled look. Janhvi responded to him, something about how they didn't speak Hindi, and he frowned in obvious surprise, before speaking in English.

"I hope you're all right, Miss. I heard you last night, but I wasn't sure if there was anything I could do, and I didn't want to wake anyone else up."

Mariam's face flushed, "I'm okay, thank you." She turned her gaze back to the last piece of the paratha on her plate—not only was she hungry, she wanted to limit conversation as much as possible. The more she or Dinah spoke to anyone here, the more likely it was that someone would figure out that they weren't Indian. While she didn't know what arrangement the office owner had made with the Iraqi soldiers, she definitely wasn't going to risk their safety for a bit of conversation, even if the man initiating it was quite attractive.

"I'm glad to hear that," he said in a quiet voice. "I'm Raj."

"Mariam."

"I'm Janhvi, and this is Dinah," Janhvi sat up straighter in an obvious attempt to take them out of the hot seat.

"Nice to meet you. I'm sure I'll see you," Raj said before he turned and sat down at one of the long rectangular tables.

"What's the matter with you, Mariam?" Dinah asked, crossing her arms. "We can't be rude to the people here—we don't want to attract that kind of attention."

"Oh…I thought I shouldn't talk to him in case he figures out who we are."

Dinah shrugged, "They'll know who we are soon enough. We just have to hope that no one turns us in. There's no way we can keep it a real secret—look at us, we can't speak Hindi, we barely know how to wear a salwar kamese. It's only a matter of time, but this is still better than anywhere else we could be right now." She turned toward Janhvi, and her voice cracked. "I don't even know how to thank you for bringing us here. You saved us, you saved us both—from the Iraqis, and from Tareq."

Chapter 41

Salmiya, Kuwait - Two weeks later, August, 1990

Raj Ghosh dropped the last bag of rice onto the kitchen floor and leaned against the wall to catch his breath. Earlier in the week, he had helped relocate the makeshift refugee camp from the office building to the nearby Salmiya Indian School. Two businessmen had taken on primary leadership of the group and had recruited him, amongst a few others, to help with the effort once they had secured permission to move to the school. Raj had primarily dealt with Sanjay, an architect-turned-businessman with whom he had dealings with as part of his construction work, but he'd been equally impressed with Daniels, more commonly known as Hyundai Daniels due to his involvement in the management of several local car dealerships in Kuwait. Both possessed a deep serenity and gravitas that had been invaluable in organizing and managing the massive group of Indians who had taken up residence at the school.

Raj picked up a large bottle of water and resisted the urge to dump half of it over his head to cool off. Thankfully they'd been able to wheel in a number of crates from the nearby cooperative—the different jamaiyas had been generous with water and basic dry food supplies—but he couldn't exactly justify wasting a bottle of water under the circumstances. The tap water was never as cold as water from the fridge though, and the bottle wouldn't stay cold. He sighed and instead of pouring it over his head, gulped it down, then went to the sink and splashed some water on his face and the back of his neck. With a deep breath, he was ready to rejoin the world, at least temporarily.

Sanjay had requested his help in several aspects of running the camp: "You're used to running a construction crew, maybe you could help resolve some of the disputes that keep coming up between the different families." Raj had agreed, but he'd had no idea that he was basically committing to climb a mountain with his hands tied behind his back. The families had only been living together for a couple of weeks, yet the number of petty disputes was multiplying at an alarming rate. When he'd had to deal with disputes within his construction crew—even though there were far fewer than the number he dealt with here on a daily basis—he'd had the ability to enforce his decisions: he could fire someone for refusing to follow his instructions, or at the very least, sanction them. Now all he could do was threaten to move them to a different room, and everyone was generally aware that that was mostly an empty threat. In the office, people had essentially been sleeping on top of one another, they had more space at the school, but their needs had increased exponentially. The father in one family wanted to make sure that there were no other men in the same room with his teenage daughter, a mother wanted her family to stay separate from the family of two boys that had gotten her son in trouble at school. Those were at least the more descriptive, perhaps even the more reasonable demands. The ones that were much worse were: "Ranvir makes the bathroom stinky so we need to put him on a schedule," or "Visab snores really loud, can he move to another room?" Raj's personal favorite was, "Everyone in that room stinks, I need a private bedroom." It had taken all of his self-control not to burst out laughing at that one in particular. *It's August in Kuwait and only some of the rooms have air conditioning—everyone stinks, including you.* He'd almost wrinkled his nose but had just managed to stop himself.

Raj sighed. The list went on and on, without any reprieve in sight. Still, there were moments he welcomed the disputes as a distraction from the slew of rumors that flew around with each passing day—every morning he heard that another building was on fire, another person had vanished, another Kuwaiti woman had been raped, and there'd been another shooting in some other neighborhood. If the rumors were to be believed, most of the country had already gone up in smoke. In truth, they rarely heard bullets after the first week. Raj saw the evidence each time he ventured outside the school grounds—the sky wasn't ablaze and there were only a handful of checkpoints manned by the few well-dressed Iraqi officers—yet it wasn't enough to silence the fear that plagued him, magnified at least ten-fold amongst the school's residents. The rumors were far more effective than reality, the fear muzzled any discussion of resistance and kept most of them into pure survival mode. Only a small pocket of resistance was centered in the Sabah Al-Salem neighborhood where many Kuwaitis lived, but from what Raj had heard they struggled with a lack of clear leadership since most of the government had fled at the start of the invasion.

Leaning his head back, Raj contemplated what he'd overheard a few days earlier: some of the other men that Sanjay had recruited to help with the move expected the invasion to be over in less than a month. They claimed that the international community wouldn't stand for it, but Raj wasn't so sure. He kept his opinions to himself, there was no point in crushing everyone else's optimism because he couldn't summon any of his own. Something deep down told him that their situation wouldn't end that quickly—as far as he could tell, prior to the occupation, no one had actually *expected* Saddam to attack. The news had been all ablaze, but in private settings, everyone had believed Saddam would fall in line. He was, after all, a long-time American ally, and he needed their cooperation more than he needed Kuwait's oil—or so they had all believed. *Now we know better.* With that in mind, Raj was willing to bet that all of the rational sentiment behind a quick end to the conflict would be for naught. He also remembered his father's stories about the Naxalite movement in Bengal—how it had grown from something small into a revolution and continued far longer than anyone could have predicted. He'd been a child at the time, but recalled the same sorts of discussions he was often privy to now, discussions that were so confident everything would turn out fine, and quickly at that. He had learned that lesson the hard way back then, he wished that he didn't have to see it in action again now.

Once was more than enough.

With another sigh he walked into one of the two sitting rooms that he supervised—old classrooms that had been turned into eating areas for the residents of the school. *Residents of the school.* He noted how odd that phrase sounded in his head. The first room was always the hardest, once he got through it and made it to the second, the worst was usually behind him, at least for that particular evening. Each of the hall monitors—as he affectionately called himself—and the other supervisors Sanjay had appointed had their own systems. Some of them did rounds and dealt with disputes on the go at the same time, others set up specific sessions for people to come to them with their issues. Really it all just went to hell most of the time since people didn't exactly respect or operate on the schedules they set, but it still helped to feel as if they were drawing some semblance of boundaries. Raj used a slight variation on his construction crew schedule: rounds in the morning and evenings, followed by short office hours in the late morning, ensuring that all discussions took place after mealtimes. During his normal workday, rounds before the meal allowed him to get his crew working faster, but here, waiting to entertain complaints till everyone was fed dampened their intensity. *No one is quite as angry on a full stomach.* He'd experimented with other times, such as late afternoon tea time, but had discovered that those were the worst. His charges were hungry and had been able to stew most of the day. Other than a few blowups at the dinner table, the new schedule was working tolerably well, now that his expectations had been recalibrated to their worst.

That thought made him chuckle. *If I can deal with this all the time, my next construction project will be a breeze—nothing like that last one.* Remembering his last construction job made a lump form in his throat, and he turned away from the sitting room door to head straight for the bathrooms.

He locked himself in and leaned over the sink to get control of his breathing.

I'll see you tomorrow morning.

That had been the last thing his wife Ritika had said to him when he'd dropped her off for her overnight nursing shift at Farwaniya Hospital the afternoon before the Iraqis had crossed the border. They were supposed to have more time together, to get to know each other, but she had disappeared. He had gone back to the hospital at every possible opportunity, taking far too many risks driving out in the roads especially in the first couple of days after the invasion. He kicked at the wall underneath the sink.

How could Ritika be gone?

And how could he care so little?

The feelings came in waves, it wasn't as if he didn't feel anything, but his parents had arranged the wedding in India only the month before. Prior to that, he and Ritika had met once and spoken over the phone twice. She had arrived in Kuwait less than a week before the occupation began, and he had been so busy with his project that he'd kept putting off spending time with her. He could count the number of real conversations they'd had on one hand, the number of nights they had spent together on the other. He felt something at her disappearance, a gap, a sense of loss, but nothing in comparison to the emotion that losing his wife should evoke.

"Damn it," he cried out as his foot connected with the wall again. This onslaught of emotions had only come on a few times, but when it did, he couldn't interact with anyone. Sanjay was the only person at the camp who he had told about Ritika and her disappearance, Raj hadn't even informed the men from his construction crew who had taken residence at the school. Before he'd left for India for the wedding, he had been so uncertain about the whole thing that he hadn't bothered to mention the purpose of his vacation. He'd figured that he would tell them when he *felt* like he was married, not when the paperwork was signed. He had hoped that he and Ritika would reach that point—his mother had always claimed that you could learn to love someone, that she and his father had fallen in love in exactly that way. It was nothing like the movies, but it could be real and true, and he had seen it in his parents' interactions, although there was much of their relationship that he wanted never to replicate. Yet, now Ritika was gone, vanished, and he had no way to find her. He'd returned to the hospital and to their old apartment, along with the one restaurant that he had taken her to the day after they had arrived in Kuwait. The restaurant was closed, their apartment was abandoned, and the hospital was full of soldiers. There was nowhere else to look, but he clung to the hope that she would hear about this shelter and come to find him.

If she's still alive.

Raj shut his eyes, and the tears returned once again, full force this time. He cursed aloud and looked up, shaking his fist at the universe. He'd been raised a traditional Hindu, but he wasn't sure what he believed. Whatever forces controlled the universe, they shouldn't be allowing this to happen.

How can she be gone? She was barely here to begin with.

He bent over the sink and fought to regain power over his emotions. *Have faith,* Sanjay had said, *you have to have faith that you will find her.* The words had sounded easy and wonderful, they'd been exactly what Raj had needed to hear, but the inability to take action made him feel as if he was walking around carrying a three-hundred-pound barbell on his shoulders. If he was supposed to have faith, then he had to be able to *do* something. How else could he have faith? What other source of hope was there? If he didn't find her, did he even have the right to call her his wife? Ritika had vacillated on whether or not she wanted to work in the long term, but had said she wasn't ready to give up her job quite yet, and he had helped her get started at Farwaniya Hospital. A job that came with overnight shifts, the reason that she hadn't been with him the morning of August 2nd.

Did I do this to her? Did I make her take that job? Another tear rolled down his cheek; he had certainly encouraged it, even if he hadn't forced her. He rubbed the back of his neck and shook his head, beating himself up this way served no purpose, but he couldn't help it. *Especially since I don't seem to think of her that often*—that was the crux of the issue, his guilt that he didn't miss his wife, that they hadn't had enough time together for him to feel that sort of emotion. Rationally, he had to believe that that didn't make him a monster, he knew that relationships and love took time to build, but he wished that their chance hadn't been snatched away.

She must be alive. She has to be.

2016

Chapter 42

Washington D.C., USA - March, 2016

Tareq looked up from the file the private investigator had shared and glanced over the details for the third time in as many minutes.

"Do you have any questions?" the investigator asked.

How could she be with anyone else? he wanted to shout, wanted to scream it from the rooftops. The information that the investigator had provided struck him to the core, Mariam was married to another man, and they had a twenty-four-year-old daughter together. *How could she?* The fact that she was living under another name hadn't surprised him, there had to be a reason he hadn't been able to find her for all these years, Nadia had confirmed as much. The realization that she had remarried explained a lot, although it made his blood boil.

How could she do this to me? He envisioned the last time that he had seen her, the last time that he had touched her, followed by the massive blow to his head when all the lights went out.

"Mr. Salem, do you have any questions?" the investigator repeated.

The question didn't register, he was still too immersed in thought. *She's been in Texas, this whole time, so close.* He had even been to Houston for a conference three years earlier.

She was right there.

"Mr. Salem—"

Tareq looked at him, his face snapping back into focus. "I don't think so. Her phone number, her address, her work information…this should be more than enough." For a moment he considered asking if the investigator had a contact in Texas with whom he could liaise, but decided against it—he had given too much away already. *I can always Google someone else.* "It will be good to see her again, she's an old family friend who I knew in Kuwait before the Gulf War," he continued.

The investigator nodded, although Tareq could tell that he didn't really buy the explanation he'd come up with on a whim. *Oh well, it's not like he cares,* Tareq tabled his concerns, the investigator was hardly going to call Mariam and warn her.

He won't spoil the surprise, and neither will Nadia.

Tareq stood with a nod and picked up the file, "I believe I have everything I need."

"Great. I'll go ahead and charge your card for the rest of my fee."

"Of course." Tareq paused at the doorway, a thought occurring to him, flashing in front of his face like a billboard in neon letters, *Mariam has a twenty-four-year-old daughter. Twenty-four….*

He turned around, "Actually, I'll need one more thing from you—all the information you can get on her daughter, Aliya."

Chapter 43

Austin, Texas, USA – March, 2016

Aliya exhaled, the gravity of what her parents had just told her descending onto her head like a one-hundred-pound weight.

Holy shit.

She locked eyes with her dad, who she now knew wasn't her biological father, her friends had always said that she looked more like her mother than anyone else.

I'm adopted.

The concept seemed so strange, so completely separate from her reality. Aliya's gaze moved to her mom, who was fidgeting in her seat, clearly nervous as to how she was going to react. It took her a few moments to form words. She had known that her mother had decided to change her name when she got out of Kuwait after the Gulf War, and that she had wanted to cut ties with her family other than Dinah Auntie. *That was heavy enough....*

"Mom, Dad, I love you, that's the most important thing," Aliya finally mustered. "I don't know what to say, all I know is that I'm shocked." She took another deep breath and looked at her mother again, "I can't believe what you went through... I'm so sorry, I wish that man wasn't my father—I mean my *biological* father—but he's definitely not my dad. Like I said, I love you both."

"Should we not have told you?" her mom asked. "You are *nothing* like him, I promise you, and you're everything like Raj," she reached out to grasp his hand.

"I know, I just wish none of that had happened to you, Mom. I'm really glad you're going to therapy."

How on earth could you think you didn't need it? That man attacked you, beat you.

"Is there any reason you're telling me now? Did something change?"

Her mom sighed and exchanged a glance with her father, "I didn't want to, maybe I even couldn't, hold on to the secret anymore."

"I understand," Aliya's eyes moved between the two of them; there was obviously more that they weren't telling her. *When did she tell Dad?* she wondered. *When she got back from D.C. a couple of weeks ago?* Something in his posture gave her an inkling that he hadn't known for long, there was a new rigidity and anger directed at the universe that she hadn't seen before. She was just grateful that it wasn't directed at her mother.

How could she have kept this a secret from him, too?

Aliya wandered over to the kitchen to make a pot of tea, anything to keep her hands occupied. She had always been curious as to why her mom had used a different name, why all of that had to be kept a secret as she'd learned in her late teens. She moved on autopilot, filling up a pot with water and adding the tea leaves along with a few whole spices: a cinnamon stick, three cardamom pods, and a pinch of cloves for the perfect masala chai. *The recipe that Dad taught me,* she relished. *He's my dad,* the corners of her mouth twitched upward, *my dad.* She had said the words to him, and she believed them, but that simple recollection made her cherish them. She finished making the tea in silence, adding only a splash of milk at the end, the way they all liked it, and served it to her parents.

They each made an attempt to change the subject—her mom described the event in D.C., about seeing her Aunt Dinah and how much fun they had had. Aliya couldn't help but smile, the truth was heavy, but clearly her mother was dealing with the secret in a new light. *At least this will help her PTSD,* she shuddered, realizing that most of her mom's nightmares probably had nothing to do with the Gulf War and everything to do with what this man had done to her.

Tareq Al-Salem, Aliya's right hand formed a fist, and her fingernails bore into her palm, *you asshole.*

For a second, she let herself envision doling a punch straight at his eye, then forced herself to focus on her mom's story. She'd obviously had a wonderful time in D.C. and was trying to extinguish the fire her secret had caused by telling them about how much fun she'd had.

Oh, Mom, I love you, Aliya thought as she half-listened.

When she reached the end of her teacup, she made an excuse about having to get to an afternoon study group that had just come up—she needed time and space to process what her parents had just told her. "I love you both so much," she emphasized. "I'm glad you aren't carrying this around on your own anymore, Mom. You shouldn't have to, no one should go through something like this alone."

Aliya hugged them both and squeezed her mom so hard she had to wriggle free, then watched them drive away. Once their car was out of sight from her second-floor window, she sank down into the couch. She wasn't sure which part was the worst, the fact that this monster was her father, even if it was just biology.

That's all it is. She'd be telling herself that for a while.

Or was it the trauma her mom had endured? The secret that she had carried for so long? Aliya wiped her eyes, picturing Tareq standing in front of her like a punching bag in her kickboxing class. She felt the impact of each blow she delivered, and the catharsis that came with it, letting the scenario play out in her head.

He deserves to pay.

After almost an hour chewing over what she had just learned, Aliya rose and changed into workout clothes. Visualizing the encounter in her head was helpful, but it would be all the more so if she could hit an actual punching bag.

At least in my head, I'll see him pay.

Chapter 44

Washington D.C., USA - April, 2016

Tareq gawked at the email attachment he had just received from the investigator.

I have a daughter?

He could scarcely comprehend it, but her birthday confirmed his earlier suspicions. Still, the concrete realization was more than he had expected. *Aliya,* he remembered that name, Mariam's mother's name. *A daughter,* as if he had needed further validation that he and Mariam belonged together. His torso quivered, the anticipation of seeing her returning in full.

His anger toward her magnified as he thought further.

When did she know? He remembered visiting Mariam in the hospital and he slammed his fist onto the table. *She must have known then, she* had *to have known.* As he continued down memory lane, another possibility struck him. *When I finally found her, she was at Dinah's...* His posture relaxed, he understood what had happened now—Mariam had never wanted to leave him, this was all about Dinah, and then this man, Raj, who had been occupying his bed all these years.

Mariam always thought we belonged together, in his mind, he could feel her beneath him again, the nights they had spent together at his home in Kuwait.

Opening another browser window, Tareq went to the American Airlines website and booked a flight to Austin. The process was frustrating, the website slow, and he longed for the days of travel agents. A few minutes later, he relaxed though, the booking was complete.

Two days, Mariam, I'll see you in two days.

Tareq reopened the file the investigator had given him—including a family photo—and leaned over to stare at it. He ogled Mariam for several moments, then glared at Raj, his face only an inch away from the photo. He took a swig from a bottle of whiskey on the table, gulping it down until he reached the last drop, then threw it at the wall. The shards landed all over the floor and he felt a release, he would have his revenge.

I've found her now and I'm coming for you.

Tareq straightened up and grinned at Raj. *Joke's on you, she belongs with me.* He concocted a picture in his head, snickering as he played out what he would do when he saw them in person. He imagined how he would torture Raj, make him pay for having his wife all of these years. Looking at Mariam, his anticipation heightened. *It will be just like before,* he wanted to say to her. His gaze moved to Aliya, only a teenager in the picture and he shrugged, he had no real interest in meeting her. *But she is proof that Mariam is mine.* He returned his gaze to Mariam and leaned back in his chair, pleasure coursing through him—she was standing in front of him now, in that maroon dress from Nadia's picture...

1990

Chapter 45

Salmiya, Kuwait – September, 1990

Raj returned to the first sitting room to check on his charges after he emerged from the bathroom, still feeling slightly unsettled. Some nights when he did his rounds, he was more active, asking questions and seeking out conversation, but this time he simply listened and maintained his distance. One of his wards needed an extra blanket, which he agreed to try to procure, although he doubted there were any extras available; another asked if he could see that the cooking didn't contain dhaniya in the future because she didn't like the taste of it. Raj found these requests relatively simple compared to what he had dealt with over the last few days and made his exit, retreating to the next sitting room, which tended to be calmer. His pulse raced when he saw her on the other side of the room, but chastised himself in a hurry.

You're married.

Raj focused on the other end of the table, this time sitting down to eat himself before entertaining requests from his "supervisees". Twenty minutes later he stood and made his way along the table, stopping twice to hear requests similar to those he had heard in the other room. When he reached the end, he greeted the three women who were usually clustered there.

"Hello, Raj," Janhvi said as he approached. "How are you?"

"I'm doing fine. You? All three of you?" he attempted to catch Mariam's gaze, but all she gave him was a quick nod and a smile.

"We're doing fine, thank you," Dinah answered, drawing his attention away from Mariam. "That curtain you set up to divide the room is really helpful, and I know Ashok and his family appreciate it. They're lovely, but it's nice for us to have a little bit of privacy, even here."

"I'm glad to hear it." Raj continued to ask Dinah a few questions to make sure that they were comfortable in the sleeping area he had allocated for them on the left side of one of the smaller classrooms across the hall. He'd set up the curtain as a personal touch since he couldn't give them a room on their own; they shared it with a family of four, whom he was sure also valued the separation. Luckily the classroom had two doors, so each side also had its own entrance as well.

After one more attempt to speak to Mariam, Raj pulled himself away, he had no business being interested in another woman when he had no idea what had happened to Ritika.

What is wrong with you? He made a quick exit, not wanting to open himself up to that channel of emotion any more than he already had, and retreated to his own bedroom. *Calling this a bedroom is a bit of a stretch,* he kicked off his shoes and stretched out on the blanket he had laid on the floor to create his "bed." The concrete was cold and hard beneath his back, but he relished its sturdiness—it would remain as it was no matter what hell broke loose everywhere else.

Raj interlocked his fingers behind his head, the only pillow he'd elected to have in favor of making sure that there were enough pillows for the elderly, the women, and the children. He was about to let himself doze off, he was exhausted from hauling in supplies and being out in the camp offered him no solace, but at the last minute decided to make a visit to the bathroom before turning in for the night. After washing his face and brushing his teeth, he emerged and turned the corner toward his room, almost running straight into Mariam.

"Hi, Raj, I'm so sorry," she said in a shy voice. "I should have looked."

Something in her tone made him look at her in concern. "That's okay. Are you all right?"

"I'm fine," she choked, then bounded off toward the bathroom.

Raj frowned, watching as she disappeared into the men's restroom without realizing where she was going. He pressed his ear to the door, then backed away immediately, his suspicions confirmed.

She stepped out a few minutes later with a dazed look. "Oh, I'm sorry," she said clearly noticing that she'd been in the men's bathroom.

"Are you sure you're all right? Did you get food poisoning?" Raj asked, ignoring her apology.

Mariam placed her hand on her stomach, "I'm fine, I guess something just didn't sit right. Good night." She moved past him, sporting an embarrassed expression and disappeared down the hall.

He watched her leave with another frown, wishing that he could do something to help her. After a moment of pondering, he went to the kitchen in search of Mylanta, a stomach remedy that he'd discovered was quite helpful. He found some in the cabinet and extracted two tablets encased in plastic.

When he got to the classroom where Mariam slept, he knocked on the door, and Dinah answered it. "Hi, err Dinah," he said and handed her the tablets with a hasty explanation.

"I don't think it'll help, but thank you."

Raj tilted his head to the side, unsure why she was so certain. He opened his mouth to ask, but she had already disappeared back into the room. He shrugged it off and returned to bed, battling his thoughts. Mariam was beautiful, mysterious, and intriguing, but he kept trying to redirect his attention to Ritika. He was already starting to forget what she looked like, he had known her such a short time and now hadn't seen her since the occupation began. Raj tossed and turned in frustration until sleep finally took hold and he dozed off despite the limited cushioning and the hard floor.

Chapter 46

Salmiya, Kuwait – Three weeks later, September, 1990

Raj's eyes followed Mariam as she left the breakfast table, then refocused on the man sitting across from him. Now that they had been at the school for over a month, the demands had eased as people adjusted to their new circumstances, but his role as a dispute moderator had amped up even more. The continued proximity had only added to some of the tensions throughout the camp. He and the other supervisors had even had to reallocate some of the sleeping arrangements to mediate two of the disputes, much to their frustration. Despite that, everyone had settled into something of a routine. Cooking responsibilities alternated from day to day, and he and some of the other men made weekly trips to procure food and supplies. The visits to the cooperative down the street had started to worry him as they had already exhausted some supplies, but thankfully the stores of rice and canned goods were continuing to be replenished, if for no other reason than to meet the soldiers' needs as well. Fayaz, the owner of the cooperative, sounded as if he had things under control, so Raj chose to believe him, especially since the alternative was too grim to contemplate. He had seen Fayaz and Sanjay having a few hushed discussions, but Raj had decided not to butt in. He had enough to deal with taking care of his charges, he had no interest in adding to his responsibilities unless absolutely necessary.

A commotion outside caught his attention, and he rushed out of the sitting room, unable to make out what they were saying from inside. As soon as he stepped out, he heard the words, "Soldiers are coming! Hide the supplies!"

Raj moved back into the canteen area and tried to make his voice portray a calm that couldn't be further from his state of mind. "There are Iraqi soldiers coming to the camp. For everyone's safety it would be best if all of you return to your quarters. We're going to hide the kitchen supplies and could use your help if you're able to lift any of the heavier bags."

He didn't wait around for a reaction; instead, he rushed toward the kitchen where three others had already gathered to grab bags of rice and lentils to hide them.

Would the soldiers really take the food? He discarded the idea before he even had the chance to process it—someone clearly thought that it would be worth the effort to hide the provisions. He heaved a giant bag of rice onto his shoulder and headed toward the bathrooms as fast as he could. Of all the places, they probably wouldn't look there. A few seconds later he stashed it underneath one of the sinks, glad that the bag was sealed. *Not the ideal place to store food.* By the time he returned to the kitchen he heard the trucks pulling in outside—he might have enough time to hide one more bag before the soldiers made it into the camp.

Raj had just hoisted the next bag of rice onto his back when someone caught his arm, and he looked up, frowning to see Mariam's friend Janhvi in front of him. "What is it?" he panted.

"You can't let them come into our room. Please."

Why on earth would I let them if I could stop them?

"Okay," he was confused, but didn't have time to argue—he would obviously prevent it if he could. The soldiers were nearby now, shouting, and he wouldn't have enough time to make it to the bathroom. Acting on instinct, he ducked into the doorway on his left, a tiny storeroom and dumped the bag underneath a pile of desks that they had stashed there when they repurposed one of the classrooms as a bedroom. Back in the hallway, he looked for Janhvi, but she had disappeared. Before he had the chance to find her to get clarification, the soldiers swept through the camp like a tornado.

2016

Chapter 47

Austin, Texas, USA – April, 2016

Mariam squinted from the reception desk of the BookPeople bookstore out into the parking lot.

You're seeing things.

She squeezed her eyes shut, opened and rubbed them, before looking out into the parking lot again, this time from directly in front of the entrance. She told herself no one was there, but remained frustrated and off balance. She returned to the reception desk and made a hasty excuse to one of her colleagues before retreating to her office.

With a deep breath, Mariam sank into her chair and looked at her desk; the to-read pile on the right had grown considerably in the last week, but she'd had trouble focusing. *I thought I was doing better,* she sighed, thinking back to her breakthrough in therapy. There was no denying it though, this was the fourth time in the week since she and Raj had told Aliya the truth that she had seen someone she'd recognized as Tareq. Clearly her mind was playing tricks on her, she wasn't ready to move on.

Will I ever be free of him? She reached for her phone to call Teresa's office and moved her appointment up from the end of the week to later that afternoon, citing a scheduling difficulty since she was hesitant to admit how much she obviously needed another session. *Just focus on work.* She picked up the first book on the to-read pile, a spy thriller called *The Spirit of Destruction,* written by a new author the store was considering stocking.

Mariam opened to the first page and had disappeared into the book for about fifteen minutes before her phone rang. She picked up without noticing the caller ID, "Hello?" she repeated three times before hearing a click and then nothing. The caller ID was listed as "Blocked". Telemarketers were a frequent nuisance, but most came up as a number she didn't recognize, rarely blocked. She checked her call log—only to confirm that she had received a total of eight blocked number calls over the last four days.

Just another telemarketer, she reassured herself. Her hands shook as she remembered the figure that she'd seen in the parking lot, and she suppressed her fears once again. *This has to stop, you're being crazy.*

Mariam reopened her book, and within a few minutes was once again encapsulated by the story, following an Iranian spy engaged in a ploy to assassinate the Kuwaiti monarch and the American agent who was attempting to foil his plans. She smiled as the plot drew her back to Kuwait, to the Persian Gulf Coast and the streets of the Salmiya neighborhood. The book's portrayal made her want to return there, it had been so many years since she had fled, never considering that she could return once the Gulf War had ended. Mariam leaned back in her chair and fondly recalled the walks she and her mother used to take along the water's edge before she'd died when Mariam was a teenager. *I guess not all the memories are bad,* she reluctantly admitted. After checking her watch, she set an alarm for thirty minutes later, when her reading break would be over, and she'd have to go back out to the floor, either to work on the display in the mystery/thriller section that she managed or return to the front desk. As she continued reading, she lost herself in the story, turning page after page, wondering where it would take her next.

Once the alarm went off, she set the book down and was about to leave when her phone rang again.

No.

She reached for it, the muscles in her torso rigid. The caller ID said Raj. She steadied herself against the desk and spent the next several minutes trying to convince him, as well as herself, that all was well. In the end she knew she'd failed and resisted the urge to hurl the phone against the wall.

Dammit! I was doing so well, but all it takes is some idiotic telemarketer for me to come unhinged.

She returned to the floor and spent an hour restacking books in her section and two others, avoiding the reception desk like the plague until it was time to head to therapy. When she turned onto the street, she spotted a man on the corner taking pictures who she could have sworn she'd seen that morning when she was parking her car.

You are really losing it, she shook her head, *but at least you don't think he's Tareq.*

Chapter 48

Austin, Texas, USA - April, 2016

Tareq hit the unlock button on his car key as the local investigator that he was working with opened the passenger door.

"I think she saw me this time," the investigator said. "I still don't understand why you wanted me to take so many pictures of BookPeople, you already know that she works there."

Idiot, Tareq thought, then answered with a shrug, "Like I told you, she's been shirking child support payments, but I had to make sure it's her before I go in and confront her. It's not like I could go in and ask."

"Whatever, man, I'm sending you the pictures now," the investigator tapped on his phone screen. "You should have them in a second, so please go ahead and transfer the rest of my fee. Will you need anything else?"

Tareq stared at his phone, waiting for the pictures came through. Once he'd downloaded them, he scrolled through quickly, zooming in on one of Mariam sitting in her car.

It's her. He smirked at the confirmation, there was no mistaking it. He'd been following her, observing her daily routine, but had been unable to get close enough without giving himself away. After four failed attempts in the last three days, he'd met with this investigator the evening before to solicit his services. She was so close, they would be together again. A wave of anticipation passed over him as he recalled the soft curve of her neck, the feel of her hair in his fingers, and the creaminess of her skin.

"Actually, yes, could you send me a few pictures of her daughter—the one that she's actually taken care of, that is. Her name is Aliya Ghosh." He handed over the family photo of Raj, Mariam, and Aliya.

"Sure, no problem." The local investigator took a picture of the photo with his phone, then looked back at Tareq expectedly. "It'll be the same fee, same arrangement."

"Right," he pulled out his wallet and handed over double the remaining payment they had discussed in cash, half for what remained on the initial assignment, along with fifty percent of the next one.

After counting the bills quickly, the investigator nodded. "I'll text you the pictures and you can drop the rest of the money at my office."

Tareq waited until the investigator was out of sight before he wandered into the bookstore. He kept to himself and moved toward the mystery section in the back. He wanted to take advantage of the time that Mariam was gone to see what she did all day. He stopped at the café and ordered a cup of coffee, grimacing at the first sip—it was a far cry from the slow brewed coffee that he made in the Bialetti at home.

Still sipping it as a distraction, he took in the books in the mystery section, noting the number of male authors and a few of the more gruesome plots, at least from what he could gather based on the book descriptions. *She's spending her time on this trash,* he wanted to spit on the books in a combination of disgust and disbelief. After stewing over the display for another ten minutes, he wandered around the store in search of the staff offices until he found them nestled on the other side of the café. With a quick glance around, he opened the door and walked past four desks until he found the one labeled with Mariam's assumed name: *Ritika Ghosh.* He could barely stop himself from grabbing her nameplate and flinging it out the window. Instead, he pocketed it and straightened out the pile of books and papers, making sure that all of the corners were precisely lined up. Tareq paused and picked up the book on the center of her desk, the cover featured the silhouette of an attractive woman superimposed on top of an image of the Kuwait Towers. After reading the back cover, his frown deepened, and he stuffed it into his other jacket pocket where it bulged slightly. He checked his watch—he had to get moving before someone saw him in there and spoiled the surprise. He grabbed a tissue from the box on her desk and ran it over the surface to pick up any dust, cringing at the black specks before he tossed it in the trash bin under her desk. Patting his pockets to make sure that he had both the nameplate and the book, he exited the staff bay quietly, not allowing himself to relax until he was safely back in his car.

Tareq relished the last sip of coffee in spite of its acidic taste, he'd found Mariam, and he felt closer to her than he had in years—he had sat at her desk, shared the space where she spent so much time.

I have to save her from all this filth. He felt even more vindicated, remembering the books on display in the mystery section of the store. *This man Raj has corrupted her, but not for much longer.* He revved the engine and input an address in the Travis Heights neighborhood into the GPS. He didn't even need to check the file from the investigator in D.C., he'd already memorized the address, 1605 Drake Avenue. The engine purred as he turned south toward Town Lake, reflecting his contentment.

We'll be together again soon, my Mariam.

1990

Chapter 49

Salmiya, Kuwait - September, 1990

Mariam huddled in the corner of her room and waited for the nausea to abate. Her bouts of morning sickness had grown more frequent over the last two months, but their severity had decreased, and most of the time she could wait it out if she sat still for a few minutes, far away from any smells that might trigger another vomiting spell. The heat didn't help, but thankfully the evenings brought some relief now that August was behind them.

She leaned her head back against the wall—the nausea was passing now, but the deep feeling of loneliness remained. If only that would pass in a quick bout as the nausea did… Mariam let out a long sigh and tried not to fixate on their plight. The school camp had given them sanctuary, and Tareq was gone, but she still lived in a constant state of fear. If she interacted with anyone at the camp more than the occasional hello, they would figure out that she was Kuwaiti and she'd be putting Dinah and herself at serious risk. She trembled, recalling the Iraqi soldiers who had raided the camp less than a week before. They had confiscated food and water but had caused more chaos than anything else. As far as she knew they hadn't been looking for Kuwaitis—it hadn't sounded like it from the shouting she'd heard while she and Dinah were hiding in their bedroom—but she'd never been more aware of the danger.

If they'd found us... the mere possibility made her shudder again. She had heard the rumors—a Kuwaiti man who had gone out to buy bread and came home to find that his seventeen-year-old daughter had been taken prisoner, the families who had vanished overnight, among others. The soldiers who raided the school had threatened to take some of the younger Indian women away...she didn't want to imagine what they would have done to her and Dinah had they been discovered as Kuwaiti women hiding out at an Indian refugee camp.

What would the soldiers do to the people here, if they found us? Mariam drew her knees into her chest, *Are we putting everyone here at risk?* An image of the soldiers coming back and executing half of the camp at gunpoint came to mind, and she tried to shake it off. She couldn't stand to deliberate on what would happen to the people who had taken them in, given them refuge, if they were discovered. Contrary to what Dinah had predicted, they had managed to keep a relatively low profile, interacting only with Janhvi, so as far as she could tell, no one suspected their true nationalities. They kept Arabic conversations to a minimum, speaking only in English, which—although it would seem odd to others at the camp—wasn't necessarily a red flag. Mariam tried to throw a Hindi word or phrase into her occasional encounters, then excuse herself for how she'd never learned to speak the language properly. Still the idea that everyone might be in even more danger, all due to her existence, haunted her.

I put Dinah in danger because I didn't leave Tareq, and now everyone here might pay the price.

Mariam's gaze wandered to the side of her bed, landing on the Mylanta tablets that Raj had procured for her, and she couldn't help but smile. The way he had looked at her, the genuine concern, the gentleness in his eyes when he had waited for her outside of the bathroom, all of that brought her comfort. She had never seen those emotions in a man before, certainly not someone outside of her family—tender moments had been few and far between even there.

Tareq never looked at me like that. Not even once in the time that they'd been married, nor before or on the day of their wedding. She squeezed her eyes shut as the memory of his touch returned, his mouth on hers, along with the sense of being so powerless and incapable of stopping him. Mariam tried to push the images away, but they came on even stronger, and she could feel his hands on the drawstring of her kamese, grappling at her underwear. Her back crashed into the wall, and the tears took hold. She buried her head in her hands and sobbed.

This will never be over. Even when he is not with me, he's always there.

When the intensity of the emotions subsided, Mariam wiped her eyes; she had considered several times whether or not to report Tareq's death. Under normal circumstances, they might have stood a chance of acquittal—Janhvi had killed him in self-defense. She could have blamed his death on the soldiers, but if there was an investigation, she knew that his body would tell a different story. Anyone interrogating her would also see through such a story in a heartbeat: she could imagine the questions about why Tareq had been killed in someone else's house. With the Iraqi invasion though, there was hardly any rule of law left, and simply by being Kuwaitis she and Dinah were already too much of a target, making them even more likely to be fingered as responsible for such a crime. Despite the constant rumors, the actual number of Kuwaiti deaths were low, especially now, and she also feared drawing too much attention to herself and the camp. The soldiers wouldn't need any other excuse to take them into custody to beat and rape them, they would be labeled criminals, after all. Even if there were some hope that they would see her side, Mariam couldn't imagine taking that risk. She placed her hand over her belly, thinking of the baby growing inside her. Besides, she couldn't do that to Dinah, or to Janhvi, both of whom had saved her from Tareq. She owed them both so much—reporting Tareq's death was unthinkable since it meant that something might happen to either of them.

Mariam collected herself, she had to find a way to get past these thoughts, they were rapidly becoming a never ending abyss.

Tareq was a monster, she reminded herself, echoing variations on phrases that both Dinah and Janhvi had used to describe him. *He's not worth your guilt, or your time.* She looked up at the ceiling and nodded to herself, then maneuvered to standing position. The nausea had subsided now, and Dinah needed her help with the laundry—that was enough of memories for the moment.

Chapter 50

Salmiya, Kuwait - September, 1990

Raj sauntered into the kitchen and poured several small cups of masala tea from the pot that one of the women at the camp had prepared. He paused and savored a sip before serving it in the sitting room. His mother had started to make masala tea for him when he was studying for his entrance exams to university. He relished the sweetness, evoking memories of how she had said she would only make it if he was studying, not if he went out to play cricket with his friends as he'd so often been tempted to do. She had thought the tea would act as an added incentive, although he already put more than enough pressure on himself—even if he had procrastinated about studying from time to time.

After two more sips he felt rejuvenated, so he grabbed the tray and made his way down the outdoor hall, moving speedily to make it out of the heat as quickly as possible. Even in late September, the Kuwaiti heat was still going strong. He walked into the sitting room, set the tray down at the table and wiped his brow before making a short announcement about the tea. He was about to retreat to his room—the level of interaction required for his job as a supervisor required a substantial amount of alone time for him to feel functional—when he noticed Mariam enter through the side door.

Raj greeted her with a small smile and stopped himself from frowning as she drew closer, her eyes were puffy, and her nose was red as if she'd been crying. "Would you like some tea?" he asked, wishing that there was more he could do.

"Sure, thank you," Mariam answered. "I'm actually looking for Dinah, I was supposed to help her with the laundry, but I can't find her anywhere. Have you seen her?"

Raj handed her a cup and shook his head. He was about to offer to help her look for Dinah when her face contorted at the first sip. "Are you all right?"

Without a word, she set the cup on the table and fled, leaving him looking after her.

Could she really have food poisoning again?

RAJ WAITED FOR MARIAM TO emerge from the bathroom, battling a sense of déjà vu. *How many times has this happened?* He'd noticed it twice in the last couple of weeks, and he couldn't help but recall Janhvi specifically asking him to keep the soldiers away from their quarters, although he had no idea how the two things could be related. He mulled over the possibility but didn't have much of a chance to reflect on it before she reappeared.

"I'm all right," she said without waiting for him to ask how she was doing. "I get a little queasy sometimes, I don't know why."

"Are you sure?" Raj's thoughts started to run away from him as he recalled a segment he had seen on the news a few months earlier about eating disorders. *Could she be bulimic?* He racked his brain, trying to recall the signs the program had described, but nothing more than throwing up after eating came to mind.

"I'm fine." Mariam brushed past him in the direction of her quarters.

For a moment, Raj debated following her, then caught up to her in a few steps. "Look, I'm only asking because I'm concerned. Are you quite sure everything's fine? You've had food poisoning a few times now, are you sure it isn't something more? Are you sick? There's a doctor coming by in a couple of days…" She met his gaze in silence, and he blurted out his worry before he could stop himself. "I saw this program a few months ago on something called bulimia, an eating disorder, it makes someone throw up everything they eat—"

"I don't have an eating disorder," she interrupted curtly.

"I'm sorry, I was just asking," Raj said, taken aback by her tone. "I'll see you later," he turned to walk away.

Mariam sighed and spoke in a gentler tone, "I'm sorry, I didn't mean it like that, but I don't have an eating disorder, and I'm not sick. The nausea is related to…something else."

"As long as you're okay," Raj raised his eyebrows, wondering if she was going to tell him what the something else was.

"I'm not sick." She swallowed before she continued. "I'm pregnant."

Raj recoiled in surprise. *She's married?* She looked so young he had never imagined that she could be pregnant. He gathered himself. "I feel so stupid. I don't know why I thought—I guess I just didn't realize you were married…" his voice trailed off and he kicked himself for behaving like an idiot. *You should be thinking about Ritika,* he censured himself and tried to remember what she looked like, but he couldn't recall a single feature of her face.

"It's okay."

"Let me know if there's anything you need," he said before he excused himself in a hurry.

That evening he drove toward Farwaniya Hospital and stared at the boundary wall for several minutes unable to move. He had already searched for Ritika there, and there was no reason to think that she would appear now, but he had to try.

She's your wife, he slammed the car door shut. *This is what you're supposed to be doing.*

Chapter 51

Salmiya, Kuwait - September, 1990

Raj knocked on the door softly and waited for someone to answer. He sighed and looked down at the bottle of prenatal vitamins in his hand, the only thing that his visit to the hospital had yielded. Farwaniya Hospital was still somewhat active, with a few staff working, coaxed on by the soldiers who patrolled at all hours. The remaining staff had continued to care for long-term patients, along with the few injured soldiers that they were forced to treat at gunpoint. Raj had managed to get inside to speak to one of the pharmacists who he had recognized from a party some months earlier. They didn't know each other well, but the recognition helped to initiate the conversation. For a second, Raj had entertained a glimmer of hope—maybe he could get some information about Ritika, but he'd still come up short. Yusuf had said that the soldiers had dragged out some of the Kuwaiti staff, but the remainder had been instructed to keep on working. Many of them were staying at the hospital, sleeping in the on-call rooms.

Raj had walked the halls one more time, searching the radiology ward where Ritika had worked, and asking anyone he ran into for information. On his way out, he stopped to thank Yusuf again. After a short exchange, he was about to leave when he'd thought of Mariam's pregnancy and asked about prenatal vitamins.

Raj glanced at his right hand, holding the bottle that he'd picked up. What made him so compelled to care for Mariam? He wasn't sure what it was, something about her demeanor, the twinkle in her eyes when she smiled. They hadn't had many interactions at the camp, she had certainly kept her distance—which made all the more sense now that he knew that she was married—but there was still a connection there. *There's something—I'm not crazy.* He rejected the sentiment, reminding himself that he had picked up the vitamins while he was out searching for Ritika.

Before he could go further down the rabbit hole, Dinah answered the door. He gave her the vitamins along with a short explanation of what they were. Her eyes widened as he spoke, and he felt himself shrinking away involuntarily to shield himself from her disapproval. Dinah thanked him and shut the door, leaving Raj outside, unsure of what was so wrong about what he had done. *Shouldn't the vitamins be helpful?* Even if she disapproved of his interaction with Mariam, a little gratitude didn't seem out of line.

Raj was about to step away from the room when he heard raised voices inside, and he straightened up abruptly. The voices weren't speaking in Hindi, or in English, or any other Indian language. Dinah and Mariam were arguing in Arabic. And not just any Arabic—a dialect that he distinctly recognized, one that couldn't be confused with any other region—*Kuwaiti Arabic.*

2016

Chapter 52

Washington D.C., USA - May, 2016

Nadia tossed and turned in bed in a feeble attempt to take a nap two hours after arriving at her parents' house. Earlier in the week, her mother had told her that Uncle Tareq was out of town and she'd jumped at the chance for a visit. As soon as she got there, she was about to explain what had happened, when her mother preempted her by gushing about how glad she was that he had decided to move in.

Since then, Nadia had struggled to work up the courage to broach the subject, how Uncle Tareq had accosted her to find out about Mariam. What he had threatened to do to her, and to them, if she ever told anyone. Every time she opened her mouth to begin her throat turned dry, the words escaped her and remained just out of reach.

I have to say something.

She flipped onto her other side once again in frustration, her pillow damp from tears. She had never felt so powerless, his threats had rendered her immobile. When his fingers had closed around her throat, she'd even tried to fight back—she had lashed out, almost hit him, but he was almost a foot taller and probably fifty pounds heavier.

What is he planning to do to Mariam?

In the two weeks since her encounter with Uncle Tareq, Nadia had hardly been able to sleep. Anytime the lights dimmed, she returned to that moment, when his hands had gripped her throat. Her attempts to scream failed. His hold on her only eased when she answered him with Ritika, the first name from Mariam's credit card. Nadia had been about to submit and blurt out the last name as well, but instead of pushing for more information, he was more interested in doling out a series of four slaps.

I have to do something. This is not who I am, she kept saying to herself to no avail. *At least I didn't tell him her full name, that has to be worth* something. *Please be worth something.*

She turned onto her back and stared up at the ceiling, she had never hoped so much for God to stand with her, to save her, her family, and her friend. Nadia tried for the umpteenth time to convince herself that there was nothing to worry about. After all, Mariam was no longer in D.C., she had returned home to Austin where she was safe. Since Uncle Tareq didn't know her full name, she would remain that way—all Nadia had to worry about was her own safety. That argument, which continued to rage on in the back of her mind, seemed to hold less water with each passing minute.

I could warn her... I should *warn her.* She felt his hands on her again.

What if he tries to kill us? She thought of her parents, of herself, and the vicious circle expanded.

Nadia wrestled with those thoughts for the next half hour, her head spinning from the internal debate along with the lack of sleep. She had read articles about it in one of her classes at university, how prolonged insomnia could literally make someone go crazy, but she had never considered that it might happen to her. Indeed, she'd never had trouble sleeping, her mother had always claimed that she'd been a great sleeper, even when she was an infant and a toddler. *I never cried then, yet now I can't stop.* Nadia bit her lip and gave up, sitting up with her head in her hands.

There has to be a way out.

She had always believed that, even in the most difficult of situations. Now, the mere notion of an escape seemed ludicrous, like a fallacy that she'd created from a life without difficulty, a life filled with privilege. The flow of tears increased, tracing her cheekbones to her chin—she had been entirely at his mercy and she was lucky that all he'd wanted to do was slap her, nothing more. Uncle Tareq was far too terrifying, she didn't dare defy him. There was no point in even trying, she couldn't risk it, she wasn't strong enough. She sank back into bed and pulled the covers up to her nose.

There is no way out.

Chapter 53

Austin, Texas, USA – May, 2016

Mariam walked out of her therapy session and looked around frantically as she reached her Honda CR-V. She pulled the door shut and hit the lock button, then leaned over the steering wheel to catch her breath.

This has to stop.

She bit her lip, wishing that therapy could have an instantaneous result. Instead, it made her feel tremendously raw, and she had never been so glad to not have to return to her office.

Traffic moved at a snail's pace, but the lack of focus needed to navigate her way home meant she could remain absorbed in her therapy session.

"Why do you think you keep seeing people that look like Tareq?" Teresa had asked.

Mariam had found herself stumped. "Maybe I'm still reliving everything that happened? I guess I'm still paranoid about people finding out about him, about holding me responsible for his death?" She shrugged, "I really thought that the worst was behind me, but I keep feeling as if he's coming for me. This last week—I can't stand it. Why can't I get him out of my head?"

As she drove home, continuing to replay the conversation, Mariam wiped her eyes and turned off of South Congress Avenue onto Drake before steering into her driveway. She switched the engine off and banged her head against her hands, her knuckles white from their grip on the wheel.

Why can't I let this go? Why can't I leave him behind? She sobbed for a couple of minutes before composing herself and heading into the house.

Mariam stepped inside and shivered—the usually warm and toasty house was a mere fifty degrees Fahrenheit. She frowned and checked the living room windows, then noticed that the door to their back porch had been left open. Confused, she shut the door and latched it, thankful that the neighborhood was safe enough for break-ins to be few and far between.

Raj never leaves the door open. She sunk into a chair at the dining table and pulled off her black cowboy boots. Aliya had bought them for her as a gift a few months earlier, claiming that her mother needed to finally get with the Austin style. Looking at them made Mariam smile, she had so much in her life to be grateful for, so much to help her to deal with and get past all of this insanity with Tareq.

I can get through this.

She munched on an apple and decided that she might as well start dinner; Raj would be home in less than an hour and she was already hungry so there was no point in waiting. After checking the contents of the fridge, she pulled out some chicken which she put to marinate in Greek yogurt, based on a new favorite recipe that Dinah had recommended. To add the spice mix, she opened her cabinet and backed away. The spices weren't in their usual spots. Mariam leaned forward to look for the Kashmiri chili powder only to find the bottle in the second row of her horizontal spice rack. Setting it on the kitchen counter, she rummaged through the cabinet, unable to see the bottle of garam masala anywhere. She looked one more time, this time noticing it two bottles to the left of where the Kashmiri chili powder had been.

Did Raj reorganize my spices? He'd been complaining about her non-existent organizational system for years—basically her spices were just thrown into the rack in whatever order she felt like on a particular day—but he had never done anything about it despite numerous declarations to the contrary. Mariam started at the top of the rack, pausing on each bottle, looking from the top left to the bottom right. *They're in alphabetical order,* she realized with a perplexed smile. *I guess he finally fixed it, but why didn't he tell me?* She rubbed her chin, normally a victory like that would have been something he crowed about for days.

Mariam added the spices to her marinade and decided to let Raj surprise her—after all, he had gone through such an effort. Her spice cabinet was something of a labyrinth and reorganizing it must have been quite the undertaking. She chuckled and practiced feigning disbelief when he told her about the effort that he'd put in.

She set a pot on the stove to make a sauce for the chicken when she noticed the Bialetti coffee maker on her counter.

It's Tareq.

She froze, and the empty pot clattered as it dropped onto the stove grill and fell to the ground.

You're being an idiot, this is insane. Tareq is dead. Her hands wobbled as she placed the pot back on the stovetop and reassured herself in vain. Raj must have taken it out of the cabinet when he reorganized the spices. *That's all, everything is fine.*

Supporting herself against the counter, Mariam looked through the rest of the kitchen cabinets, and let out a sigh of relief that everything else seemed as she had left it. After several deep breaths, she felt calmer.

Everything is fine.

Tareq always liked coffee from the Bialetti, a voice in the back of her mind piped up.

While she and Raj both enjoyed the depth of the slow brewed coffee, most of the time their impatience won out and they elected to use the standard filter coffee machine instead—the Bialetti required at least ten minutes to heat up along with supervision to make sure the coffee didn't burn. Mariam examined the old Italian percolator before setting it back on the counter, perhaps having it in sight would make them use it. That must be why Raj had left it out, she decided, still unable to assuage her fears. Her eyes ventured to her bedroom door—there was one way to know for sure. Mariam headed for the walk-in closet off of her bedroom, her heart racing as she reached for the light switch.

"Oh, thank God," she said aloud when the light turned on, her closet was in the exact state of disarray that she'd left it in that morning.

Mariam shook her head, Teresa had said that the paranoia could remain with her until she dealt with all of her emotions, everything had come to the surface following her visit to D.C.

"Your conversations with Aliya, with Raj, along with the trip, opened up a whole host of memories and emotions that you've been suppressing for years. It's only natural that there would be consequences, although the paranoia is more extreme than I would have expected. Try not to beat yourself up over it though, you've been holding in a ton of emotion, this is just your mind's way of addressing and coping with all of it," Teresa had said. "Just remember to validate that and you'll get past this. Tareq is dead, and that part of your life is behind you."

Mariam looked up and down her closet again, once again relieved at the disarray of her clothes—her laundry hamper in the corner was overflowing, and her shirts and dresses were hung without any semblance of an organizational system. When she was still with Tareq, keeping her closet in this condition would have earned her a sound beating. She'd never told Raj that was why she relished keeping her clothes in such disorder, but the entropy of her closet comforted her and reminded her that Tareq no longer had control over her. Being messy was an aspect of Mariam Qatami that he had repressed, something that she had allowed to flourish since the first day that she'd escaped him.

She heard the front door unlock, followed by Raj's voice.

See, everything is fine, she headed to the living room to greet him with a long kiss.

There's nothing to worry about.

Chapter 54

Austin, Texas, USA - May, 2016

Tareq watched Mariam with binoculars through the picture window that faced out onto her backyard; he'd been able to rent the house directly behind hers through a rental service called Airbnb. He could never have fathomed such a service, but the younger woman at his work, the one who'd told him about social media, had mentioned it when he informed his office that he would be taking his first vacation.

"Where are you going?" she had asked. When he had answered Austin, she'd started to gush about an apartment that she had stayed at through the same service, how it had been in the perfect neighborhood, and offered something so charming at a rate cheaper than a hotel.

He'd disregarded it initially, and booked his stay at the Hyatt down the street from Mariam's home. Every time he tried to get close to her house though, he found his efforts thwarted—first by a couple speeding by on one of the newfangled scooters that appeared to be everywhere, then by several pedestrians. Each encounter had amplified his frustration and finally, he'd figured it couldn't hurt to check what the site had to offer. What he had discovered was a treasure trove of places to stay, right in her neighborhood. After much contemplation, he had chosen the place that seemed the closest, despite the fact that it had been booked for another two nights.

Since his arrival a few hours earlier, he couldn't be more pleased—he had lucked out more than he could have possibly imagined. This studio was far superior to the Hyatt, he now had a self-contained unit with a fence line that adjoined Mariam's backyard. He also had a direct line of sight into Mariam's patio windows, including both her dining room and, most importantly, her bedroom.

The minutes flew by as he watched her, first cooking in the kitchen, and then as she disappeared into her bedroom. Tareq broke into a smile, perhaps he would get to see her change her clothes. The prospect of touching her again was imminent and becoming all the more visceral.

Soon, but not soon enough, he imagined his right hand grazing her leg, while the other slid down her torso.

He straightened up as she disappeared from view; good as his viewpoint was, he didn't have a line of sight into her walk-in closet. He cursed under his breath. Now that she was so close, the idea that he had to wait to approach her seemed ludicrous, what on earth was he waiting for? She was alone, right there in front of him, awaiting his arrival.

Tareq set down his binoculars and stood, almost in a trance as he contemplated knocking on Mariam's door. He could have waited for her to come home instead of hightailing it when he had. She would pretend that she wasn't happy to see him, that she was frightened and uneasy, but he knew better—deep in his core, in his soul, he knew how much she wanted him. He kept his gaze on the bedroom window as he slid the knife that he'd purchased two days earlier into the back of his waistband; Mariam might be happy to see him, but he couldn't say the same for the impostor who she was living with. Tareq's eyes narrowed as he thought of Raj, the man who had taken his place in Mariam's arms and in her bed.

I will make sure that you pay.

He was on his way out when he caught movement in Mariam's dining room as she walked out of the bedroom. On the far side of the room, Raj walked in, followed by her greeting him with an extended kiss. A few minutes later the window blinds in the bedroom came down sharply, blocking his view. Tareq's imagination started to run wild; more than anything he didn't want to visualize what they were doing, but he was drawn to it, unable to look away from the closed blinds as if he were passing a major car wreck. His breathing sped up and his jaw set, they were within his reach, but he was frozen—he didn't dare confront them, he couldn't stand to see what had to be taking place. When he revealed himself, he needed to be sure that Raj had no escape, no way of manipulating Mariam to do his bidding as he had for so many years. He wanted his first encounter with Mariam to be alone so that she could fall into his arms the way that she used to, so that he could have what had been denied to him all of these years. Tareq dropped the binoculars, they hit the ground with a resounding crack, and he clenched his fists, his knuckles turning white.

That man is never going to touch her again.

1990

Chapter 55

Salmiya, Kuwait - September, 1990

Raj made it back to his room somehow, operating in a daze. Everything made so much sense now—he'd been surprised that neither Mariam nor Dinah understood more than a few words of Hindi, and now realized that he'd never heard them speaking any language other than English amongst themselves. That had been why Janhvi asked specifically to keep the soldiers away. The truth had been in front of him the whole time, but he hadn't seen it.

They're Kuwaiti.

That was why they'd kept to themselves so much, why they had limited all of their interactions with others at the camp. Deep down he felt a twinge of validation, Mariam had kept her distance for a reason: to protect her identity, not merely to keep him at arm's length. He sighed, wishing that that validation didn't feel like such a relief.

You should be thinking about your wife. At this point though, he was almost resigned to it, he wondered if he would ever see Ritika again. He just wished that he knew what had happened to her, that her disappearance wasn't a question that continued to hover over him.

He had nearly dozed off when he heard something outside and sat up abruptly. "Is someone there?" He heard another noise, but no response to his question, so he got out of bed and opened the door.

Down the hallway, he saw a figure that looked like Mariam moving quickly away. There was a note wedged into the hinges and he opened it to read, *"Thank you for the vitamins."*

Raj hesitated, he wanted to follow her, to do so, but he was debating whether to tell her that he knew her secret. She had kept it to herself for obvious reasons, and it seemed unwise to rock the boat. At the very least though, he did want to speak to her.

"Mariam," he called out, trying not to raise his voice. Most of the camp would be sleeping at this hour, and he didn't want to disturb anyone. She turned around with a sheepish look, then walked back toward him.

"I didn't mean to wake you," she said when she reached him.

"I wasn't asleep."

"Thank you for the vitamins. I actually was almost out of them, so it's really helpful."

"I'm glad." Raj paused, "I'm sorry I put you on the spot earlier. I guess you were keeping your pregnancy quiet for a reason." He determined not to bring up her other secret.

"I don't know," she answered with a shrug.

"Your husband—do you know where he is?" As soon as the words had left his mouth, Raj kicked himself, why had he asked her that? The answer was none of his business, but he couldn't deny that he wanted to know.

Mariam made eye contact with him for a second then looked down at the ground. "He died," she finally whispered.

"I'm sorry."

After what seemed like another prolonged silence, she said, "Thank you."

Something in her tone sounded off, but he couldn't figure out what it was. She didn't seem sad, she almost sounded angry. Raj disregarded it, he had to be imagining things.

"It all feels like a long time ago," she continued, "even though it hasn't even been a couple of months. Sometimes I feel as if my life is a nightmare, and I'm supposed to wake up."

Her tone was wistful now, and he reached out and grabbed her hand, he couldn't help himself. "I feel the same way," he said in a quiet voice. "All the time, in fact."

She met his gaze and held it this time, without removing her hand from his grasp, "Did you lose someone?" After a second's pause, she added the word, "Too?"

"I did." A moment later he had told her everything before he even realized it—he shared how Ritika had disappeared, how they had only been married for a week, how he had barely known her before they got married. "I've searched for her so many times," he said once he was done. "I can't find her, and I don't even really miss her. What kind of a man does that make me?" Mariam took a deep breath, and he could tell he had said too much. "I shouldn't have told you all this, I didn't mean to burden you."

"It's okay, I just wish there was something I could do. Something any of us could do." She sighed, "All I can say is that you're not a bad man. You've taken care of everyone here, you even got me those vitamins. I don't think you should beat yourself up for… for being distracted from your wife… with everything that's going on here." She extracted her hand from his grip. "Good night, Raj."

Mariam gave him a small smile before returning to her room. Raj stared after her for a long while before finally turning in for the night.

Chapter 56

Salmiya, Kuwait - October, 1990

Janhvi saw Raj at the end of the hallway and sped up to catch him before he reached the dining area. She grabbed his arm and whispered, "I need your help."

"What—"

"Not here." She guided him away from the main hallway, turned the corner and stopped once they reached the path that ran between the school's main building and the exterior wall. Few people went there, especially during the afternoon heat.

Raj squinted at her and stepped as close to the wall as possible to take shelter from the sun, "What's going on?"

"I know you know. You must know—I saw you talking the other night. I can't keep this secret anymore."

"I must know what?"

"Do I need to spell it out for you? You know about them—about Mariam and Dinah."

Raj's expression changed slowly, but she could tell he was trying to play dumb as he said, "Mariam and Dinah? What about them?"

What if he doesn't know? Maybe I should let it lie?

For a brief moment, she hesitated, but the weight of the secret was crushing her. She had to find an ally and he was her best bet. "You know who they are."

After a few seconds of silence, Raj opened his mouth, "I do, but I'm not going to say anything."

Janhvi waved her right hand to dismiss his statement, "I know you're not going to say anything—you only seem to want to make puppy eyes at Mariam. That's not what I'm worried about—I think other people are starting to suspect."

"How?"

"Well, it was only a matter of time—Mariam only speaks a few words of Hindi and neither of them speak any other Indian language. They don't really socialize, so that helps, but I think the family on the other side of the curtain, the ones that we share a room with, might have figured it out."

"Did they say something?" Raj's tone betrayed the extent of his fears.

"They've been asking a lot of questions over the last two or three days. I told them the story that we came up with, that Dinah's a Kashmiri married to a Palestinian businessman who was away on a work trip when the invasion started, and that Mariam's lived her whole life in Kuwait, so she didn't really learn Hindi. Please, Raj. If you don't do something, I don't know—" Janhvi's voice faltered and she gave him a beseeching look.

"I'll talk to them. It's going to be okay."

Chapter 57

Salmiya, Kuwait - October, 1990

Raj waited until the evening to approach the family that shared an enclosure with Dinah, Mariam, and Janhvi. He knocked on the door to the family's side of the classroom and waited anxiously for one of them to answer, rehearsing his questions in his head.

"Hello, Raj," the father, Ashok, opened the door.

"How are you, Uncle?" Raj greeted him in Hindi, using the title as a sign of respect for his age.

"I'm fine."

After a few pleasantries, Raj broached the issue. "I wanted to come around and check that everything is okay. Is your room all right?"

Ashok shifted his weight from one foot to the other, "Yes, beta, everything is fine."

"Are you sure?"

"Well," Ashok glanced behind him and stepped outside, pulling the door shut. "It's our neighbors—there's something off about them."

"What do you mean?" Raj kept his voice as level as possible, not wanting to sound overly concerned.

"Are you sure they're Indian? Last week my daughter was taking a nap and she said that she heard them talking in Arabic, and since then I've been listening really closely—"

"And you heard them speaking in Arabic again?" Raj interrupted.

"No. They only speak in English, but their features…they don't look Indian. I know the young girl—Mariam—is supposed to be half Palestinian, but her mother doesn't look Indian either. My wife asked her when the last time they went back to India was and she said that it hasn't been for years!"

Raj nodded, pretending to hear and share Ashok's concern. "I'll look into it, Uncle, I promise. Just don't say anything to anyone else, okay? We wouldn't want anyone to get the wrong idea until we know for sure."

2016

Chapter 58

Austin, Texas, USA – May, 2016

Mariam awoke with her head on Raj's shoulder and his arm wrapped around her, holding her close. She craved a reality in which that protection didn't feel necessary. She turned her head to plant a kiss on his neck and he shifted, pulling her onto his chest. Mariam nestled back in with a bittersweet smile—in a way they'd never felt closer, now that she had told him the truth about her past with Tareq, but she had also noticed that Raj hesitated to touch her in the way that he used to. They hadn't been intimate in the two months since her return from Washington, and she couldn't help but be concerned. She had wanted to raise the issue during her therapy session the day before, but the session had been commandeered by her paranoia. She hadn't told Raj about that, she didn't want him to worry any more than he already was.

I have to stop being the victim.

Mariam extracted herself from Raj's arms and gave him another kiss before she disappeared into the bathroom. She turned on the hot water in the shower and let it wash over her. Lowering herself to the shower floor, she curled into a ball.

It's going to be okay, she said to herself, she had heard the phrase so many times. She even believed it, at least most of the time, but that morning such an eventuality felt more like a mirage. Try as she might, she couldn't shake the feeling that there was an even darker cloud looming over the horizon. Deep in her gut she had an inkling that something was tremendously wrong, that she shouldn't just dismiss her paranoia offhand.

Mariam heard the bathroom door open and she froze, her heart almost stopping at the sound.

Please, no... please.

"Mariam?" Raj's voice cut through the pattering of the water, "What's wrong?" He opened the shower door and pulled her off of the floor, then put his arms around her. He was still wearing his boxers, but he stood with her as the water rained down on them and she sobbed into his chest. Every bit of optimism from her trip to D.C. was lost in that moment, the terror had taken hold. Someday she wouldn't be a victim anymore, either in her own eyes or in Raj's, but that day had never seemed farther away.

Chapter 59

Austin, Texas, USA – May, 2016

Aliya stared at her feet, deeply disturbed by what her dad had just shared. They'd pushed her to go to therapy. She couldn't understand how something that had made so much sense could have gone so awry. Only a few days ago, her world had been simple: she had been focused on school and her biweekly kickboxing classes, with the occasional family dilemma mixed in. The most difficult thing that she'd been dealing with was whether or not she wanted to go on a date with Nick, a guy she had met at school. They were friends, and he wanted more than that, but she remained unsure if she wanted a relationship. That question had faded far into the background with the revelation that not only was she adopted, but her biological father was the kind of scum she felt should be stamped out of the earth.

Although Aliya had recommended *both* of her parents go to therapy, she had never been too concerned about what they were dealing with—after all, it had seemed only natural that they would need therapy after fleeing the Gulf War, but all of that had happened a long time ago. Her phone buzzed and she saw a text message from Nick asking if she wanted to get dinner that evening. She turned her phone over, not wanting to engage, unable to trust herself to decide on even something so minor.

She fought the urge to scream at the top of her lungs. On top of the news that her dad wasn't her biological father, he had now shared his concerns about her mom.

"I don't know what to do, she's having some kind of episode. She won't tell me what's going on, but she's jumping at everything. It's like she thinks he's coming back for her, as if he's hiding around every corner, waiting to pounce on her."

Aliya wished that she could help, but at the same time felt some gratitude for the fact that she had no idea how. Dealing with her own thoughts and emotions was already overwhelming, tackling her mom's on top of that was nigh on impossible, a sure path to a nervous breakdown.

Hoping to distract herself, she went for a long run, noticing a black Nissan Rogue parked on the corner on her way back. She frowned, the neighborhood was small and parking was hard to come by, so she rarely saw new cars appear in the street. She shrugged it off.

Don't you start jumping at straws now. Her emotions were still running on high, so she took a long shower, but the relaxation only lasted a short while before she felt on edge once again. She peered out her window and saw that the car was still there.

Frustrated, she decided to go with the flow, acting on impulse and reaching for her phone. "Can you bring over take out?" she replied to Nick, knowing full well the signal that she was sending. Her emotions were running too high to care, all she was looking for was some release. When he came over later that night, she saw that the car was gone, and felt better, but when he left three hours later, she noticed it again, in a different spot this time. She shook it off, glad that she would be leaving the next morning on her backpacking trip—she clearly needed a change of scenery, some distance to grapple with everything that was going on.

Chapter 60

Austin, Texas, USA - May, 2016

In the morning, Tareq returned to the window, checking his text messages before picking up the binoculars. He waited for the attachments from the investigator to open. The first one made him wince, a picture of Aliya out running in shorts and a tank top.

My daughter, wearing that?

His anger at Raj bubbled further, and he moved on quickly. He thumbed past the next two quickly, all they showed was her walking around, then in her apartment at her window. When he reached the last one, he gagged and had to rush to the bathroom to retch over the toilet.

She is disgusting, he wanted to scream. He had thought nothing could be worse than her outfit when she had gone out running, but he had been wrong—she had entertained some *boy* in her apartment, and there they were in the photo, *kissing*. Tareq refused to consider what had happened after that, he didn't want to know, but he did know.

After several minutes over the toilet, he pulled himself upright. When he returned to the bedroom, he watched the house for a moment, then looked over at the knife that he had purchased to take care of Raj.

I'll only get one chance at this.

He grabbed his wallet and headed for the door. To execute true justice, for what this man had done to his Mariam, for turning his daughter into an American slut, he needed something else. Something with more finality.

A gun.

1990

Chapter 61

Salmiya, Kuwait - October, 1990

Raj stood, battling sensations of being overwhelmed, overjoyed, and terrified at the same time. He had used stall techniques to quell Ashok's concerns and so far it was working—he'd claimed to have spoken to Mariam and Dinah, and that their stories checked out. When Ashok approached him for the third time, he'd reassured him again, stating that he would raise the concern with Sanjay and Daniels but there was no need to worry.

Today's news would rescue him from those excuses, which were rapidly beginning to diminish in effectiveness. Finally, after what felt like an eternity at the camp together, Sanjay and Daniels had come up with an evacuation plan. The plan was exceedingly complicated and risky: they would have to drive out to Jordan en masse, there the Indian government would hopefully issue them papers. Many of the people at the camp didn't have their passports, which had been held by their employers, so without that, they would be stuck in no man's land. Raj himself didn't have his passport—he had actually submitted it to the Kuwaiti ministry for processing of his wife's visa and had been unable to get it back after the troops had crossed the border.

It wouldn't be easy, but the possibility of an escape glimmered like a light at the end of a long tunnel, especially with the ticking time bomb of Mariam and Dinah's true identities. He couldn't help but be excited about it, yet leaving meant confronting a truth that he wasn't ready to face. If he left, would he ever be able to find Ritika? None of his efforts to locate her had provided any leads, and the fact that she could be dead had finally begun to hammer home after weeks of dismissing the possibility. He'd spoken to Sanjay about it twice, but neither of them had been able to come up with any ideas. Sanjay had made some calls to see if there were any other refugee camps where she could be hiding, but they'd all come up blank.

If I leave her for dead, what kind of man does that make me? Raj asked himself as he contemplated the idea of escape. *How could I leave her? How could I leave without knowing what happened to her?* He unclenched his right fist, noticing for the first time that his fingernails had dug deep impressions into his palm.

There was no way out of this, he couldn't miss his chance to evacuate, but he wasn't sure if he could live with himself if he left without knowing what had happened.

AFTER A FEW MINUTES TO collect his thoughts, Raj ventured into the sitting room where he would have to gather everyone so that Sanjay could brief them on the overall plan. Raj was dreading it; the plan seemed complicated enough to him, he didn't want to think about the questions that they were bound to ask, and how he would probably have to convince them to leave. At least a portion would want to stay, wait it out, rather than brave the desert and the drive, along with the uncertainty of whether the Indian government would take care of them once they crossed into Jordan. There had been two more raids on the camps in the last two weeks though, and everyone was living on edge. It was only a matter of time until the soldiers were no longer satisfied with stealing some of their food and water supplies—people would be next.

A shiver went up Raj's spine as he thought of the soldiers discovering Mariam and Dinah's real identities. *What would the soldiers do to them? What would they do to the rest of us?* He gritted his teeth, he would never divulge their secret, and he had dealt with Ashok's suspicions, but eventually, someone else would figure out who they really were. If the soldiers put them to the test, he suspected that the unspoken agreement about protecting each other wouldn't hold for long—anyone else who held similar suspicions was bound to give them up in the hope of mercy. That possibility was both too real and too frightening to contemplate, yet he couldn't get past it. *We have to get out. There is no choice.* He looked around, taking in the hallways that had given them refuge, that had offered a modicum of peace in a setting full of chaos. The school had had its place, had had its time, but now it was a tinder box on the verge of igniting.

It was time to leave.

Chapter 62

Salmiya, Kuwait - October, 1990

Raj waited to the side as his charges filed into the school auditorium. The room was full of whispers as the residents guessed at why they had all been gathered this way. By this point, they all knew each other, had gossiped together and railed at each other—and everything in between. Raj watched as Sanjay and Daniels stepped onto the stage to speak to them.

"When the Iraqis first crossed the border, we thought the invasion would be short-lived, that everything would return to normal relatively soon. We've been here, at this camp, for almost two months now, and I think we can all agree that that hasn't happened. I hope Kuwait will be liberated. I hope that the UN will intervene. But it's safe to say that we can no longer wait around for that to happen. The soldiers have raided our camp three times already, and, eventually, we won't be safe here anymore. Daniels and I have come up with a plan to get all of you out and back to India safely. That's what we want more than anything, to keep all of you safe, and to return to a normal life. If I've learned anything from this crisis, it's how precious that normalcy is, how we should cherish it. The small things in life, a smile from your wife at breakfast, a walk on the beach with your children, an evening of laughter with a friend is what life is all about. I am grateful for the grace with which you all have handled this crisis, how you have worked and lived together in harmony, resolving differences from bathroom schedules to sleeping quarters and more. You have all risen above and come through a terrible situation with your heads held high." Sanjay stopped and signaled to Daniels to take over.

"I can't echo enough how much I agree with Sanjay. You've shown tremendous grace under fire, but now is the time that we will ask even more of you. We were hoping for an easier option to evacuate out of Kuwait—we looked into getting out by sea, and every other option we could think of. After much consideration, the best option we could find was evacuating by land, through Jordan." He continued to describe the plan, the drive through Iraq and across the border into Jordan. Daniels attempted to address some of the potential objections upfront, raising his hand to delay questions from the group. At one point the audience threatened to interrupt in a spree of those questions, but the gravitas of his voice and posture kept them at bay. He made sure to tackle potential pitfalls, including how the drive to Jordan was long and would be difficult even under normal circumstances, especially for some of the elderly at the camp, but he had confidence that they could help each other through it. He explained their plan in detail, including how he and Sanjay had secured an agreement to use several abandoned school buses and cross into Iraq at night, minimizing their exposure to street patrols.

Raj watched enthralled, he had seen Daniels speak only a few times before but had never appreciated his ability to captivate people, to carry an audience. *No wonder he's a pastor,* Raj thought as Daniels continued.

At the end of the speech, Daniels rallied the audience, appealing to their inner strength as individuals who had endured more than most people deal with in a lifetime, as a group who had banded and stood together, and as Indians. Raj had never felt more patriotic than at that moment, when Daniels hammered home their collective strength and identity as one people who would stand together. When Daniels finally stepped off the stage, several people in the crowd stood, cheering for him and Sanjay.

Raj basked in the moment, floating on the high from the speech. Even as it ended though, he could feel the high slipping away, the questions that he had feared would come soon enough. He could only hope that the camp residents would stick with it when the high wore off completely.

There's no way to protect them if they stay behind.

Chapter 63

Salmiya, Kuwait – October, 1990

"Raj, could we speak with you?"

"Of course." Raj, who had been on his way to the sitting room, turned around, recognizing Sanjay's booming voice.

Sanjay led him down the hall to the adjacent wing of classrooms and then through one of the doorways. The interior was so dimly lit that it took Raj's eyes a moment to adjust after coming from the sunny hallway. Once they did, he noticed two twin mattresses set against the far corner of the room. In front of them was a chair where Daniels was seated

Daniels motioned toward two chairs on the other side of the room. Sanjay grabbed one with an attached desk and nodded toward the third seat which was farther away from the other two. Raj found his gaze scanning the room for an escape as he pulled it closer. He sat down and looked between the two of them.

"Is everything okay?"

Sanjay tapped his fingers against the desk, "Ashok has raised a very serious accusation, but he said that he brought it to you first."

Sh—, Raj stopped himself from cursing aloud. "I'm sorry, I should have come to you—"

With a deep frown, Daniels asked, "Is it true? Are two of the women that share that room with Ashok and his family Kuwaitis?"

Raj thought about denying it, justifying his actions, or using another stall tactic, but he couldn't bring himself to lie. Sanjay and Daniels had both put themselves on the line to take care of everyone at the camp—they could have left on the first Indian government attempt at evacuation, a chartered plane that had arrived weeks earlier on August 20th. Both men had more than enough money to pay the airfare but had elected to stay behind to ensure the safety of other Indians in Kuwait and had gone through some major logistical gymnastics to arrange for the buses and other necessities of their evacuation plan. Whatever happened, Raj found himself steadfast on one point—he refused to lie to them.

Here goes nothing.

"Yes."

"How could you keep that from us?" Daniels exclaimed. "You've put everyone at this camp at risk."

"I'm sorry," Raj kept his head down. "I was only trying to protect them. I thought that the fewer people that knew, the easier it would be to keep it a secret."

"No one told you to go around and tell the entire camp, but you should have told us." Sanjay paused with a grave expression, "You should have told *me*."

"I thought I had dealt with Ashok's suspicions." Raj squirmed, "What are you going to do?"

Daniels exchanged a glance with Sanjay before he answered, "What *can* we do? They're Kuwaitis."

"You don't mean—?" Raj was unable to finish the question.

"Of course not," Sanjay said. "What Daniels is saying is that they're human beings. We aren't just going to leave them here to get captured—two women on their own like that. Who knows what would happen to them?" He stood and glared at Raj, "What kind of monsters do you think we are? We told Ashok that they're one of us, that they would travel with us, Kuwaitis, Indians, or Mongolians, and whatever else in between. But you should have informed us immediately. We'll need your help to keep them from attracting any attention on our way through Iraq. They're *your* responsibility."

2016

Chapter 64

Washington D.C., USA - May, 2016

Nadia inhaled her first cup of coffee and poured herself another, then sat down in the living room with her parents. She swirled the mug, watching the pale brown liquid coating the interior to the rim. She was reminded of an old aunt in Kuwait who used to read fortunes from the leftover grounds.

Why can't I find my answers at the bottom of a coffee cup?

"Are you sure you're okay?"

"I'm fine, Mom," Nadia dismissed the obvious concern with a shrug.

You're not convincing anybody, this was the third time that morning her mother had asked her. *Moms always know.* "I didn't sleep well that's all. I'm fine, don't worry."

Her mother looked skeptical, but a look from her father made the room return to silence—he'd always disapproved of her incessant prying. Nadia wasn't sure how she felt about their questions, or lack thereof, she had asked for it so many times, begged them to limit their meddling into her life, but now she wanted them to probe more than anything else. If they broke through her walls, she wouldn't have to carry this secret anymore, even if it meant that they would all be in danger. Nadia took a deep breath, the possibility that her mom wouldn't believe her scared her even more than Uncle Tareq. Her mom had given him so much leeway, maybe that would continue? "*He's been through so much, Nadia. He was just having a flashback, an episode. We can't hold it against him. How could you even think he would hurt us? You're turning this into one of those crazy movies that you watch with your father.*" Nadia could picture her mom saying those words, each one stabbing further into her heart.

Maybe she's right.

A buzzing on the table interrupted her train of thought as her mom answered her phone. "Hi, Tareq, I was wondering if you would ever call me back," she said in a chirpy voice.

Nadia's ears perked up. She sighed and listened in as her mom and uncle exchanged small talk. Even without hearing the other side of the conversation, Nadia could tell how much effort her mom was making to force the conversation to continue; she always tried so hard to have a relationship with him without getting anything back. At one point, Nadia had considered that sweet, but now it was a curse.

Nadia stood up, she didn't think she could take much more. She was halfway to the kitchen when her mother's words made her freeze in place.

"Enjoy Texas, Tareq. We'll see you when you get back."

Texas.

Nadia dropped her coffee. The mug broke into three large pieces, the brown liquid spreading out over the beige ceramic tiles. "Uncle Tareq is in Texas?" She kicked herself, why hadn't it occurred to her to ask where he had gone?

It can't be Austin… it can't be Austin.

"Nadia, what's the matter with you?" her mother mopped up the coffee with a napkin and picked up the broken mug. "Look what you did, this was one of my favorites."

"I'm sorry," with shaking hands, Nadia took the pieces from her mother and grabbed a paper towel to join her on the floor. "Is Uncle Tareq in Texas?" she repeated.

I must have heard wrong, please let me have heard wrong.

Her mother frowned, "Yes, he's in Austin for a conference. Nadia, what's the matter with you?"

The weight of that reality slammed into Nadia's chest, she had presumed that Mariam was safe, had at least managed to convince herself of that.

Austin.

"Nadia?"

"I'm fine," Nadia answered for the fourth time that morning. "I just need to make a phone call." She fumbled her way back to her room and pulled her phone from the charger, searching for Mariam's number before she realized that she had forgotten to save it. The pressure on her chest heightened as she found Dinah's contact instead and hit the call button onscreen.

When Dinah picked up a moment later, Nadia burst into tears, unable to get control of her breathing. "Dinah, I'm coming over—there's something I have to tell you."

Chapter 65

Washington D.C., USA – May, 2016

Dinah stared at Nadia aghast, she wanted to pinch herself to wake up from this nightmare.

Tareq is alive.

The idea was incomprehensible, how in the world could he be alive? She tried to focus on what Nadia was saying, but the question continued to gnaw at her.

The last words that Nadia said caught her attention, "…I didn't want to tell him anything, but I was so scared. I didn't tell him her full name, so I figured it was okay, I thought she would be safe, but this morning Mom spoke to him and she said that he's in Austin. Dinah, he's in Austin! I don't know how, but he must have found her—I think he's going after her."

Dinah caught the armrest of the seat behind her to stabilize herself. "Oh my God," she whispered, "we have to warn her." She reached toward the coffee table to grab her phone but fell forward onto the floor before she could grasp it. "Please pick up, Mariam, please pick up," Dinah glared at the screen, willing her phone to connect faster. The ring echoed out over the speakers, once, then twice, then three times. She swallowed and steadied her breathing, she had to find Mariam, she had to warn her. After the fifth ring, she disconnected and dialed Raj's number instead.

The line connected a moment later, and he picked up, his voice disgruntled, "Hi, Dinah, this isn't really a good time. Can I call you back?"

"Raj, you need to get home right away. I know Mariam finally told you about Tareq..." her voice trailed off, unable to believe what she had to tell him. "He's alive, and he's in Austin. Get home and get Mariam. You have to run."

Chapter 66

Austin, Texas, USA - May, 2016

Mariam sighed as she parked in front of her house once again, having spent only two hours at the office before feigning sickness to head home. Raj had been driving her since the morning he'd found her on the shower floor, but having leaned on him so much over the last couple of days, she had finally convinced him that she was fine. She had made sure that Aliya left on her trip, even persuaded herself that she could venture into work without any issues. That belief had been crushed within less than ten minutes at her desk—the disappearance of her nameplate and the book that she'd been reading had seen to that. She'd asked three colleagues about both items—it had to be some sort of weird prank, an odd coincidence—but the voice in the back of her mind would not be silenced. The fact that the book was gone was even more disturbing than the nameplate: *The Spirit of Destruction,* a book that featured the Kuwait Towers on its cover. How much of a coincidence could it be that a book set in Kuwait had disappeared? Where could it have got to? She hadn't taken it home, and it was nowhere around her desk.

Mariam turned off the engine unable to stop her body from trembling. She had no idea where to go, home hardly seemed like a refuge, especially alone, but she refused to call Raj. After a slow exhale, she called her therapist and scheduled another emergency session for late that afternoon.

Now all I have to do is get through the next few hours. Mariam glanced at the clock on her dashboard as she headed home to wait it out.

You're going to be fine. Perhaps if she reassured herself enough times, she would eventually start to believe it?

Her nose wrinkled when she stepped inside, she detected a faint burning scent. After checking the stove to be sure that none of the burners were on, Mariam shrugged it off. One of the neighbors must be barbecuing. She smiled, remembering the last time that they had gone out for barbecue. Raj was still able to eat as much meat in one sitting as he had when they'd first met, something which never ceased to amaze both her and Aliya. He would turn into a college freshman, taking down one beef rib after the next, followed by a full plate of pulled pork, all as if he was consuming a standard two-egg omelet. Aliya had quoted Star Wars to him—"Impressive, most impressive"—while Mariam watched in disbelief, just glad that he didn't eat like that every day. They had both maintained their physique and health quite well, at least physical health, perhaps because of Aliya's constant hounding. She had taken far too many nutritional health classes to let any poor eating habits persist in the house, even though she no longer lived with them.

Mariam put her feet up on the couch and connected her phone to her Sonos speakers, then stretched out as "Jessie's Girl" played over the sound system. She swayed back and forth for a moment, the old 80s classic forcing her to relax.

Everything is going to be okay.

She even started to believe it.

At the end of the song, she went to the bathroom to splash some water on her face. On the way back to the couch, she caught a glimpse of the bookshelf to the left of the bedroom door and did a doubletake. There, on the second shelf was the image of the Kuwait Towers, the book that had gone missing from her office.

How on earth? She picked up the novel and felt a flutter in her stomach, she'd been so sure that she hadn't brought it home. Unless she'd forgotten? She'd been under so much stress. She tilted her head to the side and noticed that her missing nameplate was wedged behind the book against the bedroom wall.

Now I know *I'm losing it.*

Book in hand, she returned to the couch, she might as well use the free time to read until she had to leave for her therapy session in two hours.

She turned the pages and the next hour passed quickly, the story was gripping, and she found herself completely taken in. Eventually, she felt a wave of sleepiness coming on, and after setting an alarm on her phone, decided to give into it. She set the book on the coffee table and settled back with her head on one of the couch cushions.

MARIAM HEARD A NOISE AND sat up. Her eyes scanned the room, everything seemed in order, the book was still lying next to her on the coffee table, and the kitchen looked just as she had left it that morning. A draft blew in from the back porch, and her brow furrowed as she, once again, caught the smell of smoke.

Raj must have left the door open again.

She refused to allow herself to think anything else and walked over to shut it, goosebumps forming up and down her forearms—the sun had disappeared behind gray cloud cover, and it was cooler than a normal spring day.

When she got close to the door, she noticed that the firepit was glowing. Stepping outside, she checked the setting to ensure it was firmly on "Off".

He's not here, he's not here.

She had convinced herself the last time the paranoia had hit by looking in the closet, she'd do it again.

It will be just like you left it, she told herself. *Messy and disorganized, the way it always is.* Mariam covered the steps to her closet and opened the door.

It had been reorganized: color-coded just the way Tareq used to keep it. She stumbled backward, catching hold of the wall for support.

He was dead, how can he not be dead?

There was still a chance this was a dream, that this was all in her head. Only one way to tell. She grappled her way back to the bookshelf seeking out her copy of *The Godfather.* She pulled the books off the shelf and threw them to the floor, searching, but coming up empty.

Once all of the books were splayed across the floor, she grabbed the side of the bookshelf to stand and groped her way along the dining room wall toward the outside. She no longer trusted herself to stand unsupported, but she had to know....

Somehow, she found her way to the firepit and raked through the fire stones. She heard her phone ringing from the dining room but ignored it, she had to find out for sure.

Please let this be a nightmare. This has to be a nightmare.

At the bottom of the firepit, she saw it, the deep red cover, with the letters "God" still visible and the word Puzo underneath it. Mariam backed up against one of the porch columns, unable to breathe, her vision blurred by tears and slid slowly to the ground.

Tareq was alive, and he had found her. Everything about her life that she loved, her independence, her work, her family, all of that was behind her now—over.

I will never be free.

Chapter 67

Austin, Texas, USA - May, 2016

Tareq panted as he made it past the fence back over to the loft where he was staying. He wanted Mariam to realize that he was there before he finally approached her. He'd left clues for her that morning, the book with the Kuwait Towers on the cover, along with her nameplate on the bookshelf, and had returned to rearrange her clothes while she was napping. He couldn't wait to feel her excitement once she realized that he was alive, that he had found her and that they could be together again. His skin tingled, the electricity of that moment awaited.

When he saw her copy of *The Godfather* on her bookshelf, though, it was all he could do not to trash the entire house—how could she have defied his memory to that extent? He remembered their argument about the book as if it were yesterday, how Dinah had given it to her and she had brought it home that night in Kuwait. He'd had no choice but to make it clear, to discipline her for that audacity—such a book could not be tolerated.

It must be that man, this is his fault.

Tareq broke into a smile, he was so close to Mariam he could taste it. After his capture in Kuwait, he had sworn to find her, but following his release, he had searched for months only to come up empty time and again. He slammed his boot into the base of the wall, envisaging it connecting with Raj's head as he hit the same spot four times in a row before he stepped back to peer out the window once again.

He watched Mariam approach the porch door he had purposely left ajar. She paused with her head in the doorway before she pulled it shut. Through the binoculars, he caught the expression on her face, the look of fear that she had performed so well when they were living together.

It's all an act. He grinned, his toes curled, he knew that she would be overjoyed to see him. She disappeared into the bedroom, and he grunted in frustration, they still hadn't opened the blinds since the evening before and he hadn't dared open them himself in case she heard him from the living room where she'd been napping. It had taken all of his self-control not to venture closer to her, he wanted her so badly, but his intent to leave clues and watch before he surprised her had superseded that longing. She would find the evidence in her closet soon enough.

Tareq checked the magazine of his pistol, he wanted to have it just in case Raj showed up, but his preferred reunion would be with her alone. Mariam would give herself to him, he had no doubt about that, but that impostor would almost certainly put up a fight. Clenching the gun's grip panel, Tareq raised it and pointed it toward the wall, lining up the sight before he slid it into the back of his waistband.

He returned his attention to Mariam's house, frustrated by the lack of activity. A few seconds later she reappeared, emerging from the bedroom and stumbling out toward the back porch where she knelt over the fireplace. Tareq watched her rake the coals, then reel away before she crumpled to the ground.

She knows. He beamed as he watched her sob.

He grabbed his jacket and pulled it over his shoulders, now was the time to approach her, to validate her excitement. He would show her that she was right, that she could hope again. His entire body quaked in anticipation as he walked toward the door. A small hop over the fence and a few steps and he would be there, she would be in his arms again.

I will never let her go.

Chapter 68

Austin, Texas, USA – May, 2016

Raj hammered his palm into his horn at the traffic around him drew to a standstill. He hit the call button on his phone again, now for the sixth time.

Why isn't she picking up?

"Damn it, Mariam, pick up, pick up!"

When the cars in front of him started to move past the construction area which had blocked one of the road lanes, he hit the horn again, "Move, people! Drive!"

Several moments later he was speeding forward. As soon as he passed the road closure area, he made a sharp lane change to the left and sped down the street, ignoring the honking that followed as he cut off yet another driver. He turned off of South Congress Avenue and finally came to a screeching halt in front of his house.

Leaving the engine in neutral, he jumped out of the car and ran toward the door.

Please be there, please be okay.

He sprinted up the driveway just dodging Mariam's CR-V which was already parked there. He scrambled to enter the lock code, his hand was shaking so badly that he had to enter it twice before the mechanism disengaged and he raced inside.

1990

Chapter 69

Salmiya, Kuwait - October, 1990

Raj waited until well past sundown to take his car out that night. After a few hours of anxious tossing and turning in his bed, he'd given up on sleep. He squashed the emotional turmoil raging in his head—they were leaving the next evening. This would be his last shot to find Ritika. As he reversed out of the parking spot, he had to wonder how he felt about her—he wanted to find her, he had to know what had become of her, but at the same time, he could no longer imagine building a life with her. So much had happened, and their wedding seemed like it belonged to someone else after everything he had been through since the beginning of the invasion. Even if he found her—he still clung to a tendril of hope—would she want a life with him? If she were still alive, she had to have been to hell and back, too. He sighed, imagining what his mother would say under the circumstances, *You'll be able to connect based on your experience, even if it wasn't together.*

Raj took a deep breath and looked out at the deserted streets, a stark contrast to the normal activity that would have characterized them on a Thursday night just months earlier. He passed two shwarma sandwich and fatayer shops that would have been packed with cars picking up take out, then turned right by the old Naif chicken place where he would buy his rotisserie. The route he took to the hospital was a roundabout way, designed to avoid some of the larger streets which were more likely to have patrols. Although most officers that manned the checkpoints would wave him by when they saw a man with Indian features, accompanied by the words, "Hindi sadeek," meaning Indian friend, Raj still felt his blood pressure ratchet up any time he had to stop at one. Instead, he preferred to take smaller roads to avoid the officers, and nowadays, the Resistance too. While the Resistance was primarily active in the more Kuwaiti neighborhoods such as Sabah Al-Salem, he didn't want to get caught in the crossfire.

The soldiers seemed to have run out of steam though, with the street patrols fewer and far between—bored by driving empty streets since the Westerners had evacuated. That fact couldn't help but spur some resentment, the American and British embassies had evacuated all of their nationals in secret within a few days of the invasion. The Indian embassy, on the other hand, had only just started evacuation procedures out of Jordan a few weeks earlier—a momentous task, he had to admit, but a fact that nonetheless frustrated him. Raj had heard that plans were in motion, that the Indian Foreign Minister had met with Saddam to secure permission for the evacuation, but what he wanted to see was action, not promises. From what he'd been told, both Daniels and Sanjay had slaved over the process to make it happen, but the reissuing of passport documents that would be required for so many in the group remained a question mark. *We'll see what happens when we get to Jordan,* he thought, a point that Daniels had conveniently left out of his speech. Not that Raj disagreed with him, they needed to rally the residents to leave, and disclosing that they might end up stuck in a Jordanian refugee camp would do more harm than good.

At the end of the day they had no choice—remain in a time bomb or do something about it.

Raj pulled into a parking spot outside the wall of Farwaniya Hospital and stopped to buy a piece of khoobus flatbread from a hawker on the street along with a pack of cigarettes. Munching on the bread while he sucked down a cigarette eased his mood a tad as he approached the entrance despite the steep price tag that had gone along with them. Prior to the war, cigarettes had been available on the cheap, but he'd cut down considerably since then—a pack that had cost less than one Kuwaiti Dinar just a few months earlier was now priced at almost nine-fold with the reversal of the dollar exchange rate.

Stubbing out the cigarette, Raj gathered his courage to move forward. His eyes stung, the air was more sandy than usual for early October, the last remnant of Kuwait's summer. He made his way through the gate, glad that he had called ahead to see if Yusuf would be at the pharmacy. After a quick hello, Raj walked back through the radiology ward, where he asked two nurses on call if they knew anything about Ritika. He showed them a picture of her from their wedding. Both took one glance at it and shook their heads, but he pressed them. "She would look a little different since she was dressed up for the wedding."

The second one, named Talia, tilted her head to the side and scrutinized the picture closely. "I think I've seen her," she said, "but not in some time."

"Is she here? Where? Where did you see her?"

Her expression was grim as she looked up from the photo. "Come with me."

Raj followed her out of the radiology ward through several sets of interior double doors, he had no idea where she was taking him. Eventually, they exited that building and entered a second one.

"Pediatrics?" he asked with a frown. "She wasn't a pediatric nurse."

Talia ignored his question and led him down a long hallway into the pediatric intensive care unit. She stopped next to a bed where a young boy, maybe five years old from what Raj could see, was sleeping with an IV in his left arm. She touched his shoulder gently to wake him.

The boy opened his eyes, staring at Talia in a haze of grogginess before he sat up. "Yes?"

"Suhail, do you remember me? I'm Nurse Talia. I was here for a night a few weeks ago," she said in Hindi.

He nodded, and she continued, "This is Raj, he's a friend of mine. We need to ask you about one of the nurses. We're trying to find her."

She waited for him to nod again before she showed him the picture, "Is that the nurse who was taking care of you before me?"

"Yes, that's Nurse Ritika. She doesn't dress like that though, she wears normal clothes."

Raj's heart leapt into his throat.

I can find her. I'm going to find her.

Talia asked, "Do you know where she is? Has she been back to see you?"

"She was here a couple of days ago, but then she had an argument with one of the soldiers, and they took her away," Suhail answered.

His heart sank.

"They took her away?" *No...* Raj's voice caught, trying not to picture what the soldiers would have done to her. "Do you remember what the argument was about?" he could scarcely get the words out, he wasn't even sure he wanted to know.

"I couldn't understand," Suhail pointed toward the hallway, "they were too far, but the soldier was always mean to her. He came in here a few times to talk to her, but this time he forced her to leave with him. He knocked over my dinner, then he grabbed her arm and dragged her out to the hallway before he started yelling."

"Was anyone else here?" Talia asked.

Suhail shrugged, "I don't know. She never came back, though, and she's the only one who would bring me chocolate pudding. All of the other nurses bring me Jell-O, but it's not nearly as good." He crossed his arms and gave Talia a grumpy look.

Talia squeezed the boy's hand, "Thank you, Suhail. I'll bring you some chocolate pudding later. It'll be our secret, that way tonight you can have Jell-O and pudding after dinner."

Suhail's eyes lit up as they walked away. Once they were back in the hall, Raj turned to Talia, fighting to keep his voice steady. "I guess that's all there is... I just wish things were different."

She reached out and touched his arm, "So do I, but there's actually one more person we can ask. There's a pharmacy in this building that's separate from the other one—he might know something."

"Absolutely, lead the way." He wondered if he should let himself hope that he might find out what had happened. If Ritika had indeed been taken by the soldiers, she could still be alive.

Or she could be dead.

They walked to the end of the corridor and turned left, then reached a booth at the end of that hall. No one was behind the desk, so Talia reached in and rang the desk bell four times in a row. "Hopefully there's someone in the back," she said.

A disheveled looking man appeared a moment later with a frown on his face. "Yes?" he directed an irritated gaze at Talia.

Raj waited for her to introduce him, then explained that he was looking for Nurse Ritika, the nurse who had been taking care of Suhail. The pharmacist examined the photo. "Yes, I met her a few times."

"Do you know what happened to her?" Raj asked. "Suhail said that a soldier took her away."

The pharmacist's expression turned dark, "That would explain why she hasn't been back. If they took her to prison, I don't know what happened, but there is somewhere you could look…"

Raj leaned forward, "Where?"

"The construction lot down the street… I know the soldiers dump bodies there."

Chapter 70

Outside Farwaniya Hospital grounds, Kuwait – October, 1990

Raj leaned over and heaved onto the ground for the third time that evening. After the conversation with the pharmacist he had forced himself to visit the old construction site—if there was a chance that Ritika was there, he had to know. As soon as he'd parked, he had regretted that decision, the smell coming from the pit had caused him to vomit for the first time that evening. There were only five bodies, but from the stench, he would have thought there were hundreds. He finally made it down the slope, pulse racing. Of the five, only two were female, lying next to each other face down. He steeled his nerves.

I have to know.

Tears coursed down his cheeks with every step, the flashlight in his hands quaking, and the minute-long walk felt more like a day in which he was heading to his execution.

He was hyperventilating as he wrapped his hand in an old hand towel from his car and reached down to flip over the first body, overwhelmed by the smell and the flies that had congregated on top. The body was heavy, and it took far more effort than he could have anticipated. Once it was right side up the sobs grew heavier, it wasn't

Ritika, but he wasn't sure how he felt. If he didn't find her now, would he ever be able to? If she wasn't here, then did that mean that she was still alive?

Using the back of his other hand, he brushed away the tears and moved toward the other body, his head spinning from the sound of both his heartbeat and uncontrolled breathing. He gathered his energy this time and flipped the body more quickly, then fell back onto the sand, emotion racking his torso. His mind overflowed with the few memories that he had, Ritika's shy smile when he first met her at her parents' home, the brilliant azure garb she had worn to their sangeet the night before the wedding, the first time he'd brought her into his apartment in Kuwait.

The memories had been fleeting since the invasion, and many of them had eluded him when he'd tried to bring them to the forefront of his mind, but now they were there in full force. Each one felt like a knife slicing across his chest, one by one leading him to death by a million cuts.

Her face was unrecognizable, a shadow of the past they might have had together, but around her neck was the Mangalsutra he had placed there at their wedding. Even with the sand that coated the gold and black beads, there was no mistaking it—the body lying in front of him was hers. He had searched for her for months, and she had been at the hospital, right there, easily within his reach, until just a few days before. Now she was gone forever, food for the flies and the crows who dared brave the desert sun and heat.

2016

Chapter 71

Austin, Texas, USA – May, 2016

Tareq was halfway out the door when he saw his host, a middle-aged man who lived in the main house across the lawn waving to him from the garden where he was crouched over a bed of fresh soil with a set of gardening tools.

"Hello," the host called out. "I was wondering if I'd get to see you, sometimes the people who rent this little loft just come and go. I really like it when I get to say hi, though. I'm Greg, it's so good to meet you. You know, I've been renting out this loft for the last six months, and I don't think I've met more than two or three people who were staying here."

He held out his hand and Tareq shook it reluctantly, squelching the desire to shove him to the ground and make for the fence as Greg droned on about his experience with renting on Airbnb.

Tareq bit his lip and tolerated the discussion—Mariam was waiting for him, but it wouldn't do either of them any good if he got himself arrested for assault. The host shot off a spree of small talk, asking Tareq where he was from and if he had been to Austin before, what he had been up to since he arrived, and what he should make sure to go and see. "Most importantly you *must* go out for breakfast tacos, my personal favorite is Marcelino's, they have this elgin sausage that's to die for. Tourists usually go to Torchy's, which is great, but you can find it all over now. The other place you *have* to make it to is the Veracruz food truck, go to the original one on Cesar Chavez Street..."

Tareq kept his answers to a minimum, not wanting to spur any further conversation, but it still took several minutes to extract himself.

Much to his chagrin, when Greg was finally out of small talk, he turned around and went back to gardening in the same spot. Tareq hesitated, he could go for the fence now, but he risked being seen—he was lucky Greg hadn't spotted him returning from Mariam's earlier. He took a deep breath and forced himself to relax as he returned to the house.

Absence makes the heart grow fonder.

Chapter 72

Austin, Texas, USA – May, 2016

"Mariam! Are you okay? Please, Mariam." Raj had found her cowering behind the laundry hamper in the corner of their spare room closet.

She opened her eyes and stared at him blankly, from the look in her eyes and her tear-stained face he could tell that he didn't have to explain.

She already knows.

He put one arm around her shoulders and scooped the other one under her knees. "Come on, babe, we have to go," he said softly. "We have to run now, before he finds us."

For a second, he thought that she was going to protest, but then she leaned her head into his chest. Raj's jaw clenched as the dampness of her tears soaked through his shirt.

I am going to make him pay.

He shut his eyes for a second and then grimaced as he lifted Mariam. Ten years earlier it would have been easy, but although he had maintained a well-built physique, he wasn't as strong as he used to be.

Somehow, he managed to get her to the car, he had to stop a few times, once in the living room and once on the driveway, but Mariam wasn't stable enough to stand. He tried to put her down, to get her to walk, but she looked like she was about to faint. When he finally lowered her into the passenger seat, he slammed the door shut and sprinted to the other side.

Raj hit the gas pedal and they were a few blocks away before he glanced at her again. "When we get home, I better spend some more time at the gym," he said, still panting, but hoping to cheer her up.

She gripped the armrest, her face ashen and pale, "It's too late, we can never go home again."

"No, you're safe now. We're going to be okay, I promise."

Mariam looked straight ahead, refusing to meet his gaze, "I'm so sorry, Raj. Our lives are over."

Chapter 73

Austin, Texas, USA – May, 2016

Tareq's breathing sped up as he watched Raj appear inside the house, move through the living room at a frantic pace, and disappear into the back bedroom. Tareq could barely stop himself from pointing the gun at the window and ending it then and there. He tightened his grip on the binoculars. When he saw Raj carry her through the open kitchen toward the front door, Tareq flung the binoculars across the room. The plastic frame hit the wall with a thud and fell to the ground, the glass lenses shattered and spilled out over the floor. Tareq let off a spree of Arabic curse words before he knelt next to the broken glass, the binoculars had been one of the few purchases from Kuwait that he'd kept when he had moved to Baltimore twelve years earlier. It had seemed fitting that they would be what reunited him with Mariam, but that scheme had now been foiled. He swept up the broken glass into a dustpan and dumped it into the trash bin in the kitchen.

She'll be back.

Once the floor was clear, Tareq peeked out of the front window, which gave him a view of the garden patch where his host Greg had been working. The garden was empty now, and he cursed again, this time under his breath—his host had delayed him and ruined everything. Part of him was tempted to seek him out, someone should pay for scuttling his plans, but his better judgment prevailed. He couldn't risk anything compromising his reunion with Mariam. He longed to feel her breath, to see the make-believe fear in her eyes from up close. His skin was on fire, he ached to hold her in his arms. He yearned to touch her, to have her the way that he used to, to control her the way she adored so much. Tareq's breath grew shallower, thirsting for that moment for the thousandth time since he'd seen her in Nadia's photograph. He pressed his face against the glass pane looking out toward her backyard. Without the binoculars he could see the outline of her patio behind the low wooden fence but not much else.

Tareq picked up his wallet and keys from the side table next to the couch—he'd have to buy a new pair of binoculars. He needed to be ready for when she returned. A resounding calm fell over him as he made his way to his car parked outside on the driveway, the extra time would only heighten their first encounter. Nothing would stop him from getting to her.

Don't worry, Mariam. We'll be together soon.

1990

Chapter 74

Salmiya, Kuwait - October, 1990

Raj wasn't sure how he made it back to the camp, somehow, he'd managed the drive on autopilot and stumbled from the parking lot into the school grounds. He was planning to head straight for his room, but his legs carried him toward the playground on the other side of the campus—the one spot that had always felt simple and safe despite the chaos. When he got there, he collapsed onto a bench facing the basketball hoop and buried his face in hands.

She was there, right there, the whole time. How could I not get to her?

He replayed the eight separate visits he had made to the hospital, the people that he'd asked about Ritika, how he had searched the radiology ward from end to end each time. Another wave of sobs contorted his chest, and he slammed his fist into the wooden bench once, then again. Pain radiated through his fingers, but he welcomed it.

You deserve this. You failed her. She was your wife, and you failed her.

Raj slid off the bench onto his knees and braced himself against the ground. The cuts on his hand filled with sand and he dragged it across his face, the grains spilling into his mouth. He spat several times and had to rely on the bench for support as he attempted to stand.

The effort of standing was too much to bear, and he almost fell forward again—he didn't want to face the real world, he couldn't endure returning to the camp and pretending everything was normal. At least as normal as their lives could be as they prepared for the evacuation.

Instead, Raj made his way toward the bathroom to wash up, continuing on autopilot was his best option rather than engaging with the onslaught of questions that lay ahead. Preparing for the evacuation would, in a way, offer a welcome distraction. He pictured the scene, the Iraqi soldier dragging her out into the hallway and then off to be shot. He bit his lip, Suhail had said the soldier came into his room to speak to her more than once. The image overpowered him, not wanting to imagine what the soldier had done to her before she'd upset him enough to shoot her. The tears returned, and he stopped to catch his breath, using a column for support. He lumbered along and finally made it to the bathroom where he made a feeble attempt to be presentable, rinsing the sand off of his face and hands.

Raj stared at his reflection, uncertain whether he could face the camp residents; he was still on the far side of campus, so he hadn't run into anyone yet. He would need to help Sanjay with planning for the bus rides, maybe even go out again to procure extra gas, but he wondered if he would be able to function.

Outside the bathroom, Raj came to a halt when he saw Mariam in the hallway. She was sitting on the ground, her back against the lockers gazing out into space. She hadn't seen him yet, and for a moment he contemplated making himself scarce, but the sand under his feet made a crunching noise as he stepped forward.

"Raj? I thought I was the only one who came to this end of campus at night."

He approached her even though part of him felt that he should run in the opposite direction, away from his feelings.

You just found out Ritika is dead.

He blinked hard to stave off tears—he was convinced they would hit him once again—and sat on the floor facing her. "I guess not. It's quieter out here, that's why I come here once in a while," he was amazed he was able to speak at all. Even though Ritika was his wife, there was one person that he wanted to go to in his grief, and she was sitting right in front of him.

Her eyes noted the cuts on his hands, difficult as they were to see in the dim courtyard lighting. "Are you okay? What happened to your hands?"

"No big deal, I scraped them on the bench by the playground."

Mariam's frown deepened, "You scraped them on the bench?" She leaned forward and took his right hand, examining it. "That's a pretty bad scrape."

Raj wasn't sure how to react, they had crossed the touch barrier a few weeks ago, but shouldn't he pull away? He was tempted to grab his hand back, to retreat and flee, yet he couldn't seem to move. He shifted, moving his hand out of her reach, then said, "It's nothing, really." He got the last words out and thought he was home free, but the look she gave him shattered his composure. His face crumpled, and the tears returned, pouring down his cheeks as he directed his gaze to the ground, to the lockers, to anything except her.

She waited several seconds before she touched the side of his face, turning his head so that he had to make eye contact. "I'm here if you want to talk," she whispered.

"When we talked before, I told you about Ritika..."

"Your wife? Yes." Mariam's expression changed, and she inched forward, moving even closer to him, "What happened?"

"I found her."

"Was she—"

"Yes."

She wrapped her arms around him, and he leaned his forehead against her collar bone. The tears had slowed now, but he still couldn't look at her again.

"I'm so sorry, Raj."

He stayed like that, with his head on her shoulder a long while, savoring the comfort of her embrace. Once they got to Jordan, he would probably never see her again. He had no right to feel this way, but he couldn't help himself. When he finally worked up the strength, he looked up and faced her.

"Thank you," he said softly. He remained in her arms, considering what to say, but the inappropriateness of the contact already felt like too much. Ritika's memory was far too fresh and so much of him wanted to surrender to Mariam.

This has to stop.

Following several deep breaths, he extricated himself and sped toward the main part of campus, moving away from her as fast as possible.

Chapter 75

Salmiya, Kuwait – October, 1990

Mariam sat down on the stained fabric seat, waiting for the other shoe to drop. The bus was packed to the brim and the engine purred as they got onto Fifth Ring Road heading west.

Any minute now they'll decide to kick us off.

She had heard the whispers from the other side of their bedroom enclosure, Ashok arguing with his wife about whether they should risk being on the bus with a Kuwaiti. Mariam wasn't sure when or how he had found out, but she'd never been so grateful to Sanjay and Daniels. Apparently, they had insisted that she and Dinah be allowed to travel with them, regardless of where they were from. "We don't even know for sure, that's what Sanjay said," Ashok had told his wife.

Her stomach churned as they exited onto Jahra Road heading north toward the Iraqi border. She wouldn't be able to breathe again until they crossed into Jordan. She hadn't even told Dinah what she'd overheard, it was all too scary. If she repeated it, that would validate her fears, making them all the more real. Besides, Mariam didn't have the heart to snuff out her cousin's hopes—she had already spoken to John and couldn't wait to join him in London.

Mariam peered out of the window although she couldn't see much other than the occasional sign with the limited street lighting. They were, of course, taking advantage of that to drive out at night, but she was filled with an overwhelming sense of dread. She and Dinah had spent much of the night debating what they would do when they reached Jordan—Dinah could use her British passport, which her husband had sacrificed everything to save, but Mariam had no papers. Tareq had made sure that her passport was tied to his, so if she admitted to her real name, she would have to get in touch with the Kuwaiti government, currently in exile. As part of establishing her identity, she would have no choice but to address what had happened to him—a thought that magnified the pressure on her chest even more.

She had grappled with the possibilities, going in circles through all the scenarios, but the only clear part was that she wanted a fresh start.

I don't want to be Mariam Al-Salem anymore.

The idea of using Tareq's name ever again made her queasier than the worst of the morning sickness. The obvious solution was to go back to Qatami, her maiden name, but that part of her identity felt just as foreign. Dinah was the only connection she had left to that name, and although being associated with her father's family was far better than being connected to Tareq, the two weren't far apart. Besides, even if she used her maiden name, she would still have to address Tareq's death with the Kuwaiti authorities. The prospect that her baby might be tied to Tareq was unimaginable, yet she saw no alternative.

It's not like I could just take on another identity.

She searched the darkness outside for a solution to magically appear.

Three hours later, Mariam rolled her head to the side and thought of how wonderful a full body massage would feel. They were one of few indulgences that had kept her sane after her marriage to Tareq, the one small pleasure he'd allowed without her having to keep it a secret. Her mind wandered, recalling her stash of books at the back of her closet, and she sighed. She was so glad to be rid of him—even if she hadn't figured out her path forward, she would never have to see him again, never have to let him touch her. Her memory flashed to that last moment at Dinah's house, and she suppressed it. With a deep breath, she focused on her books instead, and the comfort they had brought her. While she wished she didn't have to leave them behind, she could now—finally—imagine a life with her library out in the open, she would never be forced to hide her books from anyone again. Despite how terrifying and uncertain the future was, she couldn't help but smile.

I'll finally be able to read The Godfather.

She remembered Tareq ripping up the book right in front of her. Before the troops invaded, Dinah had tried to get her another copy from the British Council library, but it was already checked out. She'd promised Mariam that John would get it for her, but that had of course been put on hold with everything that had happened.

Mariam glanced over at Dinah, who was fast asleep with her head against the bus window. John was in London waiting for her, but Mariam knew that Dinah would never leave without her. Mariam sighed and closed her eyes again. She'd come this far, whatever came next, she would be able to survive it.

I have to, for my baby.

Over the rest of the drive through the Iraqi desert, Mariam dozed as much as she could. During the daylight hours she tried to read, but the movement of the bus made her head spin, so the only thing she could do other than sleep was stare out the window and wonder what would come next.

The hours passed, and after how long the first twelve hours to Baghdad dragged out, they crossed into Jordan faster than she had thought possible. The journey had a few hiccups, including three different checkpoints, but the Iraqi soldiers had waved them through as "Hindi sadeek" and the group rallied through. Thankfully their provisions for food, water, and gasoline had been adequate, helping the journey to pass smoothly. An elderly man on the bus suffered motion sickness, but he'd been moved into one of the cars and that seemed to alleviate the symptoms. She was amazed by how well she'd weathered the journey herself, but to be fair, the frequency of her morning sickness had decreased dramatically in the last month. Mariam shifted in her seat, she already felt as if she had put on three or four kilograms from her pre-pregnancy weight, but so far, she wasn't showing through her clothes. She glanced down at the slight bulge in her belly, not yet enough to make her look pregnant.

When they came to an abrupt stop at the border crossing into Jordan, Mariam's eyes shot open.

Moment of truth.

She waited as several officers inspected the bus. In the distance, at the front of the caravan, she could make out what looked like Sanjay speaking to one of the officers next to the first car. She sat on the edge of her seat for several minutes before he returned to his car. The minutes felt like hours, but eventually, the officers allowed each vehicle through, one by one.

The bus erupted into cheers once they were past the border post and Mariam smiled, the optimism was contagious.

We're free.

She would never have to sleep on the bunk bed at the school camp again. She grabbed Dinah's hand, and they looked at each other, both struggling to believe that the worst might be behind them.

The first thing Mariam noticed when they descended from the bus was the Indian flag waving from the building in front of her. Even though she wasn't Indian, she couldn't help but be infected by the national pride that surrounded her.

"This way," she saw Daniels ushering them toward a line that led into the building.

Mariam followed the crowd, but her eyes scanned the vicinity, searching for Raj. If nothing else, she wanted a moment to say goodbye. She had no illusions that their relationship—if you could call it that—would continue past this checkpoint, but she refused to just abandon their connection. Even if their paths never crossed again, she would look back on their time together with fondness.

As if he could read her mind, he waved from the top of the stairs where he was helping an elderly woman from the camp. She watched him escort her inside, accompanying her into the building, but then he disappeared.

Mariam's heart sank, she couldn't see him anymore, and with each step, she was drawing closer to the front of the line. How on earth could she claim to be Indian? If she told the official the truth, what would happen to her? She tugged on Dinah's sleeve, and from her expression, she could tell that her cousin shared her concern.

"I'm going to get John to sponsor your visa, Mariam," Dinah whispered. "I'll call him as soon as we get inside."

Before Mariam could object, Raj appeared next to her. "Can I speak to you?" he grabbed her arm and pulled her a few steps to the side.

"I was worried that we wouldn't get to say goodbye," Mariam said with a smile.

"Of course not, but what are you going to do?"

"What do you mean?"

"I know who you really are."

His words hit Mariam like a tidal wave as she processed what he meant.

He knew? All this time?

She was grateful, in a way, that he hadn't turned her in—he'd certainly had the opportunity—but they had shared several tender moments, and he had never thought to tell her this during any of those times. "Why didn't you say anything?" she finally asked.

Raj gave her a tender look, and her anger melted away, recalling the feel of his arms around her, their connection despite the strangest of circumstances. "I thought you didn't want me to know," he answered. "You never told me."

"I didn't know how."

They stood there in silence for a few minutes until Dinah motioned from the entrance. "I have to go," Mariam said.

"Come with me."

2016

Chapter 76

Austin, Texas, USA – May, 2016

Raj looked out of the kitchen window of the house where they had taken refuge for the last two days and checked his voicemail. Shortly after their arrival, he'd called his boss, Bruce, citing a family emergency and letting him know that he'd be taking some personal time. Raj had purposely left a voicemail rather than speak to him directly—he didn't trust himself not to confide in his colleague and old friend about the situation he and Mariam were facing. A couple of hours later Bruce had returned his call, and the message brought Raj a sliver of comfort as he listened to it for the fourth time.

"Hey Raj, returning your call here. I'm guessing you're already in flight back to India, I hope everything with your family turns out okay. Take as much time as you need and I'm around if you'd like to talk."

Raj disconnected and set the phone back on the counter, glad that they had been able to buy some time by claiming that they needed to return to India. Mariam had used the same excuse to get out of her job at BookPeople, so they were okay for a few more days, but he wasn't sure how much longer they could stay put. Eventually their lives would catch up with them, and for that, they needed a plan. He breathed a long sigh and stirred the store-bought soup he had set to heat on the stove. Neither of them had been in the frame of mind to do anything but the most basic cooking, and that was unlikely to change anytime soon. *5405 Jeffburn Cove,* his gaze remained focused on the street outside—the eerie street name seemed so apt for their situation. *Jeffburn,* just saying it gave him the chills.

Raj shook off the feeling and cracked two eggs into the soup and watched the egg whites dissipate into droplets instead of remaining whole as the eggs cooked with the heat from liquid. He let out a chain of expletives, cursing the brain-fog that had caused him to err at a recipe for poached eggs he had successfully executed hundreds of times. He was tempted to pitch the entire pot down the drain, but they were already low on groceries, and Mariam was terrified of either one of them going to the store. She seemed to think that if they stepped outside, even into the front yard, Tareq would materialize right out of the bushes. Inside she jumped at every corner, but that was nothing compared to the panic that had come upon her when he'd suggested they eat out on the front patio. Raj already had the worst case of cabin fever, and he had reservations on how much longer he could take being cooped up in the house. "We can at least go out into the backyard, it's completely fenced off," he'd tried to assure her to no avail.

He tabled his frustration and set another piece of bread on the pan, then focused on the soup. Once it started to bubble, he lowered the flame and set up a saucepan on the other burner to make two grilled cheese sandwiches. Since tomato soup with a poached egg on top accompanied by grilled cheese was Mariam's favorite comfort food meal, he'd gotten quite good at making it over the years. Normally he even found it relaxing. He stepped away from the stove—everything would take a few minutes to cook now—and wiped down the counter, then focused on loading the dishes in the sink into the dishwasher. Unable to silence the debate raging in the back of his mind, he set one of the plates back in the sink and gave in to his thoughts, allowing the different scenarios to play out. If they remained in hiding, they would eventually run out of money, or they would need help to run—new identities, a new home, everything. If running was off the table, at least in the long-term, that left them only two options—either confront Tareq or go to the police. Drumming his fingers against the counter, he saw only one option available, and that was getting help, which meant going to the police.

Which would mean…

He rubbed the back of his neck and looked up at the ceiling.

There has to be another way.

Try as he might though, if there was, he couldn't see it—if they went to the police, they would have to explain who Mariam really was; they would have to admit to her real identity, that she was guilty of fraud. Before she told him why she had wanted to use Ritika's name he had resented her choice, he couldn't help but feel it was an affront to his first wife's memory, but now he understood.

That choice is what protected us for this long, and now we're going to pay for it.

A sizzling sound came from the stovetop, jolting Raj back into the moment. He pulled the lid off the soup pot and turned the burner down, watching as the bubbles at the top subsided. He sniffed the air, noticing a burning smell, and cringed, he had forgotten all about the bread for the grilled cheese. Reaching over to flip the first slice of bread, he grimaced—the bread was almost black instead of golden brown. Before he could stop himself, he picked up the scalding toast and flung it into the garbage disposal. He shouted out several swear words, a combination of the pain shooting up his fingers and the direness of their situation. Raj leaned over the kitchen counter with his head in hands, kicking at the base of the floor cabinets. It took several moments before he regained his composure, all he wanted to do was smash every breakable item in the kitchen against the wall, followed by the unbreakable ones.

Once he had sufficiently suppressed his emotions, he remade the grilled cheese sandwiches, this time not letting them toast enough, but his patience had worn thin. He carried them to the dining table next to the kitchen, but as he looked out at the yard his gaze caught the poolside table and he changed his mind. He couldn't take it anymore, they had to go outside. He'd hoped he would be able to lift Mariam's spirits with one of her favorite meals, but he had to concede that was a virtual impossibility.

We've been pretending that we can live like this, but we can't. There's only one option.

Raj picked up the plates and took them outside, a return to reality would have to start with the first step.

Chapter 77

Austin, Texas, USA – May, 2016

Mariam turned the page on her Kindle to get to the end of the chapter, realizing that she couldn't recall a single thing that had happened in the last several pages. She tapped back several times until she came upon dialogue she recognized and had started reading again when she heard Raj coming down the stairs from the kitchen. She looked up with a frown, the dining table was upstairs next to the kitchen.

"Do you want to eat in front of the TV?"

"Let's go out to the back patio."

"No, we can't," her throat went dry, the mere thought of going outside was petrifying.

"Mariam, if he finds us here, it won't matter whether we're inside, in the backyard, or on the roof."

She swallowed. *Why did he have to be right?* Mariam rubbed her fingers against her mouth, a remnant of an old habit of biting her nails, then braced herself as she stood.

If you never go outside again, Tareq wins.

She took several deep breaths before she felt able to join Raj outside.

Sitting across from him, she looked out at the stone landing with a small pool, about fifteen feet long, nested against some elaborate landscaping. "I don't think I ever really looked at the garden, I didn't realize that John had such extravagant taste in gnomes," she said, making a halfhearted attempt at a joke.

Raj chuckled, although she could tell it was forced, and picked up the grilled cheese sandwich on his plate. "It's not as good as I normally make it," he shrugged. "Sorry."

"It's okay." Mariam took a bite and chewed slowly, he was right, the bread wasn't toasted properly, and the cheese was only partially melted. "It still tastes good," she fibbed.

"You're a bad liar, my dear."

"It's still bread and cheese—there are worse things."

"That's true, I guess," he sighed.

They finished the food in silence, with Mariam making furtive glances to catch his eye. She could tell he had something to say, but was trying to work up the courage to bring it up—she had lost count of how many times he'd repeated the same behavior over the years. She had a feeling that she knew where the discussion would go. He would want to call the police—to turn Tareq in. She coughed, her fear almost sent her into a tailspin, but she also knew in her gut that he was probably right. If there was some other option, she had no idea, although she wasn't ready to admit defeat.

I never wanted to be the victim again, but after twenty-five years, here I am.

Raj set his mug of soup on the table with a soft thud, "Mariam, we have to talk."

I know, she considered saying, but instead, she feigned surprise and raised her eyebrows, "Okay, what do you want to talk about?"

"We're lucky John had this place, that Dinah could set us up here, but it's not like we can stay forever. This situation can't continue."

Mariam's heart sank even further, she wasn't sure if she could stomach what he was clearly about to say.

"We have to turn him in, have the cops arrest him," Raj continued.

"For what? For stealing my nameplate from the office? He hasn't done anything…*yet*, at least nothing that we can prove." Mariam could scarcely keep her voice steady. Everything that Tareq had done had been to another woman, to Mariam Qatami, not to Ritika M. Ghosh.

"You know that's not true. What about everything that he did to you *before*? He's a monster, why can't you hold him accountable?"

"And say what? That I was his wife, Mariam Qatami? I don't think that aligns with what's on my citizenship papers," her voice cracked,. No matter how they looked at it, their lives as they knew it were over.

Tareq has won.

"Come on, we can't live like this—we can't hide out here forever. What do you want to do? Go on the run? Have him hunt us for the rest of our lives? He knows you're alive, he's never going to stop searching for you. It's not like we could fake our deaths."

Mariam let her imagination run wild, "We could leave the country, get away. We have some money saved up, I bet we could live a decent life if we found somewhere low cost."

"And then what? When the money runs out? Besides, we're not in witness protection, we don't exactly have access to new identities. And even if we could run, what happens to Aliya? Are you really willing to never see her again?"

"We could take her with us..." even as she said the words, she knew they weren't true, that she didn't want to inflict that upon Aliya, but what else could they do?

"Come on, Mariam. We can't do that to her, we'd be throwing her whole life away. All of her education, all of her hard work? I know you don't want that for her, and neither do I." He reached across the table to grasp her hands, "There is no other way—we *have* to turn ourselves in. That man hunted you, I'm sure the police would understand why you wanted to stay away."

They won't...

"I committed fraud, Raj. *We* committed fraud—we used Ritika's name to get me new papers. We can't go to the authorities; we could go to jail." Two stray tears ran down Mariam's face. She hadn't considered that ramification of running, she had only thought about fight or flight, and she didn't believe that they could defeat Tareq if they confronted him directly. Either she admitted to fraud, or they gave into his attack, neither of which she would consider winning, but she had ignored the cost of running as well.

We would never see Aliya again.

The idea was unthinkable—even her initial choice to leave Tareq had been centered around her daughter and the life that she wanted for her, the life that she refused to impose upon her. Her chest tightened—

her daughter was everything to her. "Raj, what do we do?"

"I don't know." Raj circled the table to join her on the bench on the other side and put his arms around her, pulling her close.

Mariam clung to him, not wanting to let go as she processed their meager options. He was right. She had known it before, even if she hadn't wanted to admit it, and she knew it now. The pressure on her chest increased and she wiggled to the side, releasing herself from his grasp so that she could meet his gaze.

Before she could speak, he brushed the tears from her face and said, "It's your decision, I'm not going to push you anymore. Whatever you want to do, I'll stand by you."

A wistful smile crossed her face; in that moment, the rest of the world could almost fall away. In a way, she had never felt safer, their relationship had always been something of calm and contentment, even at the beginning in the darkness of the refugee camp in Kuwait, even when she had feared that his knowledge of who she really was might compromise her safety. From the very beginning he had stood by her, loved her, cared for her, and protected her—with him by her side, she could indeed weather the inevitable next step. She had to accept the truth: Tareq was alive, and the only way to be free of him was to turn herself in, to tell the world the truth of what he'd done to her. Perhaps Raj was right, maybe the police would be merciful given why she had lived so many years under someone else's name. Even if they weren't, this was the only way forward. Mariam leaned forward and gave him a soft kiss.

"You're right. I wish you weren't, but you're right. We have to turn ourselves in, we can't run, and we can't let him win. I'm so glad Aliya's in Banff with no service. I don't think I could go through with it if I told her beforehand."

"Tomorrow, then," he whispered. "Tomorrow, I'll go to the police."

"We'll go together."

"No, I want you to stay here, where it's safe. Please, Mariam—at least let me try to see if they'll agree to some sort of leniency. We'll come and get you afterward."

She looked away, then turned back to him again before she repeated, "No, Raj, we'll go together."

"Why do you have to be so stubborn?"

He hesitated, then agreed, before she pulled him in for a deeper kiss and whispered in his ear, "At least we still have tonight."

Chapter 78

Austin, Texas, USA - The next day, May, 2016

Tareq paced back and forth alongside the window that looked out onto Mariam's backyard.

Where in the hell are they?

He kicked at the base of the wall again, the spot was slightly bowed in from all of the rage he had vented. Tareq threw down his binoculars, careful to aim toward the bed, where they bounced once before settling onto the mattress. He'd already destroyed two sets by hurling them at the wall, so his momentary solution was just to fling them at the bed. In the last two days, he had waited for the cover of darkness and snuck into the yard twice and gone into the house once. All of the clothes, books, kitchen items, etc., seemed exactly as they were when he had left. He'd been sure that Mariam had realized that he was alive—she'd had such an extreme reaction in front of the firepit, she must have discovered the remnants of her book—so what had happened since then?

She wouldn't have told Raj about it, she couldn't have. He would stop her from seeing me...

He squinted toward the garden, there had to be a reason that she hadn't come home.

I bet he found out somehow, that has to be it.

Tapping his fingers against the back of his head, he hatched a new plan, if they wouldn't return to him, he would find them. But how? He didn't have access to tracking software for their phones—he could see if one of the investigators would do it, but that would only work if they still had their phones. Still, someone had to know where they were.

Tareq sat down on the bed and reached for the file on Mariam that the investigator in D.C. had put together for him. Moving quickly through the pages on Mariam, he stopped when he got to the list of known associates, which included some people that she worked with and the names of a few friends in Austin. At the bottom of the list was the name Dinah Qatami, along with her office contact information.

Of course.

He reached for his phone and dialed Dinah's number.

Three rings later, she picked up, "Hello, Kuwaiti embassy, this is Dinah Qatami."

Tareq winced, hearing her voice stung as he recalled the number of times that she had told him to stay away from Mariam. His throat trembled for a second before he could speak.

"Hello Dinah," he said in the most incisive tone he could muster. He was furious at her, she had orchestrated Mariam's first betrayal, and had kept him from making her see reason. At the same time, deep down he was intimidated, even petrified—she was the one who had planted the idea of leaving into Mariam's head. Before her relationship with Mariam had blossomed, Mariam had always capitulated to him, she'd always loved him even if she pretended to fear him. Tareq clutched the bedframe, focusing on his wrath. "Do you know who this is? You haven't heard my voice since I was at your house in Kuwait twenty-five years ago."

There was a long pause on the other end of the line before she replied, "Tareq—what, what do you want?"

"What do you think I want? I want to know where Mariam is, I'm sure you know. You think you know everything about her, after all."

"I don't know where she is."

Tareq chuckled, his fear of Dinah's influence dispelled, the terror in her voice was palpable from the way she spoke. "I doubt very much that's true. You're the one who turned Mariam against me, but you won't be able to keep us apart this time. She will come back to me, and once she does, I'll come for you."

"You think Mariam wants to go back to you?" Dinah's tone became incensed, her anger tangible. "Mariam chose to become someone else rather than have any association with you. Do you hear me? She hated every minute that she was with you, she was just too scared to do anything about it at first."

"That's not true," Tareq shrank back into the headboard and pulled his knees into his chest. He rejected the possibility, he knew in his bones that Mariam loved him. She had stayed with him even with his indiscretions with other women, had always listened to what he said. His voice dropped to a whisper, "She loved me, she only pretended to be frightened. She loved every minute that we were together, and we will have that again."

"You really are insane, there's no question about it. Mariam would rather die than be with you again. You'll never find her, and even if you do, she will never love you."

She will never love you.

Tareq's chest convulsed, there was no way that Dinah could be right, no way. "I will find her, and we are going to be together again."

"Give it your best try," Dinah's defiance coming through clearly over the phone line. "Like I said, even if you do, she'll never love you. Nothing will ever change that, she's not your wife anymore." The line clicked as she hung up.

Tareq's wrath bubbled, glaring at the phone. He didn't want to believe her, refused to do so, but Dinah sounded so confident.

Could she be right? Could it all have been a lie?

He thought of how Raj had carried Mariam away, how she had lived as a different person for so many years, and a feeling of hopelessness descended over him. She had indeed lived as someone else's wife all this time. His right hand clenched at the comforter on the bed, squeezing the ball of fabric in his palm—she had run away from him, hidden from him, lived with another man, and now dared to defy him by disappearing yet again.

She is, and will always be, my wife.

He reached for the phone to redial Dinah's number, which went straight to voicemail. "If Mariam doesn't come back to me, I'm going to pay a visit to Aliya. She deserves to know who her real father is."

Chapter 79

Austin, Texas, USA - May, 2016

Mariam's eyes fluttered open and slowly scanned the room. It took her a moment for the last three days to come flooding back, along with her conversation with Raj from the night before. Sitting up required an extraordinary amount of effort, her head a fog from the two bottles of wine that they had consumed after dinner. She rubbed her eyes, beginning to feel half awake.

"Raj? Where are you?" her own voice vibrated through her skull.

When there was no response, she slid out of bed, goosebumps forming on her now exposed bare legs. "Raj?" she repeated, starting to become concerned. She checked the master bathroom, then the next bedroom and the living room, and finally padded up the stairs toward the kitchen, calling out for him again, each time with more urgency.

She reached the dining table, and her stomach flipped—there was a note on the table, and it had to be from him. Reaching for it, she unfolded the piece of paper, already knowing what it was going to say. The note confirmed it. He had gone to the police station without her—wanted to try to protect her by striking a bargain with one of the officers on duty. Mariam dropped onto the bench by the table.

How many times does Tareq get to ruin my life? How many times do

I have to be the victim?

A few minutes later, Mariam pulled herself together and wiped her eyes, somehow, she had to stay strong. Her jaw set and she dressed quickly, then went in search of her phone, which seemed to have disappeared in the slew of wine and sex from the night before. She couldn't help but smile, she and Raj had behaved more like their twenty-something selves, the abandon and unlimited energy that came from knowing that this might be their last night as a "normal" married couple. Mariam shrugged. Nothing about their story could ever qualify as normal, but for the last twenty-five years they had been able to live without carrying most of the baggage of their past.

In the living room, she caught the sound of her phone vibrating, but it took a few minutes to track it down. Mariam's heart sped up, assuming it was Raj trying to call. She finally found it by the poolside, next to the open living room window. With a sigh of relief, she checked the call log and froze; there were ten missed calls from Dinah in the last five minutes.

Oh no.

She hit the call back button and waited for the line to connect, "Dinah, what happened?"

"You have to call the police. Tareq, he's going after Aliya unless you come back to him. He said he's waiting at your house—"

MARIAM BARELY UNDERSTOOD WHAT DINAH said after that, the panic that struck her took hold. She tried to call Aliya, then Raj, but neither of them picked up.

What do I do?

She wanted to scream, to bang her head against the wall. Aliya was still in Banff, she wasn't supposed to be back until tomorrow, but why didn't she have service? Mariam paced back and forth by the poolside, sweat beading on her brow, she was at a complete loss. They had already left multiple voicemails telling Aliya not to go back to her apartment. Mariam's lower lip trembled.

Should we tell Aliya not to come home at all?

How could one man wreak so much destruction on her entire world?

She had to do something, had to go somewhere, but she had no idea where. If she returned to the house, she would all but be giving herself up to Tareq, and there was no point in going to Aliya's since she hadn't returned yet.

Her phone buzzed again, and she reached for it without looking at the screen.

"Raj? Where are you?"

"Mom? Are you okay? What happened?"

Mariam groped behind her for one of the lawn chairs by the pool, "Aliya? Where are you? I thought you were still in Canada. Don't come home."

Please still be in Canada.

"What's the matter with you? We got off the trail early, so I took an earlier flight. I just listened to all of your voicemails, what's going on—"

"Aliya, don't go to your apartment, you can't go home—"

"I know, I told you I listened to your voicemails. Did my apartment get flooded or something? Anyway, I just parked, and I'm heading into the house now, let's talk about it inside. I'll see you in a sec—"

The line cut off and Mariam's mouth fell open—Aliya was at their house, exactly where Tareq was waiting.

No.

Chapter 80

Austin, Texas, USA - May, 2016

Tareq could hardly believe his luck. He was about to leave for Aliya's apartment when her car materialized in the driveway before his eyes. He ducked to the side of the house as she got out, speaking emphatically to someone on the phone.

"I know, I told you I listened to your voicemails. Did my apartment get flooded or something? Anyway, I just parked, and I'm heading into the house now, let's talk about it inside. I'll see you in a sec—"

He hit her on the back of her head with a hardcover from the bookshelf and both the phone and book fell to the ground, clattering onto the driveway. She lashed out and he fell backward against the porch railing, losing his footing. He was surprised at the strength behind her jab, but he wouldn't underestimate her again. Back on his feet, he launched forward, pinning her against the car hood, using his weight to his advantage. She kicked at him but wasn't able to get enough leverage, so the force that landed on his groin was minimal. Leaning over, he held her down and smacked her twice, then stepped back, pulling his pistol from the back of his waistband.

"Is this how you treat your elders?" he grunted. "Into the house, quietly." She spat at him and he dodged, but it grazed his cheek and he wiped it off in disgust. "It's time I teach you a lesson. You've been running wild your whole life, no idea where you *actually* belong." He spat back, but it fell short, falling to the ground instead of reaching her face.

Tareq glanced to either side quickly, glad that it was past rush hour, so most people in the neighborhood had already gone to work. He shoved her down onto one of the chairs from the dining table, used duct tape to tie her to the chair, then sat down on the couch, setting the pistol on the cushion next to him.

"I have some news which will come as a shock to you—"

"I know who you are, what do you want from me?" she snarled.

She knows who I am?

On top of that, why hadn't she surrendered to him? He deserved her respect not her defiance. "I am a man, and I am your *father*. You don't stand a chance against me, you don't *deserve* that much."

"My *father*? You think you're my father? I might have your DNA, but my dad is worth fifty of you. A hundred of you. He doesn't need to hit my mom, to bolster his own ego by putting other people down—"

"That's enough," Tareq raised his voice, brandishing the gun once more. "Mariam is my wife, she loved me, until he got into her head—"

"You're even more delusional than I thought. She may have been your wife on paper, but she would have given anything to be free of you—she gave up her entire identity so that she would never have to be your wife again. Even when she thought that you were dead—"

"You're wrong about her, about all of it!" Tareq grasped her throat, unable to withstand her insolence any longer. "You will be silent." She struggled to breathe but he held on, only releasing his grip when she blacked out.

Chapter 81

Austin, Texas, USA – May, 2016

Mariam checked her watch for the fifteenth time, ten minutes in an Uber to get home had never felt so long. She tried Raj three times on the way, each going to voicemail; then dialed Aliya's number eight times in a row, pleading to the heavens that she would pick up, that the house would be empty.

The Uber driver looked at her several times in concern, she probably looked like a crazy person, furious and panicked and crying, all at the same time. Only her adrenaline to get to Aliya was keeping her functional.

I'll do whatever I have to. If that means giving myself up to Tareq, so be it.

For a second, she contemplated calling the police herself, but she didn't dare, not until Aliya was out of harm's way.

When the driver stopped in front of her house, she leapt out of the car and burst into the living room, even more out of breath from racing up the driveway.

"Aliya?" she screamed.

Mariam's face crumpled, her fears were confirmed. Aliya was tied up in a chair in the center of their living room, her head slumped over, with Tareq pointing a gun at her from behind.

"Hello, Mariam, it's been a while," Tareq said with a malicious smile. "Don't worry, she's fine, I only knocked her out."

Mariam reeled backward, tripping over the floor joint between the living room and the entrance. She fell and used the wall for support to get to her feet. His voice cut through her psyche like a hot knife through butter—she was no longer an independent, strong woman in her forties. With a simple greeting he had turned her back into her meek nineteen-year-old self, dependent on him, desperate not to exasperate him, paralyzed and unable to move. But it was only for a couple of seconds—her daughter needed her. She stepped forward, still using the wall to stay upright.

"Tareq, let her go. Please," she whimpered, looking at him, pleading with every fiber of her being. "I'll do anything."

"*Anything*? Even come back to me? Aliya had some interesting things to say about that—she said you'd never come back to me, that you were never even mine to begin with. Dinah said the same thing, but I always knew different."

"Yes, absolutely, I'll come back to you," Mariam almost choked, but even though the words sickened her, she knew how much she meant them. She would indeed do anything if it meant keeping Aliya safe.

"I know you never wanted to leave me. Even when you pretended to be scared, or acted like you wanted to run away, I know how much you loved me," he hesitated, "how much you still love me."

Mariam opened her mouth, she should agree, she had to say something to mollify him enough that he would release Aliya. Instead, she took another step toward him, willing her legs to move forward. She advanced slowly, her heartbeat ringing through her ears, as if she were approaching her execution.

For Aliya.

A voice in the back of her mind shouted at her, urging her to come up with a plan, perhaps she could get away once he had let Aliya go?

There has to be a way to fight back.

She squashed the idea as she continued forward—there was no point, she would always be the victim, he would always have the upper hand. The only way to ensure Aliya's freedom was to give up her own.

When she was halfway across the room, Tareq set the gun down on the coffee table and bridged the remaining distance toward her. With his left hand, he reached out and yanked down on her hair, jolting her chin upward.

"You were always mine, Mariam." He smacked her, the force slamming her into the far wall of the living room and knocking the wind out of her.

Before she could catch her breath, he had pounced on her once more. His left hand threw her head down toward the ceramic tile and she only just managed to break her fall with both hands.

Mariam got to her knees, panting and sobbing.

This will never end, this is my life now.

"Get up," Tareq grunted, then shouted again, "I said, get up!"

She struggled to her feet, and he used his forearm to push her up against the wall, constricting her windpipe.

"Tell me you love me," he said in a cutting voice.

"I—, I—," Mariam tried to get the words out, they should have been easy enough to say. They would end her pain, at least some portion of it, but she had never been able to say them, not even when she was nineteen and life bound to this man. "I lov—"

"Say it!" Tareq released her throat and used both arms to hurl her to the ground. She crashed into the coffee table, and it disintegrated around her, the shards of glass piercing the skin on her right arm and face.

On the floor surrounded by glass, she recalled who she once was, the same instance from years earlier flashing through her mind. The sensation of her concussion from his attack twenty-five years before flooded over her, along with the recollection of the day in the hospital when she had finally decided to free herself. The moment that she had chosen to walk away, to end her life as a victim.

I did it then, I can do it now.

Her fingers closed around a shard of glass, and the voice in the back of her mind returned, the one that she had tamped down earlier.

Fight back, you can fight back. You don't have to be the victim anymore—

She kicked out as she felt Tareq climb on top of her, but his weight across her back pinned her to the floor. Stars flickered in her vision as his fist connected with one of her ears, and she flailed backward, attempting to stab him with the glass, but all she got was air. She lashed out several more times to no avail until she went limp, he was too heavy, and he had overpowered her.

At least it'll be over soon. She gave up.

"You know you want this," he whispered into her ear as his hands clawed at her hips.

"Mom!" she heard Aliya scream, but she sounded far away, as if from another life. "Get off of her!" She cried out again, "Mom, get up, fight back!"

Tareq grunted and pressed even more of his weight into Mariam's back, the glass fragments cutting into her face. He stood up, and the pressure on her torso eased. It took her a second to start to move, she was in so much pain, but she had to stop him—he was going toward Aliya.

"Shut up, little girl. Don't you see, you want her to fight back, but she wants this as much as I do." He approached the chair where Aliya was tied up and dealt a slap across the right side of her face, followed by another one on the opposite side. The chair tipped over and landed on the ground. Tareq kicked at Aliya's knee with a resounding crack, and she screamed, the shrill sound piercing the air.

Mariam scrambled to get to her feet, she couldn't tell where the pain stopped, and her body began. She commanded her muscles to move, she had to get up, had to move faster, when she heard a loud crash at the back of the house.

Raj appeared out of nowhere and launched himself into Tareq's side. They fell to the ground, rolling over the floor in the far corner of the living room, and dealing punch after punch at each other.

Pushing her palms into the ground and ignoring the stinging in her hands, Mariam finally managed to stand. She searched frantically.

Where's the gun?

She had seen it on the coffee table before she smashed through it, it had to be somewhere. A second later, she caught a glimpse of it at the base of the couch where it had fallen when the table shattered.

Her hands shook as she grabbed it and turned toward the corner of the room. Aliya was struggling against the rope binding her to the chair, and Raj and Tareq were still on the ground. Mariam pointed the pistol forward, but her grip wasn't steady enough to aim properly especially with how much they were moving.

Before she could process her options, a loud crack split the air. The remnants of an old glass vase from the living room side table now strewn all over the floor. Raj fell back against the wall to the left of Tareq's now limp body.

"I never liked it anyway," he said panting, looking over at Mariam.

Her hands quavered as she inched closer.

Did Raj really stop him?

Raj was safe, he was out of the way of the shot. She could end this now, end this man who had hunted and haunted her, who had tainted her entire life.

"He's out cold, Mariam."

Raj's voice was right in front of her, but she ignored it, the weight of the gun still heavy in her grip.

I wanted to be the one who stopped him.

She cocked the hammer and pulled the trigger, and the shot rang out through the now quiet living room.

She slid to the ground next to Raj, the gun going limp in her hand as he enveloped her in his arms. "It's over, Mariam, it's over. He can never hurt you again."

The pistol fell from her fingers.

It's over.

Epilogue

Austin, Texas, USA – Two months later, July 2016

Mariam was still glowing as she walked the trail running alongside the Colorado River. She hadn't stopped since early that morning when she finished her last interview at the Austin Police Department. The ordeal with Tareq was truly and finally behind her, and she could be herself—something that she hadn't appreciated properly until she'd been through a number of therapy sessions. She was winding down the frequency of her sessions, and the nightmares were rare now, holding little power over her. She had grown to appreciate herself and the life that she had built. *Even if I didn't do it alone,* she acknowledged with a smile. Her life had been the product of her own choices, combined with the impact of circumstance and many other people, good and bad. Dinah, Raj, Janhvi, Aliya… even Tareq, all of them had influenced who she was today.

And Ritika.

She stopped on one of the pavilions jutting further out onto the water from the boardwalk and leaned against the railing, soaking in the late morning sunlight.

"Thank you, Ritika," she whispered, taking in the view of the river, with the greenery and skyline superimposed against it.

You gave me my life back. You gave me myself *back, gave me the opportunity to figure out who that was.*

I never really appreciated that till now.

Mariam stood there for a few more minutes, reflecting on the events of the last year, all of which had brought her to this moment of peace.

After much debate, she and Raj had decided to tell the detective at the precinct the truth—to share who Tareq was to her, and how she'd gotten away from him during the Gulf War.

"I never intended to stay Ritika Ghosh after we got out of Kuwait," she had explained, "but I was so scared of being culpable in Tareq's death that I couldn't work up the courage to be myself again. It was just easier to stay Ritika, no one except for Raj really knew her. She was an orphan, so she didn't have a family, and neither did I. The only paperwork I had in India was under her name anyway, I didn't have a British passport or anything like that, the way Dinah did."

"Why come forward now? Tareq is dead, you could have just claimed that he was a stalker from your time in Kuwait—no one would have known he was your husband," Detective Sigmund had asked.

"If therapy's taught me anything, it's that I have to stop running from my past, I can't pretend that it doesn't exist. Our demons always find us," Mariam shrugged. "So, I decided to come clean. Besides, Ritika deserves more of a memory than that."

Mariam took a deep breath, that moment playing on loop in her head as she stood out on the pavilion. The detective had listened to her story, taking several pages of notes on a faded yellow legal pad along with recording their discussions. He'd interviewed both Aliya and Raj about her history with Tareq, along with chronicling the attack at the house, even noting how quickly Aliya progressed in physical therapy after the injury to her knee. At the end of the interview this morning, Detective Sigmund had changed his mind about moving forward.

"I have a sister who was in an abusive relationship. She never married him, but it took her over a year to leave him." He looked away, his eyes moving to the ceiling before he met Mariam's gaze again. "She couldn't talk to me about it until it was all over, but I never understood why, not until we talked about it a couple of days ago. Much like you, she said she never wanted to be that person again. That she was so conflicted about whether it was her fault that it had happened to begin with. With all of that, she never acknowledged or affirmed how much of a victory it was when she did something about it, when she finally chose to walk away."

The detective reached out and tapped a button on the recorder. "I'm not going to move forward with this. You deserve to have your life. I understand why you did what you did, why you hid who you were." He exhaled, "I'm going to get rid of this file, and you're free to go. You can still be Ritika M. Ghosh, because that's who you are now. A few years of your past shouldn't define your entire future."

Mariam stared at him in disbelief.

I'm free to go?

She couldn't fathom that her life could return to the path that she'd been on before she had found out that Tareq was still alive.

Detective Sigmund had stood up to shake her hand, "As far as I'm concerned, Tareq Al-Salem was someone who started stalking you when you were in Kuwait, and followed you to Austin after you attended the embassy event in D.C. When he attacked you and your family, you defended yourselves, and once you were able to get to his gun, you shot him in self-defense. That's what my report's going to say."

After the interview, she had walked out with a weight off her shoulders. Raj had wanted to celebrate, to take her out to lunch before they headed over to the University of Texas campus for a pre-graduation reception for Aliya, but Mariam had chosen to take some alone time by the river instead. The trail had always offered her peace, the view of the water and the sun reminded her of the walks that she and her mother used to take along the seaside in Kuwait. Mariam breathed deeply—the detective was right, she *was* Ritika M. Ghosh now, and while her life in Kuwait was part of that identity, it wasn't the only part.

She felt some guilt about shooting Tareq; he'd been more or less neutralized at that point, but if she hadn't done it, he would have kept after her for life. Those ghosts had to be put to bed, and although she wished there had been another way, reality was never that simple. His memory would continue to haunt her to a certain extent, but she had relinquished the grip that it held over her—after all, she was the one who had finally taken control of her destiny.

"I will never be a victim again," she said softly to herself. She had said those same words so many times, in her head and out loud, but this time they rang true.

A few hours later, Mariam stood in front of the mirror in her bedroom wearing a knee-length fuchsia dress with spaghetti straps and a conservative swoop neckline. Her arms were bare other than the silver bracelet she was wearing. Her mother had once worn a bracelet like that, but it had been lost with her jewelry collection after the Gulf War. The weekend before, Mariam had seen this piece, which looked similar, at a street fair on South Congress Avenue and had purchased two of them on a whim. The other one was for Aliya, a graduation present in memory of her grandmother.

After brushing out her hair, Mariam glanced at the bed where she had laid out a cardigan to wear over the dress—but decided against it. Austin had moved into full-fledged summer, and the evening was warm.

They left early so that they could stop at a nearby wine bar, where they grabbed a table outside. Mariam sipped on her glass of Nero D'Avola and waved as she saw Dinah and Nadia down the block. After the ordeal they had all been through together, Aliya had thought it fitting for them all to be at her graduation, as she moved past this major milestone.

After several hugs, Dinah and Nadia settled down across from her and Raj. Placing his hand on her shoulder, Raj looked at Mariam and excused himself.

"I'm going to go meet Aliya a little early, give you guys some time. See you there in a bit?"

Mariam nodded and once he had left for the car, Dinah grasped her wine glass with white knuckles, her voice filled with trepidation. "Mariam, what happened with the detective?"

Mariam smiled, she had decided to wait to tell them in person rather than letting them know earlier when they were boarding their flight. "Everything's okay. He's dropping the whole thing."

"Oh, thank God. I'm so glad we get to go to the graduation today with this whole thing behind us, with all of it behind you."

"Me too," Mariam agreed. She turned toward Nadia, who had remained quiet other than their initial greeting, "How are you doing?"

"Could be better, but I'll get there," she answered softly. "I'm so sorry again, all of this, it happened because of me—"

Mariam shook her head, "No, come on, we've been through this. Tareq hurt all of us, I wasn't his only victim." Her smile widened, she was able to say the word *victim* without the pain that previously accompanied it.

What happened doesn't make us weak, in fact, overcoming it means that we're strong.

"Thank you again for understanding," Nadia looked down at the napkin on her lap. "I think the trauma counseling is helping, but honestly, I'm still struggling."

"You're doing all the right things—trust me, I'm a poster child for therapy these days," Mariam said with a nod.

Dinah sighed and raised her glass, "I'm stopping all of this bittersweet talk now—to the case being closed, and Tareq being truly behind us."

Mariam clinked her glass against Dinah's, wondering if should say more.

There'll be no more victims.

She waited till they each had a sip, and then changed the subject, broaching their plans for the next few days. When they reached the venue an hour later, Mariam paused as she got out of the car, taking in the sunlight that made the grass sparkle as if it were the setting of a scene from *Lord of the Rings.* She reveled in the moment, she had accepted her past and moved on—despite her protests to the contrary, she had been apprehensive about seeing Nadia, worried that she would blame her for what had led to Tareq's return even if intellectually she knew that it wasn't her fault. Instead, Mariam found herself light and free, she didn't need to blame Nadia, and she was grateful that she could help her to move forward past the trauma of his attack. A few months earlier she had no doubt that seeing her would have put her completely off balance, but today she was ready to greet the day and celebrate Aliya's big moment.

They met Raj and Aliya on the lawn, and Mariam looked at her daughter with a teary smile. "You're finishing your Master's now, I can't even believe it."

Raj's voice cracked as he gave Aliya a hug, "You know, you're my little girl, but you grew up. I'm so proud of you."

"I love you, Dad."

Mariam watched the two of them, fighting back tears, she couldn't believe this was her life.

My family, my life.

Her eyes grew watery despite her best efforts and she smiled through them.

They were about to head into the reception hall five minutes later when they heard a stream of sirens coming down the street. Mariam stopped and looked in the direction of the sound, an ambulance and a fire engine were speeding toward them. The vehicles flew past where they were standing on the sidewalk and turned right at the next street corner. When the sound faded away after a few seconds, Raj reached out and grabbed her hand; he was trying to be supportive, he knew now how the sirens used to affect her. Mariam smiled at him—the memory of the sirens from the night of her concussion in Kuwait was still with her, but it no longer held her hostage. Nor did her life with Tareq.

That past is part of me, but it does not define me.

THE END

Acknowledgments

I often find the task of drafting the Acknowledgement page to be as daunting as the story itself. There are so many who have contributed to my writing career, making me the storyteller I am today. Without each of them, I may never have written a single word.

First and foremost, I thank you, the reader. By opening this book, you have joined me in a journey back in time when the Gulf War disrupted so many lives. While Mariam is a fictional character inspired by events of the war, I felt a kinship with her as she pushed on through difficult days in her quest to survive and emerge the victor in her own story. Thank you for believing in her and her strength as much as I do.

For my editors, Tanya Besmehn and Chantelle Osman, thank you for bearing with all of the back-and-forth communications necessary to make *Sirens of Memory* the best it could be. There were delays as I processed, reacted to, and finally worked on implementing your edits and plot-point suggestions. Together we took *Sirens of Memory* from an idea in my mind to the reality of a book in my hands.

My endearing gratitude and thanks:

To John Besmehn for designing the original cover and being patient with me as we tweaked it.

To Scott Montgomery for believing in me and this story enough to champion it, and for making the introduction that led to this book deal.

To the team at Agora and Polis for all of your support.

Finally, I want to extend my deepest gratitude to my family and friends, both immediate and extended. To my husband, Brendan Snow, thank you for your continual support and for being one of my greatest champions. To my parents, Pradip and Jayashree Guha, I couldn't do without all of your love and support, and Dad, my writing would be very different without your beta-reads and apt critiques. My list here could go on and on, so instead, I'll say thank you to the universe for bringing so many wonderful people into my life—all of them have shaped me as a writer and as a person. For that, I am grateful.

Note to the reader

Dear Reader,

I'm so excited that you read my book. Thank you so much, the fact that I have readers who enjoy my work is still quite surreal.

I would love to hear your thoughts on *Sirens of Memory*. Would you consider posting a review on Amazon? Reviews and word of mouth are invaluable to an author on a quest to succeed, and I would be so grateful for a few minutes of your time in posting. Even a line or two would be a tremendous help.

I'd also love to stay in touch—you can stay up to date on all my projects, book signings and news by signing up for my mailing list at **smarturl.it/PujaList.**

Thank you again!

With all my best,
Puja

About the Author

Puja Guha

International Development Consultant. Global Citizen.

AUTHOR.

Born into a family of acclaimed Indian architects, Puja Guha traveled with her parents as they worked on projects around the world. After graduating from the University of Pennsylvania, Puja completed her Master's degree in public policy at *Sciences Po* and the *London School of Economics.*

Today, she works as an independent consultant on international development programs - primarily in Africa and South Asia - traveling to some of the most economically-challenged countries in the world. Leveraging her scholarship, her ability to speak five languages, and her earnest goal of engendering global economic progress, she continues to learn about, support and embrace new countries.

Along her journey, she's been inspired by politics, culture and setting as her imagination enhances her experiences. Her books include the Ahriman Legacy, a series of spy thrillers, Sirens of Memory, a domestic suspense thriller, and The Confluence, a family drama, along with a number of short stories.

Puja has lived in Kuwait, Toronto, Paris, London, and several American cities including New York, Washington DC, Philadelphia, and San Francisco. She currently resides in the Denver area.

Find out more by joining Puja's mailing list at:
http://smarturl.it/PujaList
www.pujaguha.com
pujaguha@pujaguha.com

CPSIA information can be obtained
at www.ICGtesting.com
Printed in the USA
JSHW020031190621
15976JS00002B/3

9 781951 709372